"All hail to the Crown of Death!"

Though all the members of the coven cried out the words, Morgan remained stubbornly silent. Held by four demons, he seemed powerless to escape what was about to happen, yet surely he could find some magical means to avoid becoming an unwilling initiate into dark witchcraft. But as a fifth demon pulled red-hot pincers out of a nearby brazier, all hope fled.

The demon came toward him, its webby wings pulsing, its insect eyes glittering. Then the pincers bit, the pain scorched through his whole body, and his nose filled with the smoke of his own burning flesh. Finally it was over, and the leader of the coven was approaching, holding a large green-bound book and a pen. He touched the nib to Morgan's blackened, torn wound and the pen filled with his blood. Then the man gave him the pen and held up the book.

On the right-hand page was a contract straight from hell: *I hereby swear fealty to Fryga Tukhanox, the Crown of Death, to do her bidding and her work, in all ways required of me . . .*

✳

THE EYE IN THE STONE

THE EYE IN THE STONE

ALLEN L. WOLD

PAGEANT BOOKS

This book is for Lea Braff, who gave me the chance,
and for Sharon Jarvis. Thanks to you both,
for your criticism and help.

♪

PAGEANT BOOKS
225 Park Avenue South
New York, New York 10003

PAGEANT and colophon are trademarks of the publisher

Cover artwork by Charles Moll

Printed in the U.S.A.

First Pageant Books printing: November, 1988

10 9 8 7 6 5 4 3 2 1

AUTHOR'S NOTE

Readers will soon notice that I have tried very hard to avoid using "he" as a neuter pronoun. One of the conventions I have used is "they." Certain purists will object that "he or she . . . they" does not agree in number. They should also note that "he or she . . . he" does not agree in gender.

The real problem, of course, is that in English today, we do not have a true neuter pronoun, other than "it," and I think almost everyone will agree that "he or she . . . it" is an abomination. After all, we do not mean that he or she is a neuter it, but that the person we refer to is either male or female but not specified.

There is precedent for the use of "they" as a neuter pronoun, to be found in the Oxford English Dictionary.

Examples of this usage date from 1526 to 1874. "They" has been used as a neuter pronoun by both common speakers and by literary figures. It is the natural thing to do. It may be the best solution we have.

Today, only a pedant will pick on the disagreement in number, though anybody can be pedantic at moments. In current social consciousness, the problem of sexual equality and gender chauvinism is much more important. If you can think of a better solution, let me know.

I would also like to refer the reader to Handbook of Non-Sexist Writing, by Casey Miller and Kate Swift (Lippincott & Crowell, 1980). It is a calm, well thought out, sympathetic discussion of the problem, which every reader, writer, speaker, and publisher should read.

End of sermon.

This book is a dream. It bears no relationship to reality in any way whatsoever.

PART ONE

Not all social ills are caused solely by the principle of Evil, but without Evil, things would be a lot better. The very nature of life presents challenge, death, decay, so that in a world devoid of Evil, intelligent beings would still have the chance to compete with each other, make mistakes, do wrong. It would not be a literary utopia. There might still be a Ghengis Khan, but there would probably be no Hitler.

Classically, Evil, the principle of death, devolution, and destruction, has wanted to pervert mankind. Biblically, this is to "punish" God, the principle of life and evolution, for having cast the author of Evil out of heaven. When Evil tried to usurp the power of Good, to supplant God's place and power, Good removed Evil from the process of Creation.

Evil was left with only the power of Destruction and Entropy, of which it is master, but it seeks the power of Creation, in order to re-create the universe to suit itself. It combats Good, not trying so much to destroy the universe as to destroy the principle of Good. An analogy is the terrorist who tries to destroy a political structure by destroying the society that supports it. The terrorist imagines that he or she is ready to step into the political vacuum thus created, and will be able to then re-create society according to his or her own beliefs. Similarly with Evil.

The forces of Evil do not operate without re-

sistance, of course. They can work most effectively through the intellect of intelligent beings;
hence their most constant opponents are the
good people of the world who persist in being
good, according to their understanding and
their culture, in spite of temptations otherwise.

Chapter One

✦ ✦ ✦

MORGAN LET HIS Los Angeles–trained driving skills maneuver the Lotus through the heavy Thursday afternoon traffic on I-94. The highway was four lanes wide each way here, going around Harborbeach in southwestern Michigan, a community of small factories and manufacturing plants, from the sprawling suburbs of lazy Chicago toward decadent Detroit, the movie capital of the world. The flow of vehicles was anything but smooth, however. People here didn't have the same understanding about driving as they did back in California.

A large red-and-black-striped tabby cat slept in the passenger's seat. The animal weighed over twenty pounds, without a trace of fat. Morgan glanced down at it as it murmured in its sleep. It had been a long drive, and Morgan would be glad for a chance at some rest himself.

He passed the first two exits for Harborbeach, going east, and got off at the third. But instead of turning left to go into town, he took Essex Avenue east, out through the orchards and farms that surrounded this town, an island of light industry in an otherwise agricultural area.

It was three in the afternoon, and Morgan had been driving hard since leaving Glass Mountain in the suburbs of Los Angeles yesterday morning. He knew tricks to keep himself alert, some of which he'd learned during his six years in the marines, where alertness was a matter of life and death. But that still took energy. He was looking forward to a long talk with his brother, a good meal, several strong drinks, and a solid night's rest. He ran his hand through the thick black hair that persisted in falling over his forehead.

He found the sign to Scott's Gun Shop and Shooting Range, at a graveled road heading south off Essex Avenue, six miles from the interchange. It was beautiful country out here, Morgan had to admit, though not like the orange groves, blue mountains, and sparkling clean air of the Los Angeles area. This was his first visit to Michigan, and he liked it.

It had been too long since he'd seen Michael. Somehow they'd both been too busy during the last seven years, after Morgan had gotten out of the marines with the rank of captain. Morgan had gotten tired of fighting, and now had his game shop to run, and his studies, and took no holidays unless he had to. For Michael there had been that bad movie business in Detroit at first, and then the effort of making a go of the gun shop. They had kept in touch, though, writing at least once a week, and phoning about once a month.

They'd always promised they'd get together, and then two months ago Michael had announced that he'd bought a house, and this summer would be a good time for Morgan to come visit. They'd settled on a date for Morgan's trip, but during the last six weeks Michael hadn't sent any letters and hadn't answered the phone. Morgan figured that with the gun shop, his girl friend, and moving into the "new" house, his brother had just not had the time. He would chide Michael about it though, when he saw him.

The gravel road wound through orchards for a little over two miles, passing several farmhouses. At last there was another turnoff, with another sign.

The trees here were hardwoods, maple and oak and Chinese elm. As Morgan drove through them he could hear, growing louder, the sound of gunshots. Even on a weekday there appeared to be plenty of business. But then, it was June. And though Morgan's visit had been arranged well in advance, Michael had always been a hard worker like his younger brother, and wouldn't take the day off until Morgan actually arrived.

He pulled into a graveled parking lot, at the other side of which was a long, low building, painted like a hunter's camouflage jacket, with the usual fiberglass bear on the roof and several sets of antlers under the eaves. Behind the shop, out of sight, would be the shooting range. The noise was quite loud, and reminded Morgan of the time when his squad had been pinned down in Havana for three days. Beside him Phoebus stretched, yawned, and sat up. "Heeorw?" the cat said.

"Yes, we're here." Morgan parked the car away from the other eight or ten vehicles clustered near the shop entrance and got out. Phoebus jumped out after him and started for the bushes at the side of the lot. "Come on in when you're done," Morgan said. "Try not to get distracted by the wildlife." The cat said nothing but started investigating some fallen leaves.

Morgan stretched, working the kinks out of his muscles, then pulled a small cigar from his shirt pocket. There was no one to see him out here, so instead of using a match he snapped his fingers, and a small blue flame appeared on the end of his thumb. He lit his cigar; the flame went out. Then he strolled across the gravel toward the shop entrance. Though he had been out of the service for seven years, he still walked with a military erectness.

Inside there were displays of guns old and new, racks of rifles, glass-fronted cases of pistols, stuffed animals and birds everywhere. The main counter ran along the back of the shop, its glass front displaying daggers, knives, antique pistols, loading supplies. Behind it were shelves of boxes: ammunition, patches, cleaning kits. A slightly overweight man in his early forties was attending to two customers who were more interested in talking than in buying. The clerk didn't seem to mind.

Morgan went up to the counter and, when the customers finished their conversation with the clerk, asked the man where Michael Scott was.

"Who?"

"Michael Scott," Morgan said, thinking this man must be new on the job.

"I'm sorry," the clerk said, "I didn't catch that." The sound of the gunfire wasn't that loud in here, but still, Morgan thought, the clerk's hearing could have been damaged by standing out on the shooting range.

"Michael Scott," Morgan repeated for the third time. "Or George Faircloth," naming the man Michael had hired when he'd gotten the shop six years ago.

"I'm Faircloth," the clerk said.

"Michael's told me a lot about you," Morgan said slowly and distinctly, "whenever he's mentioned the shop."

"Michael who?" Faircloth asked. He seemed to be genuinely confused, rather than deaf.

"Michael Scott. The guy who owns Scott's Gun Shop."

Faircloth did a kind of mild take. "Oh, yes. Ah, what can I do for you?"

"I'd like to see Michael."

Faircloth stared blankly at him. "Do you want to buy a gun? Use the range?"

"I want to talk to Michael."

Faircloth seemed rational enough otherwise, but at the mention of Michael's name, he just stared, as if Morgan had spoken in another language.

"Doesn't Michael usually work here in the afternoons?" Morgan went on, concealing his own confusion and impatience. Dissimulation was a long-practiced art for him.

Faircloth started to say something, then there was a kind of glitch and his expression went odd. "I'm sorry," he said. "I guess I missed that. What can I do for you?"

Morgan felt the hair on the back of his neck rise up. He didn't know what to answer, but was spared an embarrassing hesitation by Phoebus, who jumped up onto the counter.

"Goddamn, that's a big cat," Faircloth said.

"He is that. Say hello to the man," he told the cat, stroking the animal's head once.

"Heorrow," Phoebus said, and sat down. Faircloth reached out a tentative hand, and Phoebus offered his chin to be scritched.

"Michael Scott owns this shop, doesn't he?" Morgan asked.

"Uh, why yes, he does." Faircloth didn't sound too sure of that. Phoebus moved his head so Faircloth could scratch behind his left ear.

"Is he here this afternoon?" Morgan went on.

"No, no, he's not." More than unsure, he was distinctly uncomfortable and confused, though Phoebus's presence seemed to be loosening his tongue a little.

"When does he usually come in?" Morgan asked, projecting his questions directly at Faircloth, in a technique he had learned that forced the other to pay attention in spite of himself and without being aware of what was being done.

"He, ah, he doesn't," Faircloth said. His forehead beaded up with perspiration and he stopped petting the cat. It was not nervousness or fear that was making him sweat, but the effort to think and respond to Morgan's questions.

"But this is his shop," Morgan said. "He's written me about it any number of times. That's all he ever talks about, except his girl friend Cindy, and lately the house he just bought."

Faircloth just stared at him. "Look, ah," he started to say, and looked down at Phoebus again. "Are you sure you're in the right place? This is a gun shop. We have a shooting range out back."

"I know," Morgan said dryly. He put his cigar butt down in an ashtray to let it go out. He let his senses spread out, but could feel nothing wrong here. Faircloth didn't seem to be lying. He had heard the words, had understood them, but couldn't make them fit in with what he knew about things.

His memory had been tampered with. Whatever was going on here, Morgan decided it would be best not to admit that he was Michael's brother, but to let his natural discretion and caution guide him.

"How long has it been," he went on, "since Michael has been in?"

Faircloth just shook his head uncomfortably, as if he hadn't understood, and didn't like not understanding.

It was almost as if Michael didn't exist. For a moment Morgan began to wonder if he really had an older brother, or if maybe he was just imagining things. This whole conversation was unreal. He decided to try once again, on a different tack.

"Do you work here alone?" he asked.

"No, sir. I have an assistant, Henry Sherman." Once again he reached out to stroke Phoebus across the shoulders. "Comes in at ten to open up, stays till four. I come in around three, close up at nine, go home at ten."

"How long has Henry worked here?" Morgan asked. Faircloth didn't seem to mind talking about anything else, as long as it wasn't about Michael.

"About five weeks now, five weeks last Monday."

"Why did you hire him?"

"Man, you gotta be kidding. This is a small shop, but it takes two to keep it open the hours, you know."

"But how come Michael doesn't work here anymore?"

"I, ah . . ."

It happened again, as if something in Faircloth's mind were shutting off. Morgan didn't detect any conspiracy or guilt there, just confusion and a strange blankness. But Faircloth was getting tired of these—to him—nonsense questions. Morgan decided not to press the issue. Until he knew better what was going on, it might be dangerous to pursue it further.

"I guess I won't shoot today," he said, as if that had been the topic of conversation all along.

"Come back any time," Faircloth told him, smiling as if indeed it had been.

Morgan picked Phoebus up off the counter, left the shop, and went back to his car.

"I think we've got trouble," he said as he opened the door and let the cat in. "As far as I can tell, Faircloth has had his mind wiped." He thought about not having received any letters from Michael during the last six weeks, the unanswered phone call last weekend. Michael had gotten in trouble before, and he'd always been able to get out of it. But this was different. Morgan didn't like it one bit. He turned the car around and drove out of the lot.

Chapter Two

✧ ✧ ✧

MORGAN DROVE BACK toward Harborbeach, stopping at an Americo station on the other side of the I-94 interchange. While the attendant was filling him up he checked the municipal map Michael had sent him two months ago, to make sure he knew the way to his brother's house. The layout of the streets of Harborbeach made less sense than in any other town he'd ever been in, and in six years in the marines' special combat forces, he'd been in quite a few strange towns.

When he was sure he knew the way, he drove south through town to the residential suburb where Michael now lived. There weren't many houses here, and there were stretches of actual forest, both behind Michael's place and across the road farther up and down.

He pulled into the driveway beside the two-story house and parked in front of the garage. The grass in the lawn was knee-high. There were several newspapers on the front porch.

He got out of the car, Phoebus following, and went up to the double front door. It was locked. He rang the bell, but there was no answer. The house felt empty.

He picked up the newspapers, yellowing with age. There were five of them, the oldest dated six weeks ago. The last time he'd talked to Michael was before that. And Faircloth had hired an assistant nearly six weeks ago.

Bushes beside the driveway screened him

from the next house toward town, the house on the other side was three lots away, and the house across the street was set far back, behind its own screen of bushes. Even if someone were watching, they couldn't see very well what he was doing.

Morgan could just go in, but he could not be sure that the house was still Michael's. During the six weeks it appeared to have been empty it could have been sold or repossessed. It didn't seem likely that Michael would have sold the house when he'd bought it just over two months ago, but if there had been a change of owner, he didn't want to try to explain how he'd gotten into the house without breaking the lock or using a key.

Phoebus padded back and forth across the porch, investigated the door, jumped up on a windowsill.

"How does it look?" Morgan asked.

"No one home," Phoebus said. His voice sounded like a bad long-distance phone connection. He would not have spoken if there had been anyone near to hear him.

Morgan went back to the drive and tried to see around the side of the garage. Bushes next to it obscured his view. He returned to the front walk and then crossed the lawn toward the empty lots at the other side. He could see more of the yard from here—two large trees in back, with a hammock, and the forest beyond.

The house looked as though Michael had just packed up and left without making any arrangements whatsoever. That wasn't like him. If he had just gone on a trip, he would have stopped the paper delivery, instead of letting the carrier find him gone. He would have hired someone to mow the lawn.

On the other hand, if he was sick or hurt, then Faircloth should have known about that, and cared. He went back to his car and called the cat, who came out from the bushes beside the house.

"Find anything?" Morgan asked.

"No," Phoebus said.

Morgan sat in the Lotus and thought about it a moment longer. He wanted answers, but he didn't want to take the chance of prying here anymore just now. He scritched the cat for a moment, then pulled out his map again.

It was after five; Michael's girl friend should be home from work. Morgan had never met Cindy Vann, but Michael had written a lot about her. Morgan had asked his brother whether he was getting serious, but Michael had always evaded the question. Morgan suspected that he was. The purchase of the house indicated as much.

He had her address, found the right street on his map, on the other side of the St. James River, which divided Harborbeach unequally, and started to drive over. He got lost twice when the map failed to correspond with the streets on which he was driving.

Cindy lived in an older residential neighborhood, in a smallish ranch-style house. Morgan knew she had a roommate, but nothing about her. There were two cars parked in the driveway, so he assumed they were both at home. He parked in front of the house, got out of the car, and let Phoebus jump up onto his left shoulder with his hind legs hanging down in back. They went up to the door, and Morgan rang the bell.

The young woman who answered the door had to be the roommate. She was about five feet tall, wearing an open-necked blouse and slacks. Her face was more what Morgan thought of as cute rather than pretty, emphasized by her short, dark hair. She appeared to be in her middle twenties, just a few years younger than Morgan. She looked up at Morgan with that expression one uses on strangers at the door, and then her attention was immediately drawn to the cat.

"Good heavens," she said. Her voice was a nice alto. "I've never seen a cat like that before."

"A rather rare species," Morgan said with a smile. "Is Cindy Vann in?"

"Yes, she is," she said, looking up at Morgan at last, "just a moment, please." She smiled at the cat again, then disappeared into the house.

While he waited, Morgan decided that until he learned more about his brother's mysterious absence it would be wise to continue keeping his true identity secret. He was cautious by nature, and indulged in certain other activities besides his game shop that made discretion a good idea.

Cindy Vann came to the door after only a moment. She was almost as tall as Morgan, dressed in blouse and skirt, with honey-brown hair framing a model's face. She was a little too thin for Morgan's taste. She, too, was fascinated by the cat, who was now purring loudly.

"Cindy Vann?" he said. "I'm Lester Van Alan." He gave her a name he'd used in the bad days of his youth, before his violent activities had made him choose between a prison sentence and joining the marines. "I'm trying to locate Michael Scott, and I understand that you're a friend of his. Do you know where he is?"

She stared at him blankly, as if he hadn't spoken.

"You do know Michael Scott?" Morgan persisted.

"Uh, yes, I do." She seemed surprised at her own uncertainty. At least her response was better than Faircloth's.

"I've come from Los Angeles to visit Michael," Morgan said. "He's not at home or at the gun shop. He's written me about you, and I thought you might know where he was."

"I'm sorry," she said, as if her mind had just cleared. "Who did you say you were?"

"Lester Van Alan. I'm an old friend of Michael Scott's."

Once again her face went blank.

"Are you familiar with Scott's Gun Shop and Shooting Range?" Morgan asked, taking another tack. He was beginning to get frightened. Phoebus just kept on purring.

"Why, yes, I am. I've been there several times."

"Forgive me for imposing, but there seems to be some problem in communicating here. Are you familiar with the owner?"

"George Faircloth?"

"Michael Scott."

"Ah, yes, I think so."

Morgan could hear Cindy's roommate calling to her from somewhere inside the house, but couldn't make out the words. Cindy called back, "It's someone asking about Michael Scott. Do you know who he is?" A moment later the smaller woman came back to the door, a puzzled expression on her face.

"Yes," she said, "I know him. Won't you come inside?" Cindy watched her roommate as if she didn't understand what was going on.

"Is the cat all right?" Morgan asked, reaching up to Phoebus as if ready to put him down.

"By all means," Cindy's roommate said, flashing a bright smile and reaching up to scratch the cat's chin as if she knew how. Phoebus stretched his neck out for more, and purred louder than ever.

Morgan followed the two women into a colorfully decorated living room, and was offered a seat on the couch. Phoebus moved to his lap.

"I'm sorry for intruding," he said, taking another look at Cindy's roommate. Phoebus seemed to be watching her too. "I seem to be having a hell of a time finding Michael." She was very nicely built, and though her face wasn't perfect, she radiated a lot of character.

"That's quite all right," she said. "By the way, I'm Dana Kirkpatrick."

"I'm Lester Van Alan. And this is Phoebus. I'm very pleased to meet you. Do you know where Michael Scott is?"

"No, I'm afraid I don't." She sat down in one of two huge armchairs at the side of the room.

He turned back to Cindy, who had taken the other armchair. "You do know Michael Scott," he repeated, trying to keep the impatience and frustration out of his voice.

"Why, yes, certainly I do," she said, but she sounded as though she didn't believe it.

"Where is he?"

She stared at him a moment, then said, "I don't know."

"Has he gone on vacation? Is he in the hospital? Has he moved away? His house has been empty for six weeks, and Faircloth has hired someone else to help him run the gun shop."

"I'm sorry," Cindy said. "I don't understand. I feel like I'm missing something." She didn't seem to be worried, except by her inability to think clearly.

"George Faircloth had the same problem," Morgan said, "when I spoke to him just an hour or so ago." He stroked Phoebus idly, and the cat curled up to take a nap. "Like you, he seemed perfectly rational, except when I mentioned Michael. Then, all of a sudden, as you have done, he became confused, as if he couldn't hear or didn't understand. It's almost as if Michael had been spirited away somehow, and anybody who knew him made to forget."

"But that's silly," Cindy said, glancing at Dana. "People don't just disappear."

"Then where is Michael?"

Once again, Cindy's face went blank. Dana watched her with very little expression.

"Think back about two months," Morgan prompted.

"Okay."

"You saw Michael then?"

"Oh, yes, of course, every day." Her face brightened with the memory.

"Then when was the last time you remember seeing him?"

Her face clouded. She seemed to be struggling with the words. "About s-six weeks ago, I think."

"And you don't wonder about that? You're not worried about where he might have been for the last six weeks?"

"I should be, shouldn't I?"

"Was Michael behaving strangely the last time you saw him?"

Again Cindy turned to Dana, who just shrugged. "I don't think so," Cindy said.

"Isn't it odd that you haven't seen Michael in six weeks, and don't even care?"

The point finally began to sink home. She tried to think about it, but Morgan could see that she was having difficulty even yet. Dana was beginning to look concerned too. Morgan wondered if she had a boyfriend.

"You're right," Dana said, "we haven't seen him in six weeks. . . . But how could we not miss him? Now that you mention it, we haven't missed him at all. How could that be?"

"I don't know," Morgan said. "But I don't like it. Faircloth didn't miss him either. Something funny is going on."

"Yes, there certainly is," Dana said. "It's . . . it's as if, whenever I try to think of him, the thought just slips away, like a dream you can't remember in the morning. That isn't right, is it?"

"No, it's not. You haven't all three been visited by a strange hypnotist, have you?" He tried to make his voice sound light and half-joking.

"No," Cindy said, not laughing at all. "At least, I don't remember any such person."

"All right, I've bothered you enough. Michael's told me about somebody else, a Gary Weiss. Do you know him?"

"Certainly. He's—Michael's best friend."

"Kind of paranoid," Dana said, "but otherwise a nice enough guy. The four of us have gone out together quite a bit."

"All right, I'll go talk to him and see if maybe he can't shed some light on this. Do you know of anyone else who might help?"

Both women tried to think. "I'm sorry," Cindy said. "Help with what?"

"With finding Michael."

"Oh. Yes. Ah, yes, Logan O'Reilley. He knows . . . Michael, I think."

"Of course he does," Dana said, sounding frustrated. "Why can't I think clearly? He and Michael shoot down at the range all the time."

Morgan got O'Reilley's address and, unable to think of a good excuse to ask Dana out, just told them he'd keep them informed, then thanked them and left. He got back in his car and started away from the curb.

"They were pretty fuddled," Phoebus said.

"They were indeed. Clear as a bell on anything except Michael. They've been touched somehow, Phoebus. I don't like it. Michael is missing, leaving no trace, and not only that, leaving no awareness of his having disappeared. If George Faircloth were the only one acting oddly, I might think he was just crazy. Even considering Michael's empty house. But with both Cindy and Dana showing the same effects, that can only mean that somebody or something has actually erased their memories. Not perfectly, but enough so that they don't even know what they've forgotten."

"Where now?" Phoebus asked.

"Supper," Morgan said, and started looking for a MacDougal's emerald arches.

Chapter Three
✛ ✛ ✛

GARY WEISS LIVED in the main residential area just south of the central business district, in a small one-story house. At this hour of the summer evening there were children playing in the yards, riding bicycles in the street. Morgan pulled his Lotus up to the curb and got out. Phoebus did not jump onto his shoulder but followed him up the walk to the front porch.

Weiss answered the door. He was slightly taller than Morgan, slightly heavier, a year or two older, maybe thirty-three.

"My name's Van Alan," Morgan said. "I understand you're a friend of Michael Scott."

Weiss just looked blank. Third time in a row, Morgan thought.

"Do you know Michael Scott?" Morgan asked, tired of asking the same question over and over again.

"Yes, I know him. What of it?"

"I'm trying to find him," Morgan said, realizing that his first assumption had been wrong. This one was going to be different.

"He lives over on South Catalpa," Weiss said.

"I know that, but the house is empty, nobody's been there for six weeks."

"You gotta be crazy." He started to shut the door.

"Wait," Morgan said. "I've been to his house, the gun shop, and I've talked to Cindy Vann. Michael disappeared six weeks ago. I was hoping you might know what had happened to him."

"Nothing's happened to him."

"Then where is he?"

"At this hour of the night"—it was about seven-twenty—"he should be at his shop. You know where that is?"

"Yes, I've been there. Michael's not there. George Faircloth hasn't seen him in six weeks."

"Look, fella, what do you want with Michael, anyway?" Morgan found Weiss's rudeness unpleasant, but at least his answers were a change from those Morgan had gotten so far.

"Michael invited me to visit him, a couple months ago. When I got here, I went to the shop. He wasn't there. Faircloth acted like he didn't even know him. He's hired someone else to fill in the hours."

"Hell, Michael owns that shop. George can't hire anybody."

Weiss wasn't really listening. For a moment, Morgan had hoped that his rude behavior was just a quirk of personality, but every time Michael came up, Weiss sidestepped the issue.

"Nonetheless," Morgan said, "Faircloth hired another clerk. Michael hasn't been in the shop in six weeks."

"Nonsense. That shop's Michael's life, that and Cindy Vann."

"I know. Neither she nor her roommate have seen him for six weeks either."

"Hell, man, Michael sees Cindy every night."

"Not for the last six weeks he hasn't."

"How do you know that?"

"Cindy Vann told me herself."

"Oh." He might have said more, but he noticed Phoebus for the first time. "Shoo, scat," he said, waving his hands at the cat. Phoebus disappeared around the side of the house. "Damn cats," Weiss muttered.

"When was the last time you saw Michael?" Morgan asked, ignoring the insult to his pet.

"Look, I don't meddle with things that aren't my business."

"Aren't you supposed to be his best friend?"

"Sure I am. I've known him since he moved here after he got taken in that phony movie deal in Detroit. Lost everything. Came into the paper where I work, looking for a job. I found him one at the gun shop, which he bought half a year later. Goddamn, that guy is bright. Never lets a thing get by him. Except for that movie deal, but what can you expect from tinseltown. Used Michael's script, claimed it was their own. Made money, too, but never paid Michael a cent. It's a racket. Don't know how he ever got into that mess in the first place."

"He and the producer were in college together."

"Is that it? Old school buddy turns cheat. Yeah, I've seen it happen before. So what do you want Michael for?"

"He invited me out to visit him, so he could show off the house he just bought."

"Yeah, he's been hot on that house for a long time. Just the right breaks. He ought to be home about ten tonight, I guess."

"He hasn't been home in six weeks."

"Seems like you said that once before."

"I did."

"What are you trying to tell me?"

"That Michael's disappeared."

"That's crazy."

"When did you see him last?"

"Why . . . who did you say your name was?"

"Lester Van Alan."

"Just what the hell are you up to?" Weiss asked, suddenly defensive.

"Dammit, I'm trying to find Michael Scott. He's missing. Has been for six weeks. Haven't you noticed that?"

"Look, buddy, I haven't got time." He started to close the door.

"Don't you care!" Morgan yelled.

"Sure I care. I care that you're yelling at me on my doorstep. I care that you're pushing your nose in where it doesn't belong. You want I should care more?"

"Where's Michael?"

"Where he always is at this time of night. At his shop."

"He's not. I've been there."

"Sure you have. What do you want with him, anyway?"

"He's a friend of mine," Morgan said quietly. The conversation was getting nowhere. Weiss was as befuddled as everybody else had been, it was just less obvious with him. "He invited me to visit him."

"Sure he did. You leave him alone."

"Look, Weiss, I drove here all the way from California to see him. I haven't seen him in seven years, not since I got out of the Marines. Nobody knows where he is. Do you?"

"The hell you say. If you don't get out of here, I'll call the cops."

"Do that. Maybe they would be some help. Where is Michael, Weiss?"

Finally he drew a blank. Weiss just stood and stared, the same confused, uncomprehending expression on his face that Faircloth, Cindy, and Dana had worn. It slowly changed to anger.

"I know who you are," Weiss said slowly, a crafty edge to his voice. "You're one of those whoosies, the people who meddle with other people's minds."

"I beg your pardon?"

"You can't fool me. I've been around. I know your kind. And I'm not going to stand for it." He raised his hands, his fingers held in odd positions that Morgan recognized all too well. Weiss wove a pattern in the air with one hand, gestured at Morgan with the other, and spoke words of a strange language. Sparks of lavender glittered in the air, tracing the pattern his hand was making.

For a moment Morgan was so surprised that he couldn't do anything. Weiss had almost finished his incantation before Morgan could recover himself. Frantically, he turned and ran for his car. Phoebus streaked toward him from the side of the house, and Morgan felt the welcome safety of an anti-magic shield settle over him.

Lavender sparks coruscated around them but didn't touch them. Morgan slammed into his car and was driving away before Weiss could try again.

"Goddamn," he said, gasping, as he pulled over to the curb a couple blocks away. "I wasn't ready for that. I don't know what kind of fire he had in mind, and I don't want to find out. What the hell does he think he's doing, using magic out in the open like that?"

"He's paranoid," Phoebus said.

"He's going to get himself killed. If anybody saw that little display, there may already be a 'witch hunt' in the making." The existence of magic was not common knowledge, for the good reason that those suspected of it were frequently killed out of fear and misunderstanding.

"I don't think there were any witnesses, but even if there were they wouldn't know how to interpret what they saw."

"I hope not. Damn, it's difficult enough keeping magic secret as it is, without lunatics like that threatening to give the whole game away."

"You just caught him at a bad moment," Phoebus said. "He'd have been lynched long before now if he were normally that careless."

"I suppose so, but I still don't like it."

"Maybe you ought to contact the Dreamer," Phoebus suggested. Morgan looked down at the cat.

"No, not yet. I haven't got this business all sorted out yet. I don't like to go running for help when I can do things myself."

"At least let your teacher know where you are," Phoebus insisted.

"I'm not going to intrude on him until I'm sure there's a good reason."

"Four people with their memories altered isn't a good reason? A paranoid magician who might uncover the reality of magic is not a good reason?"

"Just give me a little time," Morgan said. "Weiss has gone undetected so far. If we leave him alone, he might not slip again."

"Maybe not, but there's magic involved. You should have your teacher's advice and help."

"I know, I know, but there's still this guy O'Reilley. I want to check him out first." He pulled out his map again and found where Logan O'Reilley lived. Then he started the Lotus and drove through the weird streets of Harborbeach.

Chapter Four
✠ ✠ ✠

MORGAN DROVE UP and parked in front of O'Reilley's house. It was a one-story bungalow, with bushes around it and trees in the yard, much like all the other houses on the street. There was a yellow light on the porch, other lights on behind the demurely curtained windows. It was the very picture of warm friendliness. He looked at his watch. It was about nine-fifteen.

"Keep a look out," Morgan said as he got out of the car. Phoebus stood up at the open car window, watching as Morgan went to the door.

He raised his finger to the bell, but hesitated. He'd been caught by surprise once. He felt the web of magical relatedness that magicians called the Lattice, to see if any spells had been laid on this house.

There were guards, wards, charms, defensive spells of all kinds. Morgan stepped back a pace, surprised at the number and variety of spells here. Two magicians, he wondered? In a town the size of Harborbeach, he hadn't expected to find even one.

Hoping O'Reilley hadn't heard him on the porch, he went back to the Lotus and got in. Phoebus climbed up onto his shoulder. The cat didn't need to be told what Morgan had found—after all, what good was a familiar that couldn't share its master's experiences?

"What if he comes out?" Phoebus asked. "He'll see us sitting here."

"I was just thinking of that." Morgan looked around at the other houses nearby. The one across the street was dark. There were tall bushes in front of the house, large and dense enough to conceal a man. He made sure no one was watching, got back out of the car, crossed the street, and as quietly as possible moved in among the branches and foliage. Phoebus jumped down from his shoulder and made a quick trip around the house.

"Nobody home," he said when he came back.

The summer evening was warm, the neighborhood was quiet. The bushes, while letting Morgan observe O'Reilley's house across the street, concealed him completely from it. He didn't know how long he would have to wait, but he needed some time to sort out his thoughts, make plans. He hadn't come prepared for this. Two magicians in a row was two magicians too many.

He didn't know O'Reilley's habits, and didn't want to confront him until the time was right. He decided he would wait until the lights started going out. Then, when O'Reilley was ready for sleep, when his defenses were down, then Morgan would go over and knock on the door.

He waited. Phoebus jumped up onto his shoulder, arranged himself so his hind legs were comfortably dangling down Morgan's back, and purred. Morgan scritched him under the chin. The night became full dark. The streetlight on the corner, three houses up, couldn't reach them where he stood. There were few passing cars to spy them out in their hiding place.

The moments passed. He could hear an occasional muffled sound of television coming from O'Reilley's house, through an open window somewhere. He composed himself, rehearsing what he would say and do when the time came. He would ask only once if O'Reilley knew where Michael was. If the man showed the same befuddled memory as the others, Morgan would just leave. If he seemed cooperative, Morgan would carefully tell him what he had learned so far. If he became violent, Morgan would be ready this time.

He didn't mind the wait. That would give him the chance to master his fatigue, calm his fear, suppress his anxiety. Besides, it was a beautiful midsummer evening. Phoebus, sitting comfortably on his shoulder, continued purring loudly.

Only magic, Morgan knew, could explain the strange befuddlement shown by the people he had talked to so far. The mystical guards and wards around O'Reilley's house made Morgan suspect that he might be the one responsible for that befuddlement. Though Morgan couldn't know that for sure until he had talked to O'Reilley, he felt it was better to be on the safe side.

Somewhere a bird called sleepily as a vagrant breeze moved through the tops of the trees overhead. Phoebus oonched himself slightly forward on Morgan's shoulders, seeking a subtly more comfortable position.

Morgan's thoughts strayed, mostly toward Dana Kirkpatrick. He practiced a few military parade exercises to keep his muscles from cramping. Then a sound from across the street brought his wandering attention back forcibly. It was eleven-thirty. In his mind, without a movement, he went through the ritual of a magic spell.

His hands were motionless at his sides as he visualized them tracing the sigil in the air. The night was silent, but his inner ear heard his unspoken chant. Done this way, the spell could even be cast in broad daylight, since nobody but Phoebus would have noticed that anything was happening. In the darkness of the bushes, however, Morgan was momentarily surrounded by the faintest of deep purple auras.

And then the spell was done, he felt the energy he'd expended draining out of him, and the thrill that always accompanied successful magic. Usually only simple and very well known spells, such as those for opening doors, lighting a cigar, or turning on the lights, could be done completely in the mind. But Morgan had a special talent for this, that even his teacher could not match, and it enabled him to perform magic

at times when others would not dare, for fear
of discovery.

As a result of his spell his hearing sharpened
and focused. He listened intently to the sounds
coming from O'Reilley's house. Now he could
distinguish the soft thud of a refrigerator door
closing in O'Reilley's kitchen, the metallic
screech of a pop-top being torn off a can, and
the raucous song of a commercial on the tube.

He'd wasted his energy on an inconsequential
event. The strain of his long two-day drive, the
frustration of the day's investigations, his concern for his brother's whereabouts, and his apprehension of the coming interview were all
interfering with his thinking. He should have
known that O'Reilley had just gone for a beer.

He let himself relax. His hearing returned to
normal, and the night was once again silent. It
took energy to cast even small spells like that,
and more energy to maintain them. It was fool-
hardy to tire himself further now. He might
need all the energy he could muster later.

Car headlights coming up the street made him
take a step back, deeper into the tall bushes.
Phoebus, balancing perfectly, kept on purring.
The car passed, the street became silent and
dark again, and he returned to his place.

Nothing had changed at O'Reilley's house.
Morgan felt he shouldn't have much longer to
wait. In anticipation, he started the first part of
another spell.

As before, he did it all in his mind. He visualized the signs, the gestures, the words, making them as real-seeming as he could. He felt
the subtle changes in the Lattice as the spell
took hold. The aura that surrounded him briefly

was red this time. But just before he finished, he stopped short, holding back the last little bit.

Casting a spell took time, sometimes just seconds, more usually a moment or two, and sometimes, if it were complex enough, as much as several hours. By holding back this way—by leaving the last digit undialed, as it were—however long it took to prepare a spell, he could finish it in a fraction of a second.

And if O'Reilley behaved as Weiss had, that might be all the time he would have.

Across the street the living-room light went off. Morgan steadied his mind, made sure his incomplete spell was secure in its corner. He could lose it if he was sufficiently distracted, and could not hold more than one spell at a time that way.

Another window went dark across the street. There were no cars coming. He left his hiding place calmly, quickly. As he did so, Phoebus made like the Cheshire cat, slowly faded, and was invisible by the time Morgan mounted the steps of O'Rcilley's porch. The yellow light over the door flicked out. He rapped at the door frame.

His timing was perfect. The light came back on at once and the door opened. A man in his early thirties looked out, about Morgan's height but quite a bit heavier.

"I'm looking for Michael Scott," Morgan said. The smell of beer was almost overpowering. Morgan stilled his anxieties, kept his expression bland, calm, pleasant, and watched O'Reilley's eyes as the other considered him.

"He's not here," O'Reilley said. His almost-handsome face showed just the barest sign of

irritation. But there was no trace of befuddlement, other than simple intoxication.

"I didn't really expect him to be," Morgan
said, "but I thought, since you're a friend of his,
that you might know where he was, or how I
could get in touch with him."

"No way," O'Reilley said. He started to close
the door. Morgan put his hand against it and
stopped him.

"Just a minute, please. I've talked to all his
other friends. George Faircloth doesn't know
anything. Cindy Vann doesn't know anything.
Even Gary Weiss doesn't know anything.
They've all had their memories fuddled, but not
you, Mr. O'Reilley. Let's talk about it."

"Sorry, friend," O'Reilley said, "you've just
hit a dead end." His eyes narrowed with concentration, his fingers started to twitch, and his
lips moved in the first syllables of an incantation.

It was for this that Morgan had prepared his
spell. All it needed for completion was for him
to specify the target. As the air around O'Reilley's hands started to shimmer, Morgan pointed
his finger, felt the drain and the thrill, and
O'Reilley convulsed in galvanic shock. At the
same time, O'Reilley's body was surrounded
momentarily by a quick flash of lavender aura,
which revealed the fiery nature of the spell that
he had been preparing.

O'Reilley fell and lay twitching on the floor of
his entrance hall. The shock Morgan had given
him was not intended to kill, only to incapaci-
tate the victim for a moment or two. O'Reilley
would come around soon enough.

Morgan entered the house with two quick,

tense strides. He closed the door behind him against the possibility of prying eyes, then knelt over the twitching man.

"What kind of person attacks another without provocation?" Morgan asked. "The only reason I had a spell waiting was that I was attacked just a few hours ago by another magician. I don't mean you any harm. Can't we just talk?"

O'Reilley's eyes, which had been staring in opposite directions, came into focus. "You're a magician," he said, "and you're not of the Lodge. I'm not talking to you." His voice was thick with shock and intoxication, but he was recovering quickly.

"Yes, you will talk to me," Morgan said calmly, though the mention of the Lodge made his hackles rise. "You know about this. Where is Michael Scott?" He prepared his spell again, quickly, hoping that the light in the foyer was bright enough to conceal the faint aura it generated.

"You gotta be kidding," O'Reilley said, snickering. Morgan thought he saw the shadows around him move subtly. O'Reilley could work spells in his mind too, even while drunk, and that was a frightening power. But Morgan's spell was ready. He touched O'Reilley's temple. The man convulsed again. As before, he was surrounded briefly by the aura of a dissipating spell, but this time it was black, an entropy spell.

In spite of his intoxication, O'Reilley was too fast, too strong. Morgan's heart thudded as he prepared the shock spell one more time. If O'Reilley hadn't been drunk, Morgan would have been dead by now, and that realization made him break out in a sweat. Again he left the spell unfinished, saving the last gesture until he should need it.

The jolt he had delivered directly to O'Reilley's head would keep him out for considerably longer than before. Morgan dragged the twitching man into the living room, turned on a table lamp, and looked around. It was a perfectly ordinary, middle-class bachelor's home.

He heaved O'Reilley up and sat him in his own easy chair near the light. He went to sit on the couch opposite, and let himself tremble a moment. The vague outline of a cat appeared on his left shoulder.

"Now?" Phoebus asked.

"Not now," Morgan said, waiting for O'Reilley's twitches to pass.

He was waiting too long. The shock should have worn off by now. In a panic he flung out the last gesture of the spell, even as O'Reilley's gleeful eyes opened.

He was barely in time. Again the other man flopped as the shock ran through him. O'Reilley discharged a red aura this time, an electric spell. The light of the lamp had obscured the telltale signs.

In sudden anger, Morgan hit him with the shock again, and then again. Then, sweating and trembling with reaction at the nearness of his escape, he went and found the bathroom and threw up in the toilet.

He was going to have to be more careful. He finished retching, flushed the toilet, then rinsed his mouth out at the sink.

"He's stronger than you," a distant catly voice said in his left ear.

"I know," Morgan answered. "And a better magician."

He was dangerously depleting his remaining energy, and his fear and anxiety were making the accompanying thrill painful instead of pleasurable. Only surprise and O'Reilley's intoxication had given Morgan the upper hand so far. If he ever lost it, he wouldn't stand a chance, physically or magically. He was sure O'Reilley would kill him if he had the opportunity.

He made sure O'Reilley was still unconscious when he came back to the living room. He was determined he would not be fooled again. He prepared the shock spell yet one more time, went back to the couch, and waited.

O'Reilley's use of magic was proof to Morgan that the other was an Initiate, not just a Novice. Also called Servants, they were Satanists of a sort, organized into groups they called Lodges. They were people who had sold their souls to the Intelligence which personified the forces of entropic dissolution and ultimate death. The rest of the world called that Intelligence the Principle of Evil, or simply, the Devil. Morgan had other names for it.

He made himself relax, made sure O'Reilley was still unconscious, made sure his spell was secure. He didn't want to have to use it again if he could avoid it. Hitting O'Reilley with shocks all the time wouldn't accomplish anything, and could damage him physically or mentally. The question was, how to make the man talk.

Morgan knew no spells specifically designed for that purpose, though there were one or two in his grimoire that might serve. But his grimoire was still out in his car, and he dared not take the time to go get it now. He'd have to figure out a method of interrogation from the spells he could cast without its help.

Perhaps hypnotic suggestion, he thought, augmented by magic. But he was too tired to do both that and keep the other spell in his mind at the same time. He let the shock spell dissipate in a brief red flicker, and twisted his hand into the classic position, known the world over because of its use in bad movies and television shows.

He started to trace the sigil that would open the telepathic aperture. He was sure O'Reilley would have some idea where Michael was, what had happened to him. The thought of his brother, and the anxiety he felt for him, distracted him a moment, and he did not get his arm up in time to deflect the blow from the table lamp that was suddenly in O'Reilley's hand. His head exploded in a million colors, and he felt himself falling. But not to the carpeted floor. There was gritty sand underneath his hands.

Chapter Five
✤ ✤ ✤

THE SURFACE ON which he lay was rough and sandy. Light shone through his closed eyelids. The throbbing in his head gradually changed from a distant perception to a present pain. Slowly his thoughts cleared as the immediate effects of the concussion wore off.

He should be dead. That he wasn't was not completely reassuring. He made himself relax, to hasten his recovery. When he opened his eyes his vision blurred for a moment. Then he was looking along an expanse of coarse, dry sand. It was so quiet he could hear his own heart beating, his watch ticking.

He raised himself up on his elbows. The effort made his head throb, and his vision blurred again. He sat up and waited for the pain to pass.

There was no sign of O'Reilley or the lamp base. There was nothing but the sandy plain, the sky that looked too blue, an impossibly distant horizon, and his cat, sitting a few feet away. Morgan got to his feet with the somehow certain feeling that he was not on Earth.

He turned around, scanning the emptiness. Directly behind him was a smudge of smoke rising from what looked like a burning building. It was impossible to tell just how far away it was, since there was nothing else with which to compare its size, but he guessed it to be several miles.

He looked down at the ground at his feet. Except for the disturbed place where he had lain,

and a few pawprints near Phoebus, there were
no marks of any kind on the dry surface. He'd
gotten here without traversing the physical
space between this seemingly infinite plain and
O'Reilley's living room. Morgan was not capable of performing a feat like that.

He looked for the sun. There was none. The
too-blue sky brightened overhead, but there was
no solar disk, nor any clouds to conceal it.

His head hurt, so he sat back down and gently probed at the wound on his scalp. The skin
was unbroken, but there was a growing lump,
just on the hairline on the right side. Even
though it would be a drain on what little magical energy he had left, the casting of a healing
spell seemed more than justified.

He put his hand in the Life position—thumb
tip touching forefinger, the other fingers extended. In this fashion he "grasped" those
strands of the Lattice that affected the life processes. He laid his hand over the swelling on his
head to direct the influence of the magical warp-
age. Then he chanted the incantation, the
words vibrating in the Lattice, generating the
resonances of the Heal Wound spell. *"Raelaengie-
raerietsah,"* he said.

It was a simple spell. At once the pain in his
head went away, as did the nausea he hadn't
been aware of, and the swelling started to go
down. It would still be an hour or so before he
was back to normal. The only drawback was
that, in spite of the pleasure of the successful
casting, his reserve of magical energy was now
even more depleted.

He took out one of his little cigars and
snapped his fingers. The tiny blue flame ap-

peared on the end of his up-pointing thumb. Even this small spell had its accompanying thrill. He lit his cigar; the flame went out. Phoebus climbed into his lap and lay down.

He petted the cat idly as he thought about his present circumstances. In spite of the seeming solidity of the plain on which he sat, he knew he was in some astral realm, a place not separated from the world by time or distance, but by other dimensions he did not understand.

"I guess O'Reilley was a lot more powerful than I thought," he said.

"Or someone else is helping him," the cat purred.

Now was not the time to try to figure out how he'd gotten here; that could wait till later. His immediate problem was how to get back. He was not an experienced astral traveler, and had no idea of the direction to take. The only thing he could do was to ask for help. He hated to do that, and his independence had more than once gotten him into trouble with his teacher, and with their patron demigod, known as the Dreamer. This time, however, there seemed to be little other choice. That didn't make him any happier.

He pushed Phoebus off his lap and got to his feet again. He held out his hand in the proper position, traced the sparkling, pale-yellow sigils in the air, and chanted the incantations for Deity Communion.

There was no response. Energy was consumed, but there was no thrill of pleasure. Morgan was disappointed, but not surprised. Calling up those noncorporeal beings people called demigods was difficult at best, and Mor-

gan was negligent about practicing it. It didn't
help any that he was exhausted and magically
depleted, or that he was angry with himself for
having gotten into this mess.

He made himself relax for a moment, and
tried to clear the anxiety and frustration from
his mind. Then once again he put up his hand,
with the first two fingers extended. He traced
the sigils and chanted the words. Still no response. More energy wasted.

"You're out of practice," the cat told him.

"I know, Phoebus," Morgan said.

He wasn't thinking clearly. The Dreamer was
a being of considerable power, not just a nature
spirit, numen, or genius loci. It would be better
and easier, he thought, to call up one of those
lesser beings instead. He knew the basic spell,
though it was not an area of magic he was very
fond of. He threw down his cigar butt.

He forced himself to be calm, and tried to
clear his thoughts again. He took his time, re-
laxing, getting control of himself. He made the
sign, traced the sigils. The air sparkled. He
spoke the incantation: *"Hlaedae Meloy, Kehdae-
tsehshah Meloy, Shahrie-daerieshie Meloy."*

As he spoke he gestured first with one hand,
then with the other, then both together. He
traced the figure of the sigil in the air, a loop
to the right, a hook, then diagonally down to
the left, and this time there was a thin thread
of pale-yellow and lavender fire in the air as he
did so. The exhilaration of success made his
heart beat faster.

The air shimmered in front of him and the
glittering humanoid form of a *meloy* began to
take shape. It was one of the golden ones, tall,

bright, its scales glittering, its wings arched, its eyes fiery and knowing, its claws and great teeth glinting white. After just a moment the dragon-angel, what most people might have thought of as a kind of fire elemental, stood before him, almost painful to look at.

"Why have you called?" the *meloy* asked. Its "voice" was a crystal bass chime that hurt Morgan's ears. Phoebus rubbed up against its scaley ankles.

"I need help," Morgan answered simply.

"So it would appear. You are far from your own world."

"Yes, please. Can you help me get back home?"

"You have been fighting with your fellows again. You do not want me to take sides in this affair, I hope?" the *meloy* asked, its voice terrible. Phoebus purred.

"Of course I do, but I'm not asking that."

The *meloy* laughed, and if the sound hadn't been so beautiful, Morgan would have cried out in pain.

"Very well," the *meloy* said. **"I shall return you to whence you came—approximately."**

Without transition, Morgan was standing in the shabby lobby of an old hotel, his suitcase by his feet, facing the reservation desk.

PART TWO

There are two kinds of life in the universe, the life we know, and the Other Life, which includes all the demigods and demons, and other forces of nature less easily classifiable.

Other Life came first, born out of the hot gasses and radiation when the first stars were forming. It has evolved for far longer than planetary life, but that evolution has been a lot slower. Its life processes are different; they do not breed and die the same way we do. The creatures of Other Life have no physical bodies. They are beings of pure energy, without mass.

Planetary life is roughly divided into viruses, fungi, plants, animals, and so on. Other Life is similarly divided, though not at all related to planetary life. And while there is every gradation of complexity, from something analogous to a virus, to beings roughly comparable with humans, some forms are unique, a species with only one member. Other species are as numerous as ants. They do not fill space the way mundane life forms fill their planets, and for all practical purposes, each individual is immortal. Like planetary life, Other Life occasionally achieves intelligence.

Some of these Other Intelligences live between the stars and galaxies, and visit the Earth, or other similar worlds, only seldom. Others live near the Earth and visit it frequently, though usually unperceived by men and women. They are intangible, noncorporeal.

Yet when they do appear to humans, they seem to have a form, each characteristic of its own kind. It is only by these illusory forms, and by the things they sometimes do, that they are known to human beings. When they are perceived, they are called gods—or demons.

On Earth there are very few intelligent species, but among Other Life there are hundreds. They, like Earth's great apes, cetacians, and humans, range in intelligence and ability, and some are beyond us. While those who are sentient have great power, in their own way, that power is not unlimited.

The gods, demigods, angels, demons, and all the other forms of Other Life are as much a part of the real universe as are stars and humans.

Chapter Six

✛ ✛ ✛

WELL, MORGAN THOUGHT, the *meloy* had said "approximately." He stepped up to the desk, looked at the register for the name of the hotel. It was the House of Aaron in Harborbeach. His suitcase was right here beside him, with Phoebus sitting on top of it. His car was probably still at O'Reilley's house. Might as well check in, he thought, though this was not the kind of place he would normally have chosen.

There was nobody in the shabby lobby or behind the battered desk. He glanced through the double doors to the street. It was still night outside. The clock above the pigeonholes said one-fifteen. He reached for the bell on the desktop and rang it.

A tired-looking man, as gray and dingy as the hotel lobby, appeared from a back room behind the desk and raised his eyebrows in mute inquiry.

"A single," Morgan said. "For a week."

"The cat, too?" the clerk asked.

"Ah, yes, I hope it's all right."

"That will be ten dollars extra." The clerk turned to the pigeonholes and from one of them took a key. He handed it to Morgan and indicated the register.

Morgan had concealed his identity up to now and, in light of what had happened to him since arriving in Harborbeach, he thought it more important than ever that he continue to do so. O'Reilley would have friends, other Initiates and Novices in the Lodge, and they would be certain to hear about Morgan's visit. They might be able to trace him here, and if they found his real name on the register they'd have a powerful advantage over him. So, instead, Morgan signed the register with the name he'd used earlier that day: Lester Van Alan.

"Ninety-seven fifty," the clerk said. Morgan paid, took the key, picked up his suitcase, let Phoebus jump up onto his shoulder, and went toward the elevators. A faded sign, reading "Out of Order," was taped across the doors.

His room was on the seventh floor. He sighed, found the stairs, and started up. Phoebus eased his burden by jumping down and climbing the stairs under his own power.

It was a miracle that the hotel had passed any safety inspections. The stairs, spiraling clockwise around a square stairwell, were steel-framed wooden treads, bolted to the wall. But the bolts were loose, and the stairs shook with every step. The light was dim, the railing was loose, some of the stairs sloped, and in places there was a noticeable gap between them and the wall, which seemed none too sound itself. The paint was dingy, dark, gray and brown, scarred and stained by time and thousands of people.

With every upward step he was afraid the whole construction would go crashing down. In spite of his apprehension, however, he made it to the seventh floor. He followed the arrow along the corridor to the left.

The floors were not level. The walls were bowed. Doors hung crookedly in their jambs. The ceiling lights were feeble, the carpet was worn, and a smell of ... darkness hung in the air.

He found his room, let himself in, and switched on the light. Phoebus prowled around, checking into all the corners.

A bed, chair, dresser, small table, lamp, and throw rug were the only furnishings. There was no television, no phone. There was a closet, and a tiny bath, for which Morgan was thankful. He'd been afraid it was going to be at the end of the hall or something like that.

He put his suitcase down and lay on the bed. Phoebus jumped up and curled up in his armpit. For a moment Morgan was tempted to just go to sleep, but there was too much to do. Though Michael had been missing for six weeks already, further delay in finding out what had happened to him might make a difference. When he felt the black fuzziness of sleep trying to overwhelm him, he forced himself to get up and start unpacking his suitcase.

"Do you think O'Reilley's being a Servant is just a coincidence?" Phoebus asked.

"It could be," Morgan answered, "but I don't really think so."

"Then the Lodge as a whole is involved."

"Well, this one in particular, at least, though I can't imagine what they might be up to."

"Even if O'Reilley knows," Phoebus said, "he's not likely to tell you."

"And if you think I'm going to ask him, you're crazy."

"You're afraid of him."

"I am that," Morgan admitted. His years in the marines had taught him all he needed to know to defend himself from gun, knife, or fist.

And his magical training would have made him more than a match for any Novice, or even most Initiates. But ... "Logan O'Reilley is just too strong," Morgan went on, hating to admit it, "and a better magician. And from the nature of the spells he attempted, I'm sure he would be less hesitant than most Servants to just kill me out of hand."

"But he did hesitate," Phoebus pointed out, "and he had plenty of chances."

"I know, and that bothers me because I can't explain why."

"So what are you going to do?"

"I don't think I could learn anything from O'Reilley by direct confrontation, even if I dared. That means I'll have to work on the sly."

"You could hurt yourself if you use spells you're not familiar with," Phoebus cautioned.

"More than likely they'll just fail, but I'll be careful."

"Like you have been so far?"

"I know, I know, but that's just because I'm tired."

"So get a few hours sleep. That will make everything easier."

"There's no sense putting off what has to be done. And besides, early morning is the best time for stealth. The longer I wait, the more likely it will be that O'Reilley can counter my efforts." He picked up the journal, which had been the last thing in his suitcase.

This was his grimoire. It contained, besides those spells he knew, others that he had copied but not yet completely learned, including several for astral projection. He guessed he'd have about a seventy percent chance of success on the first try, given the difficulty of the spell, its complexity, and his own level of scholarship—reduced, of course, for his mental fuzziness and fatigue.

He turned the pages until he found the spell he wanted, one that simply projected his astral self from his body, allowing it to travel invisibly. It was a simple chant: *Rahdierah-tsehshah.* He had not practiced it, and could only guess at the proper intent, frame of mind, and degree of concentration. But his guesses would be educated ones. He had been studying magic for over ten years.

He put the grimoire on the dresser, locked the door, sat in the chair, made himself comfortable, and cleared his mind.

Working magic was really quite easy, once one had the knack of finding and feeling the Lattice, but Morgan didn't know this spell and had to devote his full attention to it. He concentrated on the words. He didn't have to actually say them if he could think them clearly enough. They were syllables of a language older than the Earth. It wasn't the words themselves but the resonances they set up in his mind that affected the Lattice.

Nothing happened. Phoebus, from his place on the bed, looked at him.

"You should consult the Dreamer," the cat said.

"It's all right, I'm just going to look around a little bit." He thought the words again. Still nothing.

"You don't want to get the Dreamer angry with you," Phoebus cautioned.

"I know, I know." He tried a third time, this time saying the words out loud.

He felt the thrill this time. He felt light, weightless, disembodied. He looked down and saw his body seated in the chair. The spell had worked at last, though it had taken him three tries, and cost him three times the energy it should have.

Astral travel was not without its dangers and difficulties, especially for someone in Morgan's depleted state. But if he was careful he should be able to do what he wanted without coming to harm.

He floated, intangible and invisible, across the room to the window. Only the all-but-fictitious silver cord connected his astral self with his seemingly sleeping body. He passed through the glass and out over the city below. Phoebus would have to stay behind this time.

This was only the most elementary form of astral travel. He had not left the mundane planes. An adept could pass on into strange realms, such as the sandy plain from which the *meloy* had rescued him, or exist in astral form for extended periods, or affect the mundane world from his or her astral position. Morgan would have to be satisfied with drifting, and would have to return to his body within a few hours. He could touch nothing in the mundane world, and nothing could touch him. Or almost nothing.

He floated up into the night air to get a bird's-eye view of the city and to get his bearings. After a moment of looking around, he figured out where he was and drifted over the dark, crooked streets, the bizarre architecture of the central business district, toward the residential area where O'Reilley lived. His progress was not fast, but he had time enough.

He found the street he wanted and drifted up it, just inches above the sidewalk. There were still a few cars out this late at night. Their headlights shone through him. A solitary pedestrian passed through his intangible self and shivered, then walked on. Morgan came to O'Reilley's house. His car was not where he had left it.

The house was all dark now. Morgan drifted in through the closed and locked door. It was pitch black inside, but in his astral form Morgan could see, even so. Everything was black on black, yet perfectly distinct. Had the curtains been open, letting in the pale glimmer from outside, that would not have helped, nor hindered.

The living room was as he'd last seen it, but the smashed lamp was now lying on the floor in front of the couch.

Morgan went to the bedroom, but O'Reilley wasn't there. He searched the whole house, but the man was gone. He went back to the bedroom.

On top of the dresser, in front of a mirror, were the usual toilet articles, including a brush with hair in it. With just a little bit of hair a properly trained magician could learn a lot. Even Morgan could learn something. The only question was how to get the hair back to his hotel room.

He was so tired that it took him a long moment before he thought of trying a teleport spell, to move not himself but just the hair in the brush. It was a spell he had not perfected, but there was no harm in trying.

He went over the spell once in his mind. Then, with one hand in Space position, he traced the sigil; up, down, loop and hook. With the other hand occupying the same space as the hairbrush, though he could not feel or touch it, he chanted the words inaudibly, concentrating on hair and hotel room at the same time. It worked on the first try, though the sensation of pleasure was muted by his astral condition. The brush was still on the dresser, but now clean of all hair.

His exhaustion was numbing now, but he floated through the house one more time. He didn't really know what he was looking for, and finding nothing of interest, he at last gave up.

He left the house, thought of his own body, and let the natural attraction pull him along, the silver cord glimmering in front of him. He floated through the night-lit city, back to his room, over to his body, sat down in it, and felt the click and jar as he returned to himself. Clutched in his left hand was a tangle of hair.

"Enough?" Phoebus asked from the bed.

"Enough," Morgan said.

"Will you call your teacher in the morning?"

"Yes, Phoebus, I will."

He could no longer deny his need for rest. It was after four in the morning. If he was going to be at all effective the next day, he'd have to get some rest now. He put the hair in a dresser drawer, took off his clothes, fell into bed, and was asleep even before Phoebus could curl up in his armpit.

Chapter Seven
❖ ❖ ❖

HE AWOKE SHORTLY after nine, much refreshed and anxious to get to work. He washed and dressed quickly, put Phoebus on his shoulder, and left the room. Phoebus accepted the ride this time as he went down the rickety stairs to the lobby in search of breakfast.

The hotel had no dining facilities, not even a coffee shop. Morgan asked the day clerk, who named several fast-food places nearby.

He went out to the street. The cool air of morning was remarkably clean for a town that lived on small industry. He found a McDougal's just two blocks away. He left Phoebus at an outside table, went in to order, and bought an extra Mighty Mac for Phoebus. They ate outside, Phoebus drawing attention as he always did. As they left the restaurant, Phoebus got back on Morgan's shoulder and purred into his left ear, reminding him of his promise to call his teacher.

"It's too early in the morning back there," Morgan protested, keeping his voice low so the pedestrians wouldn't hear.

"You're just being stubborn," Phoebus said in a near whisper. "Do you think you can handle a Lodge of Servants all by yourself?"

"Dammit, you know I hate to ask for help."

"So don't ask for help," Phoebus insisted. "Just tell him where you are, and what you've discovered so far. There's a phone booth across the street."

Morgan walked stiffly to the corner and crossed. He knew Phoebus was right. He went back to the gas station where the booth was located and fished in his pocket for change. He could call collect; his teacher wouldn't worry about reversed charges.

He dialed the operator, placed his call, and waited while the phone at the other end rang. After ten rings the operator told him nobody was answering. He thanked her. "I'll try again later," he said, and hung up.

"How about Starkpoole," Phoebus suggested, "or Valentine," naming other magicians Morgan knew.

He tried them. The results were the same. "I guess nobody's at home," he said. He found the lack of success oddly disconcerting.

"This is too much of a coincidence," Phoebus started to say and then suddenly shut up. A woman was approaching the booth, as if she wanted to use the phone. Morgan stepped aside and started walking back to the hotel. "I'll try again later," he reassured the cat.

On his return to his room Phoebus made himself comfortable on the bed while Morgan got the mat of hair from the dresser. He looked at it for a long moment, familiarizing himself with its color and texture. Then, grimoire in hand, he tried a psychometric reading.

On the third try the spell worked, but all it told him was that O'Reilley was thirty-four, an alcoholic, a bachelor, prone to violent fits of temper, deceitful, overly proud, and lots of other things that might have been interesting but weren't very helpful.

"If you're going to do things like that," Phoebus said, "you should talk to the Dreamer first. Besides, if you can't contact your teacher or your friends, you may really need help."

Morgan sighed. It was only pride, he knew, that made him reluctant to do that. "Might as well," he said at last. He put the hair down on the table beside his chair, closed his eyes, and went through the spell for Deity Communion.

After the fourth futile attempt, he gave up. Each time he cast the spell he expended more energy.

"I can't get through," he said. Phoebus jumped up on his lap. "It's almost as if something were blocking me."

"Not the Lodge," Phoebus purred.

"No."

"Your own anxiety."

"Probably." He picked up the hair again. His failure to communicate with his patron, after he had decided to do so, discouraged him. He turned the hair over and over in his hands.

There was another spell he'd seen done once before, which summoned a fragment of a person's soul, using hair like this. It wasn't in his grimoire, which meant he wouldn't be able to perform it without all kinds of paraphernalia— simple stuff, but things he didn't usually carry with him. He tried to remember it as he'd seen it done.

He hadn't participated in the ritual, merely observed as his teacher had gone through the spell the long way. The hand positions, sigil tracings, and chants that Morgan regularly used were the product of much refinement, after a spell's basic elements were determined and codified. Morgan had developed a few such spells himself—none very important—such as his cigar-lighting trick.

He visualized the Soul Summoning ritual, then made up a shopping list. He put the hair back in its drawer, in case the maid came in while he was out. It wouldn't do to have her throw it away. Then, with Phoebus in his usual place on his left shoulder, he went back down to the street.

He found rubbing alcohol, an aluminum dog dish, and a box of crayons at a nearby drugstore. But he couldn't find the small candles he wanted, and by the time he decided to get large ones instead and cut them down to size, it was after one. He had lunch, then tried calling his teacher and other fellow magicians again. Still nobody was at home, even an acquaintance named Andrade whom he'd met only once. By the time he got back to his room, it was nearly two.

He cleared off the top of the dresser and, with Phoebus sitting at one corner watching him, drew a pentagram across its surface, using a crayon of a medium shade of purple. This was the color of Spirit, the major component of the spell.

Then, using a darker purple crayon, he drew a fylfot cross in the middle of the pentagram. This was to affect Space, to bridge the distance between him and O'Reilley.

"Should you really be doing this?" Phoebus asked.

"O'Reilley knows what happened to Michael," Morgan said grimly, "and I'm going to find out."

"Meddling with other people's souls is dangerous," the cat warned. "Your shocking him is probably why you can't reach the Dreamer."

"I know."

"And if the Dreamer is *really* angry with you, that may be why you can't reach anybody else."

"I know, I know!"

He put the dog dish in the middle of the pentagram on the intersection of the arms of the cross, then cut the candles short and stuck them on the cross's ends. Then he poured alcohol into the dish and dropped in the mat of hair.

Without a formalized spell, he had to write out the incantation in full and translate it into Raen, the language that was used for all magical chants. He would have to use the full procedure instead of the short forms to which most spells had been reduced.

He pulled the blinds closed on the window to darken the room as much as possible. Then he put the paper with the long incantation against the mirror behind the dish, where he could read it while working the rest of the spell. He snapped his fingers, through the Fire position in the special way he had taught himself, and the little blue flame danced on the end of his thumb.

He touched the fire to the four candles, then to the dish of alcohol. A bright blue flame leapt up from the dish, almost two feet tall. Phoebus's eyes glinted iridescent green in its light. It was a good thing there were no smoke alarms in this building, Morgan thought, or the alcohol flame would have set them off.

Remembering the hand positions was the hardest part. They were all very similar, fingers folded or extended, pressed together or separated, in various combinations. With his left hand he took the Spirit position, with his right the Command position.

Now the sigils, the looping movement through the air, one for each hand. With his right he traced Psychometric Trace. With his left he tried Spiritual Analogue. Purple and violet sparks marked the lines of the movement.

"Psychic Analogue," Phoebus corrected. "Both hands in Command position."

"Right, right." He tried again, both hands with fingers and thumbs outstretched. "Then objectification and a command to obedience," he said to himself. He held his palms toward the flame, moving them through the patterns of the sigils. Again, thin threads of fire, all violet this time, followed his movements. He read the incantation propped up against the mirror behind the flame, focusing his attention on the results he wanted.

Nothing happened, though he could feel the energy flow out of him like water down a drain. Magic wasn't free; the energy was used even when the spell didn't work.

He read the syllables again. This time his whole body thrilled with the ecstasy of successful magic, strong because of the strength of the spell. The flame jumped, condensed, wavered, and formed into the image of a little man, all blue fire, shimmering and shifting, but with the unmistakable features of Logan O'Reilley.

"Where are you, Logan?" Morgan demanded. The flame figure grimaced, threw out its hands, and a tiny voice moaned. Except for the continuing exhilaration of the spell still in operation, that was all.

"It's not going to work," Phoebus said, staring at the flame figure.

Morgan ignored the cat. "Logan," he said again, "where is Michael Scott?"

The little flame figure twisted, its face anguished, its limbs contorted. This wasn't the way it was supposed to respond. Morgan had gotten the Psychic Analogue; it should answer his questions. He repeated the part of the incantation that demanded obedience. The alcohol level in the dish was getting low, and some of the hair was burning. The figure in the fire looked at him and cried out meaninglessly in its tiny voice.

"Logan, tell me, where are you?" Morgan commanded again. The image's only response was to go through an odd kind of transformation. Morgan felt intense disappointment and bitter frustration. It would be useless to question the image further.

"I told you so," Phoebus said.

Morgan didn't bother to answer. He let his hold on the Lattice dissipate. The sensation of thrill faded to a subtle depression. He blew out the alcohol fire and the candles, opened the window blinds, and threw himself on the bed. Maybe O'Reilley had known where Michael was, and maybe not, but it was now beyond Morgan's power to extract that or any other information from him. Logan O'Reilley was dead.

Chapter Eight

✢ ✢ ✢

MORGAN WAS NOT a master magician, though he had been studying magic for over ten years, since his third year in the marines when he'd met his teacher. He benefited from having a natural flair and the ability to hold a spell in his mind to be used at a later time, and he was adept at unconscious manipulation. That didn't help him at the moment, however. He lay on the bed, staring at the fly-specked ceiling, going over the few choices he had left.

If he could just get Weiss to listen to him for a moment, he might be able to elicit the man's aid, maybe even learn something about what was going on in this town. But Weiss was paranoid. Morgan did not think he could be of much help.

Weiss should have known that O'Reilley was a Servant, that there was a Lodge in Harborbeach. Instead, Weiss was probably completely unaware of O'Reilley's existence. Otherwise, they would have fought it out long before. Morgan thought all the less of him for his lack of perception. Still, Morgan would have to try to talk to Weiss again sooner or later.

Phoebus jumped up on the bed, and lay down stretched out along Morgan's chest, his face just inches from Morgan's chin. Morgan petted the silky red and black fur idly as he thought about O'Reilley's fire image.

Its transformation had indicated that O'Reilley had died, but not by disease or accident. He had been taken, his body destroyed, and his soul, or spirit, or psychic residue, whatever one wanted to call it, had been put in a kind of prison. Bottled, was the term.

It was as if someone had known that Morgan would be trying the very thing he had tried. O'Reilley's self-awareness had been carefully preserved, and gagged more effectively than simple death could ever have done. No decent magician would do that kind of thing. That was the work of a Servant of Death.

Morgan thought it over and over as he lay on the bed. The strain of the last two days had not been completely eliminated by his short night's rest, and he drifted off into a light sleep. He woke when the lowering sun struck his eyes through the window.

"Time to get up," Phoebus said from the windowsill.

"I know, I know."

He got out of bed and tried again to contact the Dreamer. Again he had no success. Phoebus watched him, and though his familiar didn't say anything, Morgan knew what the cat was thinking, that his fight with O'Reilley had not helped things any, and that his attempt to query O'Reilley's soul had cut him off from the Dreamer even more.

"How about some supper?" Phoebus suggested.

"Right, but first I have to find out what happened to my car."

"Check the parking lot."

"I left it at O'Reilley's house," Morgan protested.

"Was it there when you visited last night?"
Phoebus asked.

"No, it wasn't."

"Well, then? The *meloy* brought your suitcase; maybe it brought the car too."

"Whatever you say," Morgan said. He put
Phoebus on his shoulder and went down to the
hotel parking lot. His car was there.

He climbed in behind the wheel and lit one of
his small cigars while Phoebus made himself
comfortable on the passenger's seat. Then Morgan drove through town to Michael's house. He
didn't stop when he got there but drove on by.
There were too many people around now. It was
early evening, and there were barbecue fires going next door.

That, and a few words from Phoebus, reminded Morgan why he had come out in the
first place. He drove back into town, had supper, and bought something extra for the cat. Another try at calling his teacher and his fellow
magicians proved fruitless.

Phoebus ate the hamburger as they drove
back to Michael's house. They got there just as
the streetlights were going on. He pulled into
the driveway beside the house and parked in
front of the garage. The whole front yard was
deeply shadowed. That suited Morgan just fine.

He got out of the car, and with Phoebus walking beside him went up onto the porch. Morgan
stared at the double front door. There was a
faint glimmer of deep, olive drab as it opened
to his simple, unspoken spell. The cat preceded
him into the house, the door closed behind him
and locked. Another silent spell created a pale
pink luminescence around him that would en-

able him to see but that would not be visible to anyone glancing at the windows from outside.

He was standing in an entrance hall. Coats hung from a bar on his left, over a trunk. A dresser stood against the far wall. On the right was another door, standing open. He went through into a living room.

The familiarity struck him, though he'd never been in this room before. Yet this house seemed like a place he'd known for a long time. It was as if he had grown up here.

"That's an illusion," Phoebus said, standing near his feet.

Morgan was just perceiving a form of psychic residue, Michael's aura imprinted on the house and all its furnishings. However long their separation, he and Michael had always been close.

He glanced at the chairs, the couch, the end tables, the pictures on the walls. The pale ghost light he emitted just barely enabled him to make out a few details. Phoebus prowled, quickly and cautiously.

It looked as if Michael had just gone out for the evening. He'd owned this house for only two months, had lived in it for only a couple of weeks if he had disappeared when Morgan thought he had, but the furniture had been his before he'd moved in. And there was a huge emotional investment here, enough to make up for years of living.

At the back of the living room was an open stair going up to the second floor. But first Morgan wanted to check out the rest of the ground floor.

On the left was a wide door into the dining room. Morgan went through and stood by the

table with its four chairs. There was a china
cabinet to one side. Again, all was normal. On
the far side of the room were two more doors.
Phoebus went over to one of them.

"Cellars," the cat said.

Morgan opened the other door. Beyond was
the kitchen. There was food in the refrigerator,
cans on the shelves, all normal, all as it should
be. Except that it hadn't been touched for six
weeks.

To the left was the door to the back porch.
Another door led to the garage, inside of which
was Michael's Chevy truck, some tools, a lawn
mower, a hose, some boxes, a stack of old newspapers.

He went back through the kitchen to a laun-
dry. There were clothes in the dryer.

"Cellars?" Phoebus asked.

"Yes," Morgan said. "Now the basement."

He went back to the dining room and through
the other door. The stairs down were open on
the right. Phoebus ran down ahead of him.
In the main room below were the furnace, water heater, a workbench, more tools.

There were two smaller rooms, one set up as
a shop for loading shells and working on guns.
The other was filled with junk and stuff too valuable to throw away but not good enough to
use.

"There's nothing wrong here," Phoebus said,
as if confused.

"I know," Morgan said. "It's all too damn
normal."

There was no clue here as to where Michael
had gone. Morgan suppressed his anxiety and
frustration, and went back up to the first floor,

through the dining room to the living room, and up the stairs to a second-floor hall.

The bedroom on the right was obviously a spare. Phoebus just glanced in, and immediately lost interest. Another room on the left was Michael's; Morgan could feel his brother's aura through the closed door, where Phoebus was waiting expectantly.

"We'll save that for later," Morgan said.

Next, on the right, was a bathroom, then two more bedrooms opposite each other. Though Michael had never admitted it, his purchase of a four-bedroom house confirmed his serious intentions about Cindy Vann. But that made his disappearance even more disturbing. It was unlikely he would have gone off of his own free will.

At last it was time to visit Michael's room. It was just a bedroom, with bed, dresser, chairs, a desk, photographs on the wall.

Some of the photos were of Morgan and Michael before Morgan had gone off to join the marines thirteen years ago. There were other pictures, of their parents, now dead; of Cindy.

Clothes hung in the closet, were neatly folded in the dresser. There were few empty hangers, no vacant places in the drawers. Michael had left with only the clothes he'd been wearing. And there was still nothing to give any clue as to where he had gone. Nothing physical, anyway.

Morgan lay down on his brother's bed. Phoebus, knowing his intentions, did not join him.

There would be a strong psychic residue here, where Michael had slept, much stronger than anywhere else in the house. If Morgan could get in touch with it, that residue might tell him something, even though Michael was no longer here.

He lay back, closed his eyes, turned off his ghost light, and let himself become attuned to the traces of Michael's mind that whispered around the pillow. Morgan was not an expert dreamer, but in dreams were the answers, he hoped. He blotted out all sensory input, and let the images come.

Chapter Nine

✤ ✤ ✤

HE SLEPT. He dreamed of a dark parlor, opulently modern with square, heavy furniture. The windows were black, the light dim and without source. Dark frames hung on the walls. He couldn't see the pictures they contained.

He stood in the center of the room. There were several people standing around him in a circle. He tried to count them but kept losing track. They moved now. Some went to sit on square chairs, some on square sofas, some on round cushions. They were dark, shadowed, cloaked, unfriendly, mocking.

Poor Michael, someone said. Another chuckled. *Michael wanted the house so badly*, a third person said. He tried to figure out which one. He tried to see their faces, but even though their heads were bare, their faces were obscured.

The house, they said. *Michael wanted the*

house. And we got it for him. Now he owes. And then they were all laughing, soundless, motionless, yet moving in a jeering circle. Eyes in the wall stared. *Michael owes,* they said, and another voice spoke.

"What will you pay for the shop, Michael?"

"Anything," Michael answered. "Almost."

Almost? they jeered. *It's yours now. You owe. Briarly is dead, his heirs have sold. Aren't you grateful?*

"For the shop, yes; for Briarly's death, no. Of course not."

"They're one and the same, Michael," the other voice continued. "You wanted it so badly, and he wouldn't sell. Now he's dead, and you owe."

"Owe? What for?"

For the shop, Michael, for the shop. Old Man Briarly would have gone on for another twenty years. You didn't think you were just lucky, did you?

"Of course, what else—?"

It was us, Michael. We did it for you.

"No, that's impossible."

On the contrary, it's quite possible. And it's true. We put a strain on his heart. Such a simple thing to do. And we did it for you.

"Now, wait. Come on. I never asked—"

"But you did, you know," the voice said. "Deep down inside."

"But I never meant—"

Too bad. You coveted. You got. And now you owe. And for the house, too. Surely you don't think that was just more luck? If Mrs. Frost hadn't had those huge medical expenses, she

*never would have sold. So you owe us for that
one too, Michael.*

"My God, you can't mean that! How could you
do such a thing?"

*It was easy, Michael. We couldn't kill her; her
heirs are a bank and a lawyer, and they wouldn't
have sold either. But a bit of cancer, thousands
of dollars in bills, and—*

"But why, why did you do it?"

"You wanted it, Michael. Don't you remember? You wanted it so badly. And now you
owe."

"But I never told you that. I never told anyone about—"

*But we knew, Michael, all the same. We knew.
Aren't you grateful?*

"No!"

"Too bad, Michael, you still owe. You must
sign the contract."

"I'll give it all back."

"To whom? Briarly has been dead for six
years. Mrs. Frost is in a sanitarium. The deeds
have been done, Michael, and it is for what we
did, not the shop or the house, that you owe."

"But why did you do this to me?"

*We need you, Michael. To get the stone. You're
in trouble, Michael. They can trace the poison
to you. We made sure of that. But we'll help you
if you help us.*

"You're monsters!"

Now, now, Michael. They laughed, and moved
away.

He stood there, as the people moved off into
the trees. From somewhere in the forest he saw
the light beaming, a long way off. He started
toward it, walking between the huge trees. He

had to step carefully here; the roots were thick and treacherous. They seemed to twist deliberately to catch his feet.

As he walked, another level of awareness grew. Remembrance came, slowly, that this was a dream. It had all been a dream, and not his own. He should wake up now, wake up and—

He stumbled. He was standing between the house and the woods behind. Shivering, he turned back to see the back door of Michael's house, swinging open behind him. The hammock between the two trees swung idly in an evening breeze. He felt a tug, urging him toward the woods instead.

For a moment he felt panic as, against his will, without his volition, first one foot stepped toward the forest, then the other. But as he remembered more of the dream of the dark parlor, anger replaced the fear. They—whoever they were—had caught Michael in a double bind and sealed it with the kind of obligation Michael would have felt compelled to meet, no matter what.

"They." Though he didn't know their names or faces, he knew that they were Servants, members of the same Lodge to which O'Reilley had belonged—before his death.

They had wanted Michael to sign a contract, to exchange his soul for the "favors" they had done him, so that they could force him to serve them. They had set him up so that, in his own mind at least, he would have no choice but to do what they wanted.

Morgan entered the woods now, holding back just hard enough to give himself time to think. The spell that was pulling him was not all that strong, now that he had a chance to feel and gauge it. One gesture and he could break it.

But he would not do that just yet, nor would he call Phoebus to help him. He wanted first to see where the enemy would lead him. He'd play along for a while.

That was what Michael had done, apparently. He would have yielded on the surface, pretended to do what they wanted, and waited until he got his chance to strike back. He would pay the debt, but not without taking revenge for being put into such a horrible situation. The strength of his resistance to the dream taunters told Morgan that much.

That was where Michael had gone wrong. Michael knew nothing of the occult arts; he could not have known what to do, how to extricate himself from the trouble he was in.

Michael was not the kind of person who went looking for trouble, as Morgan had been in his youth. At the same time, if trouble ever found him, Michael faced up to it without hesitation. He didn't believe in things psychic, in magic. He didn't even know that Morgan was a magician. But he knew how to take care of himself and had always managed to get himself out of any predicament he'd gotten into.

Up until now. If the Lodge had forced him to sign a contract, Michael was in desperate need of help. Morgan hoped that his disappearance was because he had not yet signed, and was being held until he did. That meant Morgan had to work fast, now, because there was no telling how long Michael could hold out. But at the moment, he had other things to worry about.

He saw the clearing up ahead, dimly lit by

moonlight. It was just a small clearing. In the middle was what looked like a mausoleum.

He stepped from the trees, his feet still guided by the spell, and saw the small stone building more clearly. It looked like a more or less typical mausoleum—marble, with verdigrised bronze doors. There was something carved into the lintel overhead, and other markings on the door. Morgan slowed his footsteps, resisting the spell. He wanted to see what those markings were before he entered.

The upper carving was simple, just a single eye. Not an Osiris eye but a Cyclops one, like the mark of some demon.

Morgan struggled against the spell which moved his feet and made his hands undo the latch on the bronze door. He could now see what had been carved on the door, even as the heavy panel swung outward. It was a hollow mark in the shape of a dagger, with a thin, straight blade and a large, round pommel. It looked as though a real dagger had once been embedded there.

He resisted the spell, but only as any normal person would. He didn't know why "they" wanted him in this mausoleum, but if he broke the spell now he would never find out what they wanted with him.

He was sure that they thought him just a simple intruder into Michael's house. Had they thought otherwise their actions toward him would have been more direct and deadly. The longer he could keep them thinking that way, the longer he'd have to prepare himself for his defense later, and the more he'd learn about his destination.

He entered the mausoleum. Sealed niches lined the side walls, three rows of two on each side. At the far end was an ornamental brass urn, three feet tall on a stone base. The chamber was illuminated by a dim light that seemed to come from the air.

His feet moved him toward the urn where, perhaps, someone's ashes lay. As he neared, the marble base slowly slid to one side, revealing a flight of steep stone steps descending into the earth. He came to the steps and started down.

When his head was below floor level, the stone overhead moved back into place. The dim radiance persisted. After a few more steps the stairs turned to the right and still went down.

He hung back as much as he could without revealing his strength. He estimated that he was about twenty feet underground when the steps came to an end in a smooth, featureless, stone-walled corridor. He went on for another twenty feet, then more steps down. If he was going to prepare himself for whatever lay ahead, he'd better get started now.

He needed a strong spell, but the strongest one he could think of required gestures and incantations. He was afraid that if he started it he wouldn't be allowed to finish it.

The steps ended, and he passed two doors set into the stone walls, one on either side, both closed. They were single slabs of slate, carved with strange symbols. It was hard to tell how old this place was, but it looked a lot older than the twentieth century.

Whatever spell he chose, he would have to do it all in his head. He finally decided on one that he had gotten from his teacher, that he hadn't mastered completely yet. There would be a risk, a chance that it wouldn't work.

The corridor ended in a door, and his hands were reaching for the latches. He concentrated his thoughts even as his hands mechanically pulled the door open. He let himself step into a large room with paintings and carvings on the walls, and three other doors opposite him. He hung back as much as he could, but otherwise let the spell move him, concentrating instead on visualizing the positions of the hand, mentally tracing the sigil. He crossed the room to the middle door and let the spell make his hands open it. He thought the words of his own spell as he entered the crypt beyond. The dim light that filled the catacombs was not enough to obscure the red aura of his magic.

There were bodies here, lying mummified on their couches on either side of the narrow chamber. He passed between them and neared the dead end at the far end of the crypt.

He finished the spell, thrilling with exultation, just as the cul-de-sac opened up to disgorge a swarm of white man-shaped things with tentacles. A great bolt of lightning leapt from his outstretched hands and crashed through the half-demonic monsters that had been sent to take him prisoner; smashed the concealed door off its hinges; flashed down the hallway beyond, charring the stone walls black, white, then black again.

The pull on his body ceased.

Chapter Ten
✤ ✤ ✤

HE SAT DOWN hard on the cold stone floor. He felt reaction rush over him, and he let himself shake until the worst was over. There was still a dim radiance in the air. It wasn't much, but it was enough to let him see the charred fragments of the white bodies.

There must have been at least a dozen of them. The smell of the burned flesh made his gorge rise, but he forced his stomach down. Now was not the time to be getting sick, and any traces of himself he left behind, even vomitus, could be used against him.

After a moment or two Morgan felt enough in control of himself to get to his feet and approach the corpses. He'd learned of creatures like these from his teacher, but he'd never seen one before. They were humanlike in some ways, so utterly alien and degenerate in others.

Beyond the blasted door through which they had come was a long passage, where more of the monsters might be lurking. He listened but couldn't hear the telltale wet rustle that signified their presence.

"Phoebus?" he whispered.

"Yeow," the cat said, picking its way fastidiously among the charred fragments and puddles of ichor.

"Do you know where we are?"

"No. What *are* these things?"

"*Tsedik.* Half-breeds, part demon, part human."

"Ahhh, I've heard of them. They stink."

"They do that."

"Did they build this place?" Phoebus asked.

"No, they don't have the intelligence or the technology to construct anything like this. They do build their own caves, but usually where the stone is softer, though they're obviously living here now."

Phoebus moved from one body to another. He did not sniff. "Their eyes seem suited to the dark," he said.

"They can't stand the light of day," Morgan told his cat. "They don't ever come up to the surface, as far as I know. In fact, they shouldn't be even this close."

"Then what are they doing here?"

"That's what I'd like to know. The only thing I can think of is that the Master of the Lodge called them. But if that's true, he or she is far more powerful than I'd thought. *Tsedik* don't just come to anyone's calling."

"On the other hand," Phoebus said, "if the Lodge Master is using monsters like these, then the spell that brought you down here must have been cast long distance."

"How so?"

"If it weren't, the Lodge Master would have been here in person. The spell could even have been automatic, triggered by anybody getting too close to your brother's secret."

"I guess that makes sense," Morgan said, examining the white-burned wall of the tunnel. "In any event, this isn't a healthy place to be under the best of circumstances." He turned to leave.

"Wait," Phoebus said, peering into the darkness beyond the blasted door. "Michael was here."

Morgan turned back and let his magically trained senses perceive the catacombs on a different level of reality. Phoebus was right; Michael had been here, and not long ago. Not just in this tomb, with the mummified human bodies in their niches, but in the passageway beyond the once secret door. It was just a trace, but Morgan could still feel it.

He broke out into a cold sweat. "If Michael is down here somewhere," he said, "he's in very bad trouble indeed."

"Didn't you catch his trace before?" Phoebus asked.

"I was too busy resisting that psychic pull and preparing the Lightning Bolt spell." Without further hesitation, he picked his way over the blasted and now oozing bodies and started down the alien corridor. Phoebus trotted at his heels.

A little way farther on the corridor was crossed by another, but Michael's trail led straight ahead. The trace was a little clearer here, away from the char of the thunderbolt.

Steps led down another twelve feet or so. Then he passed through a tomb complex almost identical to the one above. First, two doors opposite each other, then a larger room with three doors on the far wall. This large room was a kind of antechamber where mourners could sit and contemplate their dead, who would be lying in one of the three vaults beyond.

"Which came first?" Phoebus asked.

"This one," Morgan answered, "the one above was built with this as a model." He went to the central door of the three, but there lost Michael's trace.

"Here," Phoebus said, standing in front of the door on the right. Morgan went to it, found the trace again, opened the door, and stepped through.

There were mummified bodies here, as in the tomb above, but in a much greater state of decay. They were human bodies, as far as he could tell from what remained. But they must have been there a long time, for the dried flesh was turning to powder.

Morgan could see, in the workmanship of the walls, where stones of even older construction had been moved and changed to make this vault. The familiarity of the structure nagged at him, but he could not place it. The antiquity of the vault oppressed him, and he wanted to leave, but his concern for his brother was stronger.

At the end of the vault the trace stopped. Morgan suspected another secret door, as there had been in the upper crypt. The Unlock spell was so easy for him he only had to think of it and the door opened at his command. More stairs led down, as he had suspected. He descended to a lower hall that opened into the side of a great wide passageway running right and left. And Michael had been here.

The trace, and now footprints in the thin dust, led to the right. After a bit another great corridor crossed the one he was in. The trail led straight ahead.

"It ends here," Phoebus said.

Morgan tried to reject the implications of this dead end, but dread was a heavy thing in his stomach. "Michael," he called softly. "I'm here."

And Michael was there too, face wild, eyes frantic, hands pleading.

"Michael!" Morgan cried, and reached for his brother. The image wavered, receded from him. It was not really his brother, but only an apparition. Morgan took another step toward the figure, and again it shimmered backward, away from him. But as it did so, it became calm, though not untroubled. The hands relaxed, the face became still, though there was yet torment in the eyes, and the mouth formed Morgan's name, silently.

Morgan didn't know if this was an apparition of the living or of the dead. He hoped desperately that it was the former, but its sudden appearance, here where Michael's trace ended, did not bode well.

"Michael," Morgan said again, though he could not breathe. And now he could see that his worst fears were realized. The apparition had responded to him, but Michael was not here. This was just an image, imprinted on the flux of the world by the intensity of Michael's will.

"It's too late, isn't it?" he asked. He felt his chest contract with anguish. His brother was dead, and beyond all hope of help.

This apparition could tell him nothing. It just nodded, and faded as it raised its hand, as if to say good-bye. At least there was no odd transformation at the end to indicate that Michael's soul had been bottled.

"I'm sorry," Phoebus said.

Morgan did not answer. He was numb. After

a while, the numbness was replaced by an intense, cold anger.

"I don't know who killed him," he said, "or why. But I'm going to find out. And when I do, Michael, I swear to you that they will pay." Then, with an icy calm, he turned and went back the way he had come.

PART THREE

The Principle of Evil is that which people have always thought of as the force of ultimate dissolution and entropic death. Most people call it the Devil. To magicians it is known as the Tukhanox, the Throne of Death.

Evil itself is only a principle. The Tukhanox is merely the Intelligence of it. It is like a god, but it is nonetheless limited. It is insane. It exalts the exercise of power above all things. It wishes to wield total power over all creation.

The Tukhanox cannot be everywhere at once, but it isn't alone. There are other Intelligences on its side, forming a hierarchy of power and control.

Below it are the archdemons, beings that have full awareness, but their interest is cosmic—or at least planetary. Below them are the demons, sentient but much more limited in power, and usually restricted to certain astral zones in the world. Below them are the things that might best be called demidemons. These last have no self-awareness, though they might be intelligent.

In the normal course of events, when one comes up against the Forces of Death, one deals with the lower orders. Typically, those would be the mortal Servants, or occasionally the halfbreed creatures, partially corporeal, bred on Earth, but unintelligent, or at best marginally so.

The subordinates of the Tukhanox are widely

scattered, its agents among the mortals influencing all things. This is not to say that everything evil that happens in the world can be laid at the feet, as it were, of the Tukhanox. But some of the more spectacular events can. Something as small as the Manson murders. Or as great as Nazi Germany.

Chapter Eleven

✠ ✠ ✠

MORGAN PULLED HIS car over to the curb and parked in front of Weiss's house again. The lights were still on in spite of the late hour. Even if they'd been off, Morgan wouldn't have hesitated to disturb him. Phoebus jumped on his shoulder and then, as he had done at O'Reilley's house, faded to invisibility as Morgan got out of the car.

There was nobody else on the street to see the telltale aura as Morgan, his mind icy calm, his body tight as a string, cast a complicated anti-magic shield around himself before he mounted the steps of Weiss's front porch. Now he was safe from all magical attack, as well as certain other forms of assault. The only drawback was that the anti-magic shield wouldn't let *him* cast spells through it either.

Ready for trouble this time, he rang the bell and waited. Weiss answered the door after a moment. Morgan advanced on him and forced him to retreat into his own foyer.

"Hey," Weiss protested, his fingers twitching, "what's the meaning—"

"Shut up, you stupid son of a bitch," Morgan snarled. Weiss's lavender fire magic just coruscated harmlessly off Morgan's shield. "You're a real stupid jerk," Morgan went on, his calm totally lost. Weiss turned and strode into a neat if cheaply furnished living room. "Michael's dead," Morgan yelled as the other man pulled open a drawer in a table and took out a gun.

Weiss hesitated. Morgan felt Phoebus's invisible claws in his shoulder, heard the cat's whisper to be calm. He leaned against the doorjamb, folded his arms, and tried to regain his shattered composure. He watched the man who supposedly had been Michael's best friend.

"What did you say?" Weiss asked belatedly, the .45 automatic not quite pointing at Morgan.

"I said, Michael's dead." He had control of himself now, in spite of his anger. "How come you didn't do anything about it? I thought you were a buddy of his."

"You killed him," Weiss said, and the gun came up. The report was deafening in the confines of the room, but the bullet fell harmlessly, undistorted, at Morgan's feet.

"Come off it," Morgan said acidly. "Why would I be telling you about it if I had killed him?" He nudged the bullet with his toe. It rolled an inch or two across the carpet. Where it had lain was a scorch mark. "Let's hope your neighbors didn't hear that and report it to the police," Morgan went on, looking at Weiss. "You don't think I'd come in here without very careful defenses, do you?" Phoebus, still invisible on his shoulder, began to relax.

Weiss stared stupidly at the bullet at Morgan's feet for a moment, then met his eyes. "You did kill him, though, didn't you?" he asked.

"No, Weiss," Morgan said, shaking his head. "I didn't kill him."

"Then how'd he die, dammit?" Weiss yelled, and brought the gun up again.

"I was in California at the time," Morgan said. He kept his voice calm, his face expressionless, though inside he wanted to scream.

"That was six weeks ago. You were here, you tell me."

The gun in Weiss's hand drooped and pointed toward the floor. "I don't know anything about it;" he said. "Are you sure he's dead?"

"Come on, Weiss," Morgan said, gesturing toward the gun. "Put it down. My defenses protect you as much as they do me." Weiss tossed the gun back in the drawer and flopped in a chair. "And yes," Morgan went on, "I'm sure. His death apparition came to me just a little while ago.

"Now, listen," he said, and his voice got hard again, "I tried to tell you yesterday that Michael was in trouble. It was too late then, but I didn't know that. You wouldn't listen to me, and just be glad that your bullheadedness had nothing to do with Michael's death, or I'd be killing you right now. Are you listening to me?"

"I'm just wondering what kind of plan you've got up your sleeve," Weiss said. His grin was supposed to display perceptive cunning, but to Morgan it just looked foolish.

"You're paranoid," Morgan said.

"Maybe you didn't kill Michael," Weiss said, "but you're sure as hell going to take advantage of his death, aren't you?"

"There's a Lodge of Servants in Harborbeach," Morgan said. "Did you know that?" He was gratified to see Weiss blanch at the mention of the enemy. Phoebus whispered to him. "How long has it been since you saw your teacher?" Morgan asked, following his cat's all-but-inaudible suggestion.

"Huh? Ah, about eight or nine years. Why?" Weiss reached into a shirt pocket, took out a pack of cigarettes, lit one with a match, and blew a cloud of smoke at the ceiling.

"It's obvious," Morgan said. "You've gotten sloppy. You cast spells where people can see you. It's hard enough keeping magic a secret as it is, without people like you being careless."

"Nonsense. I'm always on the alert—"

"You don't even know what's going on around you," Morgan interrupted. "Did you know Logan O'Reilley?" He took out one of his little cigars and rolled it between his fingers.

"No," Weiss said. "Who's he?"

"How alert," Morgan sneered. He put the cigar in his mouth, snapped his fingers, and lit the cigar from the small blue flame dancing on the end of his thumb. "Logan O'Reilley was Michael's second-best friend." He blew smoke across the room at Weiss, who had watched his performance with a strange expression. "And you didn't know him?"

"Hell, I don't know everybody Michael associates with. What of it?"

"O'Reilley was a Servant," Morgan snapped. "How come you didn't know that? You don't have to know all Michael's associates, but how come you never met his second-best friend? Michael spent more time with O'Reilley than with anyone except you, or Cindy Vann. How alert you've been! How aware! How stupid!"

"Hey," Weiss said, his face getting red, "now wait just a minute—"

"No, you just sit there and think about this for a while." Morgan blew smoke at the ceiling. "Michael was taken in by the Servants. They'd been working on him for years. They got him that gun shop six years ago, and the house just about two months back. During all that time there must have been some opportunity for you to have suspected that something nasty was going on. If you were so alert for enemies, how come you never noticed that?

"There's a whole damn coven of them here, Weiss. O'Reilley wasn't alone. The Servants got Michael hooked into their system; they put him in a double bind and were going to force him to play their game. He needed help. How much help did you give him, huh?"

"I don't understand," Weiss protested. His coloring had returned to normal, but his expression was confused.

"That's obvious," Morgan said.

"All right, dammit," Weiss barked, crushing out the stub of his cigarette. "Tell me how it happened." He got to his feet and came halfway across the room toward Morgan. At last the fact of Michael's death was beginning to sink in.

"Go to Michael's house," Morgan said, "and dream in his bed, like I did." Weiss just stared at him blankly, as if he hadn't understood.

"Michael dreamed," Morgan tried to explain, "and the Servants got to him in his dreams. It's all there, everything that happened. Just be careful, when you wake up in the woods, to break the spell before you get to the mausoleum." Weiss still didn't comprehend. Morgan's words meant nothing to him.

"Michael's dead," Morgan persisted. "He's been missing for six weeks, and now he's dead. You were his best friend, you were here. And you are a magician, you should have been aware of the Servants tampering with your memory.

Why didn't you help Michael when he needed it?"

"I didn't know," Weiss said weakly.

Morgan sighed, stood away from the doorjamb, and looked down at the end of his cigar. The inch-long ash fell and landed precisely on the charred spot on the carpet where the bullet had lain.

"You didn't know," he said softly, and looked up. "Stop playing games, Weiss. Open your eyes and take a look around you at the real world. You could do a lot of good out there. Why don't you give it a try?"

"I don't know what you're talking about."

"No, of course you don't," Morgan said. He turned away before Weiss could answer and left the house.

Chapter Twelve

✥ ✥ ✥

THE NEXT DAY was Saturday, clear and promising to get hot. After breakfast at McDougal's, Morgan drove over to Cindy Vann's place. Phoebus ate the ham biscuit on the way, and climbed onto Morgan's shoulder as he got out of the car.

Morgan went up on the porch and rang the bell. Dana answered and smiled when she saw who it was. But maybe, Morgan thought, the smile was for Phoebus, who now purred loudly.

"Well, Lester," Dana said, reaching up to scritch Phoebus under the chin, "good morning. Come on in." She led him into the living room. "What can I do for you?"

"I've been asking around about Michael." Phoebus stopped purring.

Dana looked at him sharply, as if she had forgotten their previous conversation. "Oh . . . yes," she said hesitantly. "Have you had any luck finding him?"

"I'm afraid I have. Is Cindy in?"

"Sure, just a minute. I'll go get her." She left him there, and a moment later came back with her roommate.

"Hi," Cindy said. "Sorry we were so confused the other day. I can't understand it. Dana and I talked about it after you left. It was the strangest thing, not being able to think about . . . Michael like that. I still can't make my thoughts come clear. I seem to remember you saying that Michael had been missing for six weeks. But that couldn't be right, could it?"

"I'm afraid it is," Morgan said. He'd never had to break news like this before.

"Did you talk to Gary and Logan?"

"Yes. Ah, their memories have been tampered with too."

"But you've learned something," Cindy said. Morgan just nodded.

"He's in trouble," Cindy went on. "He's been hurt, or arrested."

"He's dead," Morgan said softly. Cindy stared at him uncomprehendingly, but it was no memory-tampering this time that caused her confusion. "Are you sure?" she asked, her voice strained.

"As sure as I can be, when there's no body."

"Michael? Dead?" The color drained out of

her face. She stepped backward, as if she were going to sit in her chair. Dana, her face shocked, came up and guided her into it. Cindy sat down heavily, then leaned back and closed her eyes, visibly trying to retain her composure. Dana just watched Morgan, her expression both angry and concerned.

After a moment Cindy spoke, her eyes still closed. "How did it happen?" she asked. "When?"

"I don't know yet," he answered, "but I'm going to try to find out."

"Should we call the police?"

"You can if you want to, but it won't do any good."

"What do you mean?" Cindy asked, opening her eyes and staring at him.

"The people who killed Michael are too well organized. The police won't find anything, not even a body."

"Killed him? You mean he was murdered?" She sat forward on the edge of her chair. Dana put out an unsteady hand to calm her. "But—it wasn't a shooting accident?"

"I'm afraid not." He felt awkward standing in the middle of the room. "It was murder, but there's no body, no evidence, nothing to prove even that he's dead. Like I said, you can call the police if you want to, but it may cause more trouble than it's worth. All you can do is report him missing, and they'll wonder why you didn't do that six weeks ago. If they ask me about it, I can tell them what I know, but I can't explain how I know he's dead. If I tried, they wouldn't believe me. I have no evidence, nothing for the police to work with."

"What do you mean, no body, no evidence?"

"The people who killed him are too clever. They've covered everything up very nicely."

"You mean, like the Scandia?"

"Ah, something like that." Putting the blame on that underworld organization was a better lie than any he could have thought up on the spur of the moment.

"My God, the Scandia!" She fell back in her chair, her hands half covering her face. "How could it have happened? Are they watching me?"

"No, I don't think so."

"I don't dare go to the police," Cindy mumbled through her hands. She started to shake. Big tears formed in her eyes and slowly rolled down her cheeks. "Oh, God," she moaned, "poor Michael."

"Why don't you go lie down for a while," Dana suggested. Her face was white too, now, but there was an unspoken question in her eyes.

"They never gave him a chance," Cindy said brokenly, following some thought of her own.

"Come on," Dana urged. "Let me fix you a good stiff drink."

"I don't want a drink," Cindy said. Her face crumpled, and she started to cry. Dana took her arm and made her stand up, then led her toward the back hall. At the doorway Cindy paused, tried to pull herself together, and turned back to Morgan.

"I'm sorry," she said. "I shouldn't be behaving like this."

"Of course you should," Morgan said. He wished he could let his own grief out.

"Thank you for telling me," Cindy went on.
"I'll do whatever you think best."

"Just get some rest now, try to come to terms
with it."

Cindy opened her mouth as if to answer, but
only sobs came out. Dana gently turned her toward the door and led her away.

"That hurt," Phoebus said softly.

"It did that," Morgan agreed. "I think she was
in love with him."

"No question," Phoebus said.

A few minutes later Dana came back alone.

"She'll be all right," she said. "It will take a
while, though. That was quite a shock. She and
Michael were talking about getting married."

"I kind of suspected as much," Morgan told
her. "I mean, what does a bachelor want with
a four-bedroom house?"

"You said something about memories being
tampered with," Dana said, walking slowly toward Cindy's empty chair. "I guess that's true,
though I've never heard that organized crime
was capable of such a thing." She rubbed her
hand along the upholstery of the high back, then
turned to face him. "How do you explain it?"

"It can be done, by certain people, if they have
the right knowledge," Morgan answered non-
committally. "Not the Scandia, obviously."

"It sounds like magic." There was something
in her voice that made Morgan think she knew
more about that than she was willing to admit
to a stranger.

"I think it was," he said. "Does the phrase
'Servant of the Lodge' mean anything to you?"

"It does." She turned away. "It does indeed.
There is a very powerful Lodge in Harbor-

beach. Powerful enough, in fact, that there is no other organized crime in Harborbeach at all. If the Lodge had anything to do with Michael's death, that would certainly explain how our memories of him got fuddled."

"How come there are so many magicians in a small town like this?" Morgan asked. She turned back to him.

"Besides myself, you mean?"

"Yes. Weiss is a magician, did you know that?"

"I suspected it. I've gone out with him quite a bit, mostly doubling with Cindy and Michael, but not always. I guess you could call us good friends, but there's been very little real communication between us."

"Did he never try to find out whether you were a magician, like I did just now?"

"No. And I wouldn't have admitted it to him in any event. I kind of like him, and sometimes I get the feeling he's rather stuck on me, but he never says anything about that, and I don't want to encourage him. He's got some odd quirks, and I never trusted him that much."

"In Weiss's case, discretion is certainly wise. He's more paranoid than you think. He attacked me twice, once with a fire spell, once with a gun."

"I guess I shouldn't be surprised, though he's never been violent around me."

"But then, you've never let him know you were a magician, and that's where his paranoia lies. But Weiss is just a complication. He's unstable, he's convinced he's secretly defending the world from dire enemies, while at the same time he can't see the real enemies right under his nose. But Logan O'Reilley is another matter. He was a magician too, did you know that?"

She hesitated. "Y-yes."

"He was a member of the Lodge."

"Yes, I know that. You say he was?"

"He's dead too. I don't know if it was the same people who killed Michael or not, but it may have been. It was the work of the Lodge, in any event." He told her about his attempt to question O'Reilley by means of magic, and the frustrating results he'd obtained.

"Serves him right," Dana said, throwing herself into the other armchair. Morgan sat on the couch and let Phoebus down into his lap. "O'Reilley was always reckless," Dana went on, tucking her feet up under her. "A drunk. I was always afraid he'd do something magical that couldn't be explained away as a hoax or hallucination. There was nothing I could do about it, though. I'm not surprised his own people finally turned against him, especially if there was any danger of him revealing the Lodge to you. You've found out a lot in a rather short time," she finished.

"I wasn't handicapped by a fuddled memory. But if you're a magician, how come you couldn't counter that?"

"I didn't know my memory had been tampered with until you brought it forcibly to my attention yesterday. When I began to realize what it meant, I first thought that you were responsible. It was so hard to think clearly about it at all, that I couldn't even remember what you'd said or I'd said, whenever we were talking about Michael." She crossed her arms as if hugging herself, as if that would ease the pain of Morgan's news.

"I've been working on recovering my memory," she went on after a moment, "but I haven't got it all yet. Just enough to know that I really haven't seen Michael in six weeks, as you said. When was he killed?"

"I don't know for sure, but I suspect it was shortly after he disappeared, though it might have been as recently as a few days ago. I saw his dying apparition last night." He felt his face go wooden.

"You were fond of him, weren't you?" she asked softly.

He didn't have to answer. He knew it showed on his face.

"So what are you going to do?" Dana asked.

"I haven't figured that out yet. But whoever killed Michael is going to regret it."

"You don't strike me as the type who'd go looking for vengeance."

"Don't I? I guess that's good. Maybe I'll fool them too."

"Not looking like that you won't. Would you like some coffee?"

He took a deep breath and sighed. "Yes," he said, "I would."

"I'll be back in a minute." She got up and went into the kitchen.

He leaned back on the couch, closed his eyes, and forced himself to be calm.

"She's on your side," Phoebus purred from his lap.

"So it would seem."

"You kind of like her, don't you?"

"I'm getting to like her very much," Morgan

admitted, knowing he could not conceal his interest from Phoebus. "I just wish I'd met her under better circumstances." It was difficult for a magician to find someone they could develop a real relationship with, and Dana was reacting to him in all the right ways.

She came back after a moment with two steaming mugs. She handed him one, then went back to her chair. There was an ashtray on the coffee table in front of the couch, so he took out a little cigar and asked permission with a gesture.

"Go ahead," Dana said. He snapped his fingers and lit up. She arched an eyebrow. "Do you always light them that way?" she asked.

"Not in public," he said.

"How did it happen?"

"The murder? I don't know. And I don't know why, either. But I do know that the Lodge was directly responsible for Briarly's death, so Michael could buy the gun shop."

"That was six years ago," Dana said. She held her mug with both hands. "Have they been working on Michael that long?"

"Apparently. And then they gave Mrs. Frost cancer, so she'd be forced to sell the house to pay her bills. And then just recently they told Michael about it all and demanded payment for services rendered."

"God, how horrible. But how did you find out about that?"

"I dreamed his last dream in his bed last night." He blew smoke at the ceiling. "They told him that it was his covetousness which was responsible, that they did what they did because he wanted the shop and house so badly. Then they insisted that he owed them for it. They said they wanted him to get some kind of stone, whatever that was. And they wanted him to sign a contract."

"But that's the wrong way around. The contract comes first, and then the 'favors.' "

"I know, but Michael wouldn't have sold his soul for anything. But this way, you see, they had him in a bind, even if it was a swindle. He'd feel obligated to pay for what he'd already received and used.

"It's my guess," he went on, "that he gave in to their demands, at least provisionally, and secretly planned to get back at them once they believed they had him on their side."

"But then, why would they kill him? If he didn't sign the contract . . . or did he?"

"I don't know. I suspect they killed him because he was too dangerous for them. There wasn't anything he couldn't do if he set his mind to it—short of magic, of course. He always had contacts. He knew people, had friends everywhere, could get things done. The only time he failed in anything was seven years ago, with that movie deal in Detroit. And who knows but that the Servants weren't involved in that too."

"They seem to have gone to a lot of trouble just for one person, even one with as much potential as Michael."

"True. But look, if they could pervert him, then teach him magic, make him a full-fledged Initiate in the Lodge, then he would have been terrifyingly powerful. The Servants were aware of his potential, but I'm sure they didn't realize how dangerous an enemy Michael could be until it was too late for them to back out gracefully. He'd have been a valuable member on any team, in spite of the fact that he rejected anything mystical. He never knew I was a magician, and wouldn't have believed it if I'd shown him. He was a total materialist. But he could take advantage of situations even if he didn't believe in them. It would be just like him to get accepted into the Lodge and then try to destroy it from the inside."

"You seem to know an awful lot about this situation, in spite of everything. Did you get all this from dreaming in his bed?"

"Only the most recent events. The psychic residuum was pretty strong. I think they probably talked with him in his dreams, for the most part, instead of while he was awake. The main advantage there is that their identities were completely concealed by dream images."

"I guess I'm surprised you had access to his dreams like that. Is that where you saw his dying apparition?"

"No." He told her about his forced visit underground and what he'd found there.

"I've never heard of catacombs like those around here," she said. "There are some strange caves in the mountains north of Tucson, where there shouldn't be, and there are places on the East Coast. It bothers me that we haven't heard about those catacombs' being here before now."

"I agree. When I'm through with the business at hand, I'm going to investigate them further. They should be sealed. It wouldn't do to have some archaeologist go exploring down there; there are too many secrets to be revealed."

"So what will you do now?"

"Try to find out who the other members of

the Lodge are. O'Reilley wasn't alone. Whoever
killed Michael is going to pay. And there's the
question of that stone or whatever it was they
wanted him to get for them. Needless to say,
whatever their plot is, it should be stopped. As
if I needed any other reason to put this Lodge
out of business. I'll destroy them all if I have
to, if I can."

"You can't do it by yourself."

"I can try. Will you help me?"

"I can't, Lester. I'm not strong enough." She
was also afraid, he saw. "But there's another
magician who might help," she said. "His name
is Jerry Pickard. He lives on the north side of
town."

"Yet another one? All right, I'll look him up
this afternoon." He was disappointed, but he
couldn't blame her for wanting to stay as far
away from the Lodge as possible.

"You knew Michael pretty well, didn't you?"
Dana asked.

"Yes, I did." He thought about admitting his
relationship, and decided against it. If Dana
didn't know who he really was, the Servants
couldn't pry the information out of her. "But
listen," he went on, "that's not the worst of it.
I suspect the Lodge is getting some demonic
help. There was a sign over the mausoleum
door." He told her about the eye.

"I see. I think. Not conclusive, but certainly
indicative. That would fit in with some of the
things that have happened in Harborbeach in
the past. If there is a demon involved with the
Lodge here, it would explain a lot."

"Someday you'll have to fill me in on what
kind of things need that kind of explanation."

He began to relax. Dana seemed to be comfortable talking with him. He thought he'd pursue the acquaintance further while he had the opportunity. "How did you become a magician?" he asked her, changing the subject to that end.

"How did you?" she countered. She had truly green eyes.

"There was a gentleman at the chess club near the base where I was stationed when I was in the marines. He was the only one who'd play faerie chess with me. We talked."

"It was one of my father's old army buddies," Dana said. "He'd visit often. He was a bachelor, and we were the only family he had."

"Strange how it works."

Chapter Thirteen

✜ ✜ ✜

JERRY PICKARD WAS listed in the phone book. He was in real estate and insurance. Morgan drove over to his home on the north side of Harborbeach on the bluff overlooking Lake Michigan, after lunch in town.

It was a well-to-do neighborhood, with large houses on manicured lawns. The hedges were well trimmed, the trees tall and stately. There were people out on riding mowers going over the perfect grass. Once or twice, as he drove slowly by, he heard the sounds of children playing.

He found the right address, parked in the long

curving driveway and, with Phoebus discreetly invisible on his shoulder, went up the steps to the broad front porch. He rang the bell. After a moment a well-dressed woman in her mid-fifties answered the door.

"Is Mr. Pickard in?" Morgan asked.

"He's around in back," the woman said with a smile.

He thanked her, stepped off the porch, and followed the brick walkway to the back of the house, where he heard sounds coming from a large shed.

He knocked at the shed door, and a male voice told him to come in. Inside he found a solidly built man, a year or so older than the woman, wearing jeans and a work shirt, putting a rear wheel on a ten-speed bicycle.

"Jerry Pickard?" Morgan asked. "My name is Lester Van Alan. Dana Kirkpatrick referred me to you."

"Ah, yes, Mr. Van Alan," Pickard said, smiling and wiping his hands on a rag. "How can I help you?"

"I came here last Thursday to visit a friend of mine, Michael Scott. When I got here I discovered that he'd disappeared about six weeks ago. The people who knew him, including Dana, had had their memories tampered with. It was as if they had forgotten he had existed; they weren't even aware he was missing. Just yesterday I learned he'd been killed."

The smile left Pickard's face and he came away from the partially reassembled bicycle. "You imply that there was, ah, magic involved in this disappearance and murder."

"Yes sir, I'm afraid so. One of the people I

talked to was an Initiate in a Lodge here in Harborbeach."

Pickard's face hardened. "Are you sure he's a Lodge member?"

"He intimated as much. His memory had not been tampered with. He attacked me without provocation, and would have killed me if I hadn't been prepared. He's dead now, as far as I can tell, killed by his own people."

"Sounds nasty. Okay, Mr. Van Alan, what can I do?"

"I'm convinced the Servants of the Lodge were responsible for Michael Scott's death. I'm seeking justice, Mr. Pickard. Do you know who any of the Servants are?"

"No, I'm afraid not, though I know there are Servants here. If I knew their identities, I'd have neutralized them long ago."

"There also seem to be an inordinate number of magicians in Harborbeach. There's yourself, Dana Kirkpatrick, and at least one other. Not counting the Servants, of course. Do you know of any others?"

"One or two. But I must be discreet; I don't know who you are."

"I understand. My teacher used the name 'The Fourth Nail' on occasion."

"Ah, yes, I've heard of him. If you're a student of his, I'm doubly glad to meet you."

"Thank you. Could you tell me who these other magicians are? And why there are so many in a small town like this?"

"I'm sure you're aware that I can't just go around revealing identities. I'm not exactly pleased that Miss Kirkpatrick told you about me. She may have some reason to trust you, but let's not go too fast here. What do you propose to do with these other magicians?''

"Visit them, find out what they know about the Servants. Find out if any of them might have been involved in the trap that resulted in Michael Scott's death.''

"That could be very dangerous.''

"I agree, but if my suspicions are correct, Michael Scott was just one piece of a larger scheme.''

"Perhaps we'd better go into the house,'' Pickard suggested.

They left the shed and went in the back door of the house. Pickard led the way through the spotless kitchen and expensive if blandly furnished living room, and ushered Morgan into a comfortable study with book-lined walls, a huge desk, and two leather chairs on either side of a low table.

"Will you have a drink?'' Pickard asked, going to a concealed bar behind a set of bookshelves.

"Yes, please, scotch on the rocks, if you have it. How many magicians are there in Harborbeach?''

"Five that I know of,'' Pickard answered, dropping ice into two glasses, "including myself and Miss Kirkpatrick.'' He poured scotch into one glass, bourbon into the other. He handed Morgan the scotch, added water to his own drink, and motioned Morgan into one of the two chairs in front of the desk, then took the other.

"Plus, of course, the Servants,'' Morgan said, surprised at Pickard's information. "The one I spoke to was named Logan O'Reilley.''

"He was a real magician? Not just a Novice?"

"No doubt about it, and stronger than I. I was lucky to get out of our encounter alive. I take it, then, you didn't know about him."

"No, I didn't, I'm ashamed to say. Had he been here long?"

"Eight or nine years, as far as I could figure." He sipped his drink. It was good scotch.

"That bothers me, Mr. Van Alan. The Servants don't kill off their Initiates lightly. You say he was involved in your friend's death?"

"Yes. Perhaps not directly, but he knew something about it. I tried to question him by means of a fire image, but he was already dead by then, and his soul had been bottled."

"God, how awful." He tossed off most of his drink at one gulp.

"You see what I'm getting at. You didn't know about O'Reilley, yet he was a longtime resident here in town. And he was careless, a heavy drinker, and attacked me magically when it wasn't necessary. It may have been lapses like that that got him in trouble with his own people. It was late at night, he'd had a few beers, his guard was down. But it was stupid of him to have exposed himself so badly. And yet you never knew about him."

"It's most disturbing," Pickard said. He went back to his concealed bar and poured himself another drink. Morgan declined a refill. "But finding the Servants won't be easy," Pickard went on.

"All I need is one name," Morgan said, "and I can start from there. Given enough time, I might be able to find them on my own. But who knows how long that would take? Can you think of anyone who might be a Servant, or who might know the identity of a Servant?"

Pickard went back to his chair and thought a moment, sipping his drink more sedately this time. "As I said, I can identify no Lodge members, and I don't know if anyone else can. I suppose you could question the other magicians whom I do know."

"I'd like to do that. But I'm surprised at the number of magicians here," he said again. "I wasn't aware this town was that magically important."

"It's not," Pickard said. "Yes, there are a lot of magicians here, but let me tell you something about Harborbeach." He got up from his chair and went to sit down behind his desk.

"This"—he reached out to point at a spot in the middle of the polished oak surface—"is the center of my desk. But you'll notice that what's important about this desk is kept locked in drawers, or is off on one side or the other." He touched phone, recorder, a set of reference books, a stack of papers.

"The desk itself," he went on, "is kept clear. That's what Harborbeach is like. There are a lot of magicians here, and a lot of work is done here. But Glass Mountain in California, or Churchill, North Carolina, Tucson . . . even Forgone, North Dakota, they are all much more important than we are. Each in its own way, of course.

"We're a backwater, Van Alan. If anything is going to happen, it happens elsewhere."

"This time it didn't," Morgan said. He felt as if he'd missed a point somewhere. He tried to puzzle it out as he told Pickard about Michael's dream, and the catacombs.

"The people in Michael's dream mentioned a stone of some kind," Morgan said when he'd finished. "Does that mean anything to you?"

"No, I'm afraid not. That's the problem with living in a backwater; you get complacent. You're right, there seems to be a serious problem here. But fortunately, you also seem to have volunteered to look into it. All right, I'll help however I can. What do you want?"

"Quite simply, I want the person or persons who killed Michael Scott," Morgan said. "That's all."

"You sound as if you take it personally."

"I do."

"And when you 'take care' of your friend's murderer, what about the rest of the Lodge?"

"I will, of course, do what I can about them, but my main concern is Michael Scott's killer."

"Do you know what you're getting into?"

"I have a pretty good idea."

"Indeed. All right, then. What do you want from me?"

"The names and addresses of all the magicians in Harborbeach, or anywhere nearby."

"I see. And then what?"

"And then I check them out one by one, to see if any of them know anything about the activities of the Servants."

"And then?" Pickard persisted.

"If and when I find a lead, I'll follow it. I may have to pretend to play their game to do so, but if I have to, I will."

"My God, man, do you know what you're saying?"

"Yes, I think I do. What little I've learned so far seems to indicate that the Lodge here is up to something big, and I intend to find out what it is. The Lodge must know I'm here, and they may try to either kill me or convert me. My best bet is to anticipate their move if I can."

"You're putting an awful lot at risk, Mr. Van Alan, especially considering you're not familiar with the conditions here in Harborbeach."

"It's those very conditions that have me worried," Morgan said. "I'm surprised that in a town with, what is it, five or more magicians, the Lodge is allowed to exist at all. It seems more should have been done to have neutralized it."

"Maybe it's because the Servants are not as much of a threat here as you think they are. After all, I've lived here all my life; I know this town very well. I have no reason to believe we are the subject of one of the Lodge's typical plots.

"But if I'm wrong," Pickard went on, "if things are as bad as you think they are, then you'd be putting yourself in terrible danger. I do know something about how the Servants work. People once in their clutches don't get out again. Think of your friend as an example."

"Michael wasn't a magician. I am."

"Pretty young to have learned much. Now, listen to me. I'll give you the names you want, but you be careful. The Lodge is nothing to fool with."

"I know. I've seen more than one example in my time. Look, I appreciate your concern, but I'm going to follow this through. My chances of success, let alone of survival, will be a lot better if you help me."

"All right, then." Pickard took a key ring from his pocket and opened a side drawer in his desk, from which he took a slender notebook.

"Here they are," he said, opening the notebook and handing it across the desk. Morgan looked at the names. Pickard had not included himself, of course. Dana and Gary Weiss were listed, and two others. Another list included seven names.

"Who are these?" Morgan asked.

"People who I suspect might have some magical knowledge. I don't know whether they are magicians, Servants, or just natural talents."

"I see. I'll check them all out." Logan O'Reilley's name was not on either list.

"You're serious about this, aren't you?" Pickard asked, taking back the notebook and locking it away.

"I am," Morgan said, getting to his feet. "And you had better be serious about it too. Thank you very much for your time."

"You're certainly welcome," Pickard said. "But please, be careful."

"I will be," Morgan said, and left the house.

"What did you think?" he asked when he got back in the car and Phoebus had become visible again and taken his place on the seat beside him.

"I couldn't tell a thing," the cat said.

Chapter Fourteen
✤ ✤ ✤

THE AFTERNOON WAS as hot as the morning had
promised it would be. Morgan checked his map
for the addresses of the two magicians he had
not met yet and started for the first one. It took
a while to find her apartment building. He had
trouble again with the map of Harborbeach not
corresponding exactly to the city, and the fact
that the streets were all laid out oddly.

Her name was Dona Beloin, and she turned
out to be an aging actress, retired to Harborbeach from New York ten years ago. Her behavior was odd, but he attributed that to her to
age. She didn't seem dangerous to Morgan, and
he could detect no charms in her apartment.
She had completely withdrawn from magical
practice, knew nothing about the Lodge, and
didn't want to know. Morgan cut the uncomfortable interview short.

The next was a man who lived in Brookstone,
an unincorporated area several miles south of
Harborbeach. Morgan wasn't received warmly.
The man, Edmond Bergholm, was in his mid-
forties, and something of a hermit. Magicians,
as a rule, were by nature a solitary lot and they
didn't like being addressed and questioned too
openly. Bergholm was particularly suspicious,
especially when he detected the invisible cat on
Morgan's shoulder. Morgan didn't learn much,
but was sure Bergholm had no connections with
the Lodge. Phoebus confirmed this when they

went back to their car, after only the briefest of meetings.

That took care of the confirmed magicians—at least those whom Pickard knew. There were seven others, unconfirmed. Morgan had supper at a Chicken Deluxe, then went to visit the first of these. The woman, a housewife, was just eccentric.

He had time for one more before it would be too late to go calling on strangers. The man was a bachelor, living in a small house on the east side of town, and was a natural talent. That is, he didn't know that his "good luck" was due to his unconscious magical abilities. Morgan kept the interview brief.

Before going back to his hotel, he tried again to place phone calls to magicians who might be able to help him. But as before, his calls rang unanswered. "It can't be the Lodge that's doing this," he muttered to Phoebus as he collected his unspent quarter.

"It hardly seems likely," Phoebus said. "The only thing I can think of is that the Dreamer is responsible."

"But why?"

"Balance. And perhaps as a punishment. Your pride kept you from calling the Dreamer or your teacher when you first knew something was wrong here. You wanted to do it all yourself, and now you have to."

He slept late Sunday morning, catching up on his rest for the first time since leaving home nearly a week ago. He treated himself to a large lunch at a restaurant in town, then went to check out the next of the five remaining names on his mental list.

This was a man named Nick Jones. Morgan drove through the maze of the city to the man's house and parked.

"Be careful," Phoebus warned as he made himself invisible before they got out of the car. "There's magic here."

Jones answered the door when Morgan rang. He was holding a napkin, and still chewing his dinner.

"Mr. Jones," Morgan said, and stopped cold. There was a glint and a smile in the other man's eye. Morgan could feel Phoebus's invisible claws digging into his left shoulder.

"You'll be Van Alan," Jones said. He was a tall, very slender man in his late thirties. He looked over his shoulder into the house as if to see if his family was watching. Then he came out onto the porch and closed the door.

"Word spreads fast," Morgan said, trying to conceal the sudden rush of fear that Jones's use of his alias inspired.

"It does," Jones said. "It does that. We've been aware of you for some little time now. And we're curious." He wasn't at all unfriendly, and his very pleasantness made Morgan even more fearful.

"You know why I'm here, then?" Morgan asked. He tried to formulate a spell in his mind, but he was so nervous he couldn't keep track of it and the conversation at the same time.

"Not exactly," Jones said. "I know you're interested in Michael Scott. You've been over at his house at least once. We learned that from O'Reilley. He was a fool, I'm sorry to say. He should have talked to you, instead of attacking you. But then, that's O'Reilley for you. I also know you've been thrashing around here in a most disconcerting way for the last three days or so. You're stirring things up, Van Alan. Maybe you're not aware of just what kind of mess you could be getting into."

"Michael Scott is why I'm here," Morgan said, ignoring the implications. "Is there somewhere where we can talk?"

Jones indicated the porch swing. Morgan sat, and Jones leaned on the porch rail. The air was warm, the sun bright, and two houses up a man was pushing a mower across his lawn.

"It's too bad about Scott," Jones said. He sounded as if he meant it. "Was he a friend of yours?"

"Yes, we grew up together." The naturalness of the setting and the calmness of the conversation did nothing to alleviate his apprehension.

"I see. I'm sorry. I wish there was something we could have done to have prevented his death."

"Can you tell me anything about how it happened?"

"Not much. I know that it happened, and that it shouldn't have. I wouldn't know even that much except that your being here has stirred things up considerably. Word has gone out through the Lodge to be on the lookout for you. That's about it."

"And what happens," Morgan asked, disconcerted that his actions had been so closely watched, "now that you've found me, as it were?"

"That's entirely up to you, but I see several possible alternatives. One, you could accept our heartfelt apologies and go home. That would really be the best thing to do. I know how you feel about us, and I wish I could make you believe we're really not your enemies, regardless of differences in philosophy. But I also know you wouldn't believe me, no matter what I said. You've already decided we are at fault regarding Scott's death, so there's no sense my trying to change your mind. But if you stay here and try to 'seek justice,' as it were, you can only stir things up worse, and make trouble for everybody. Going home would really be the best idea."

"I can assure you that I have no intention of leaving Harborbeach until I have learned a lot more about why Michael Scott died, and how."

"I was afraid it would be like that." Jones stared moodily at the porch floor for a moment. An occasional car drove past on the residential street. "All right, I'll give you my second suggestion. That would be to talk to one of our officers, and explain your position."

"And how do I do that?" Morgan asked.

"Just keep on talking," Jones said with a smile.

Morgan concealed his surprise. Jones pulled a cigarette from a pack in his shirt pocket. Morgan took out one of his little cigars, snapped his fingers, and lit their smokes with the flame at the end of his thumb.

"Very well, Mr. Jones," he said, exhaling a cloud of blue smoke. "It's like this. Michael was an innocent caught in a trap not of his own making. Your Lodge tried to enlist him, and when that didn't work, instead of just letting it drop, had Michael killed instead. What I want is just what you suggested, justice. I want Michael's killer.

"I dreamed Michael's last dream the other night, so I know how your people trapped him and tried to bind him with a contract. And I know that somebody in your Lodge killed him when he proved more than they could handle. He's still more than you can handle, Mr. Jones. I will do whatever I have to do to avenge his death."

Jones stared out over his lawn at the street for a long moment, the cigarette dangling from his lips. His front door opened and a child stuck her head out.

"Your dinner is getting cold," she said.

"I know, Doll, I'll be there in a minute." He sucked on his cigarette once, blew smoke, sucked again.

"Thank you for your openness and honesty," he said at last, dropping the butt into the bushes beside the porch. "But I hope you don't hold our whole Lodge responsible for the actions of a few misguided individuals."

"Are you saying you didn't want Michael to join you, to perform some service for you?"

"On the contrary, we wanted him very much. He was a powerful person, and would have been of inestimable value to us. But we assigned his recruitment to certain people who maybe shouldn't have had the job. They bungled it, and made Michael worthless to us. As for who killed him, I can't answer that."

"Or won't?" Morgan asked. He was finding it hard not to be taken in by Jones's sincere and friendly manner.

"Both. You must understand, we cannot violate the integrity of the Lodge for any reason whatsoever. The incident was unfortunate, but I can say no more than that. To do so would be to reveal too much about ourselves to you."

"What if I offered to exchange services?" Morgan asked. Phoebus's claws dug into him, in warning. "Isn't there something I could do for you, in payment for the name of Michael's killer?" The claws dug harder. He ignored them.

"Mr. Van Alan, why would you ever want to do anything for us? You already have magical talents; you can get whatever you want on your own stick. No, Van Alan, I can't accept that."

"I want to find Michael Scott's killer," Morgan persisted. "To be quite frank about it, Mr. Jones, I'm willing to put myself at the disposal of the Lodge in exchange for that information." The claws dug hard. He forced himself not to wince.

Jones took a deep breath, and let it out very slowly.

"This really has you bugged, doesn't it?" he asked.

"It does. How about it?" His repressed anger and grief forced him to continue with the proposition, in spite of the very real danger to his soul that it represented. "Is that kind of deal possible?"

"I don't know," Jones said. "I can't make decisions like that. You'll have to talk to our Lodge Master. I'm only the Marshall."

"All right, how do I do that?" Phoebus's claws, he realized, were no longer grabbing him in warning. The cat was terrified.

"You'll have to trust us for a bit, Mr. Van

Alan," Jones said. "And you'll have to understand that you'll be restrained from certain actions during the interview."

"I understand. Just let me know whenever
you're ready." He stood up from the swing.

"I'll set it up right now," Jones said, and as
at their first meeting, the strange light came
into his eyes.

Chapter Fifteen

✛ ✛ ✛

BEFORE MORGAN COULD move or protest, it was
done. He was suddenly standing in an am-
ber-colored room, cubical in shape, with amber-
colored "furniture," strange shapes that stood
here and there seemingly at random.

There was no obvious source of the golden-
colored light that softly illuminated the room.
There was no smell to the air. There was no
sound. And there had been no sense of transition. The shift had been perfectly done, and the
resonance of the Lattice rapidly damped away
to nothing.

And Phoebus was not with him.

The room was about twenty feet on a side and
twenty feet tall. There was something like a
hassock behind Morgan's knees. He decided
he'd better sit down if he didn't want to fall
over. The "hassock" seemed to be an integral
part of the floor, as did the three or four other
objects, whose shapes were completely mean-

ingless to him. The hassock thing had a plasticky feel to it, in spite of its metallic amber color.

In the middle of the room was what appeared to be a narrow spiral stairway, going from ceiling to floor, with a round trap door at top and bottom. There was a closed door in each of the four walls.

There were no sharp corners anywhere. The corners and edges of the room were rounded, as were those of the doors, the stairs, and of the other objects that seemed to have grown out of the floor like warts. Everything was of the same bronzy amber color as the walls and floor and ceiling. Even the sourceless light was deep gold.

If it really was light, he thought. It wasn't a radiance as he knew it. There were no highlights or shadows. There didn't seem to be anything mediating his direct perception.

The more he thought about it, the more he doubted he was really using his eyes at all. It was more like hearing, a radarlike business, because there seemed to be a quality of sound to the room. The perception of golden light could just as easily be described as the perception of a soft musical tone. Thought of in that way, the whole room took on a different aspect.

Because in that case the room was pitch black. Or rather, sight had no meaning, and sound was the only way by which one could know one's environment. He could hear the radar echoes from the walls, from the objects he decided to call furniture. The sounds echoing off the central stairway were oddly complex. He wasn't sure now that it really was a stairway.

It was a novel experience, as if he were a bat. He wondered that he should ever have thought of this mode of perception as seeing. Vision, as a concept, was totally foreign to this place.

The whole room was flooded with a soft, pure sound that provided the medium of his perception. He had no idea where the sound came from, and it didn't seem to matter. His audio discrimination was fantastic, a thousand times better than it had ever been before. He could hear the differences in texture between the smooth walls and the soft floor.

Except that it wasn't exactly that way either. His hands slid over the plastic surface of the thing on which he was sitting. It was an odd sensation. He only called the feeling plastic because he didn't have any other word for it. There was no sense of temperature, only of a smooth and somewhat resilient surface.

As he thought about it he realized that he could feel the distant walls directly, without moving from his seat. It wasn't by hearing but by touch that he knew this place. He could feel—without using his hands—the banisters, rails, and treads of the spiral staircase. Now he knew that while that object might serve as a stairway, it was not like anything he had ever perceived before, in spite of the closed trapdoors at top and bottom.

There were no sharp corners, because they would hurt. There was no sight or sound, really, because they weren't necessary. He could feel everything, as if his nerve endings extended out from his body to the wall. He concentrated on this for a while until he noticed the peculiar taste of an object across the room from him.

He'd gone the whole synesthetic cycle. His smell-taste sense sharpened with growing awareness as his sense of touch disappeared. With no other sense to guide him, he surveyed the room from where he sat, smell-tasting the furnishings, the doorways, the walls and floor, even the distant tang of the ceiling. He knew objects by their odor, knew where they were by the direction of their scent, how far away by the intensity. It was not so very different from sight after all.

With that realization sight, as it were, returned. But now he knew he was perceiving this place not by any one of his accustomed senses, nor by all of them together, but by some other means entirely. His brain was simply interpreting these percepts in familiar terms, and sight was the sense he found it easiest to deal with.

He'd lost track of how long he'd been here; there was no sense of time at all. For all he could tell, time might not even exist here, regardless of his sense of duration.

At last the surprise of newness abated. Supposedly he was going to meet the chief of the local Servants' group, but there was nobody else in this "room," as far as he could tell.

He got up from whatever it was he was sitting on and went to the nearest door and opened it. As he did so he realized that "up" and "sitting" and "went" didn't really describe what he'd done. As sight was just a familiar analog for an unfamiliar mode of perception, so his sense of movement and place was an analog for an unfamiliar state of being. Nothing in this place was as it was in his own world.

He "opened"—an act that did not move anything—the "door"—an object that did not close anything—and "looked"—a sense that had no meaning here—"into"—a direction that served no function—the other "room"—a place that was not a place or a time or an idea.

The other room was identical to the one in which he was standing. At the far side was another door, and at it was a man, his back toward Morgan, peering through into another room, identical with this one, at the far side of which was an open door at which stood a man peering into another room at another man peering into another room, and so on into infinity.

Morgan froze. He was not looking into a mirror. If he were, he'd be seeing his own face at least half the time. He looked back over his shoulder and saw that the door on the other side of the room was open. Just beyond it was a figure looking over its shoulder at another door and another figure, and so on again.

The other figure looked just like himself, seen from the back. It was himself. He watched himself as he closed the door, and then he was alone again. But then, he always had been.

He stood dizzily for a moment, leaning against the closed door for support. The two opposite walls were in fact the same wall, and there was only one room and one him. It was just a very small universe. He had been looking all the way across it, around its curvature back to the starting place.

He went to the door on his right, looked through, and had the same experience. If there were only one room in this universe, and he were the only living thing in it . . .

But there were still the trapdoors in the floor

and ceiling, at the foot and head of the thing he might as well call a spiral stair.

Almost reluctantly he went to it. The round door at his feet opened downward, the stairs continuing through the opening without a break. How that was done he didn't know, and didn't really care to speculate. Below him was a completely different room, and the trapdoor at the bottom of this next flight of stairs was closed.

With a sigh of relief, he started down. There really weren't treads. But then, he really didn't have hands and feet. But if he thought about it, he became paralyzed. The only thing to do was to let his brain supply him with analogs, however false they might be, and go on with it.

This room was a very different place from the one above—given that "below" and "above" hadn't any meaning here. The objects in it were different, the overall arrangement was different, but the size of the room was the same, a cube twenty feet on a side. Except, of course, that "cube" was a translated concept too. More than that, there was a different feel to the room, as if it served a different function. It somehow made Morgan feel a lot more comfortable.

Now that he thought about it, he realized the room above had given him no sense of function at all. This room did. Without being able to recognize or name any of the objects in it—or guess for what purpose they might be used, from something as small as his fist to something the size of a bed—they nonetheless gave the room the definite atmosphere of an "office," whatever that might be in this place. The room above, on the other hand, was as functionless as empty space. It hadn't even had the feeling of closet or storage. It was just there, not used for anything at all.

As in the room "above," there was a door in each of the four walls. Almost fearfully, lest he find this part of the universe as small as the other, he went to one of the doors and opened it. A completely different room lay beyond. And there was somebody in it.

It was a person, though it "looked" nothing like the image of himself he had seen. His brain interpreted the sensory input as a humanlike male, but beyond that he could determine nothing.

The being had what was analogous to a body, without actually having one, supported somehow with parts that might serve as arms or might not, and a place that was its center of perception but was not a head. As Morgan looked at it he kept losing track of what part was which, and ended up being uncertain that there were any parts at all. The harder he tried to really "see" the being for what it was, the more confused he became. If he just relaxed and took his perceptions for granted, he got the distinct impression of a "man."

The being was not facing him, but then, that was also just a matter of interpretation. The figure had no back or front; it was just not attending to Morgan right now. It was . . . doing something, occupied with certain of the objects in the room.

This room had the feeling of "bedroom" to it, though he could not have said why. He didn't think "sleep" or "privacy" had anything like the same meaning here as they did back on his own world.

"Excuse me," Morgan said, aware that his "words" were not vocal, visual, tactile, or gustatory, but something quite different. The other being stopped its activity, and without changing its position was now facing him. Rather, it was now directing its attention toward him.

"OH, HERE YOU ARE," the being said/flashed/touched/odored, except it was more like "WHAT ARE YOU DOING HERE?" or "IT'S ABOUT TIME." Except, of course, what it had said didn't mean any of those things at all.

"I'm sorry to disturb you," Morgan said, as it were. "I was sent here."

"I KNOW/ANOTHER ONE?/TAKE IT EASY/WELCOME," the being answered, with more meanings in its "words" than that. Morgan just couldn't catch them all.

"I'm supposed to meet someone, I think," Morgan said.

"I UNDERSTAND," the being answered, in effect. "WE'VE BEEN WAITING/IT ALWAYS TAKES SO LONG." The being went to the foot of the spiral stair in the center of the room and waited until Morgan resolved his uncertainty and went to join it. Or him. Then the being went down the stairs through the floor, and after a moment's hesitation, Morgan followed.

The room below was different from the previous three. It had an air of "lobby," or "living room" to it. There were several other beings present. They were similar to the first one, but now he knew they were not really humanlike at all. He wondered what they would look like if they were ever to come to his world.

One of the other beings was a male, like Morgan's guide, but doubly so, or so it seemed. Another was female. A third was a bit of both. The concepts of male and female were only further interpretations of qualities he did not truly perceive or understand. Whether those qualities had anything to do with gender or sex or reproduction was beyond him to determine.

Chapter Sixteen
✜ ✜ ✜

THERE WAS ANOTHER person present, one who was truly human, like himself. Morgan could have distinguished him from the others simply by the fact that this one had a front and a back, whereas the others didn't. But more than that Morgan could not say. He could no more identify any details about this person than one could distinguish the verbs in a language one had never heard before. This person partook of the same ambiguity and multiple sense/meaning everything else here did. Morgan suspected that, to this other person's perception, he appeared the same.

Morgan looked down at his own body. Now that he had another human with which to compare, he saw he was correct. Up there in that first room, he had seen himself as himself only because he had known no better. That was what he had unconsciously expected to see, in spite of the surprise of the endless row of open doors.

To a stranger he would appear as this stranger now appeared to him, as a human but with no way to recognize any identifying characteristics. If he met this man again back home, he would never know it.

"As you can see," the person, undoubtedly the Lodge Master, said, "this miniature universe is a perfect place to meet face-to-face while retaining total anonymity. I know it's you, Van Alan, only because these people tell me so, and because I was expecting you. Otherwise, I couldn't have told you from my mother—except for the difference in sex. If it's any comfort, I find this place as confusing as I know you must."

"It's fascinating," Morgan said. He had to keep that fascination from distracting him from his purpose here. "Where are we?"

"At the very edges of reality. If you have the opportunity, you should come back here some time and explore. It is quite a small universe, really, as you must have suspected upstairs. A whole universe, only two hundred eighty feet in diameter, taking the longest measure. Of course, that's trying to describe it in terms with which you and I are familiar, and while I think the analogy is a good one, I'm not sure it is accurate—its dimensions are not the same ones as in our universe.

"For example, you arrived in one of the rooms where this universe is only twenty feet wide as it were. At the other places it's sixty feet, or two hundred eighty, or one hundred forty. Its 'size' differs from place to place. It truly is a miniature. And its whole population numbers exactly fourteen individuals. They are separate beings, but sometimes I think they might once have been just one person, and at other times that originally there were maybe three or four dozen of them.

"I've spent a lot of time in this miniature universe, just trying to figure it and its inhabitants out. Fortunately they don't object to me, and I've been very careful not to antagonize them. It's a challenge.

"Oh, and another thing," he went on. "Try a little magic."

Morgan hesitated, wondering what kind of a trap he would be walking into—as if any further entrapment were necessary.

"Go ahead," the Lodge Master said. "It won't hurt. Just try it."

Morgan tried the easiest spell he knew, the trick of making fire appear at the end of his thumb. But when he didn't really have any thumbs . . . and there was no such thing as fire . . . and sigils were meaningless, and chants made no sound . . .

"Magic just doesn't work here," the other person said. "With the one exception that one can enter or leave by a particular spell. Even that doesn't work *in* this universe, only in getting to or from it. Otherwise, this place follows its own unique laws. It's all very simple. And very, very safe. You can't do anything to me, nor I to you. Even if we *could* figure out a way to damage each other, these people wouldn't let us.

"So, now, let's get down to business. As I understand it, you are willing to perform a service for us in exchange for the identity of the person who killed your friend, Michael Scott. Is that correct?"

"It is."

"I understand that you want vengeance, 'justice' as you call it, but that is up to you. We would not even consider giving you the identity of Scott's killer had not he—or she—bungled things and thus be deserving of punishment. If you achieve your vengeance, that will suffice. If you die in the attempt, that person will, in some measure, be restored to our good graces. The rest of the Lodge will neither hinder nor help either of you.

"You must understand that we regret Michael Scott's death almost as much as you do. He could have been a most valuable Servant. As an indirect result of his death—which deprives us of his services—we have lost another member, a faulty one it's true, but an Initiate, nonetheless. And now you propose to eliminate yet another member or so, in order to satisfy your desire for revenge. There aren't all that many of us, after all, Mr. Van Alan, and where would that leave us? Not only without Michael Scott, but also without at least two other Lodge members."

"You can't blame me for O'Reilley," Morgan protested.

"Oh, but we can. If you hadn't come to Harborbeach, he wouldn't have been put into the position he was in. Had he never met you, he would have served us usefully for many years to come. But be that as it may, the person you seek is a member of our Lodge, regardless of how badly he or she may have bungled the recruitment of your friend.

"What's done is done. The point remains, you will have to perform a service that will compensate us in significant measure for the losses we have incurred, and may continue to incur if you succeed in your plans. Do you understand that?"

"I do." He refrained from pointing out that they wouldn't have lost anybody's services if they hadn't tried to pervert Michael. They were not amenable to that kind of logic. "What do you want me to do?"

"You have, I believe, seen the mausoleum behind Scott's house?" The tone could have been dry and sardonic, but Morgan couldn't tell.

"I have," he said.

"You saw, no doubt, the mark of a dagger on the door of the mausoleum. That was where a real dagger once was fastened. It has been put away someplace, where we can't get to it. Apparently, no member of any Lodge can. You are not a member of a Lodge, so you should be free to go there. It is possibly a dangerous place, but that's beside the point. If you will retrieve this dagger for us, that will, we feel, compensate us for the information you seek."

"I see. And how am I to do this?"

"It should not be too difficult. We can't go there, but we can send people there, just as we sent you here. All you have to do is find the dagger and bring it back to us. There will be no difficulty in returning to the real world—once you have the dagger. When you bring it back to us, you will be told the identity of Michael Scott's killer and be free to pursue your vengeance."

"All right. I'll agree to that. But how do I

know you'll live up to your end of the bargain, after I have brought you this dagger?"

"You'll have to trust us. Unless you want to sign a contract."

"No, no, I don't want to bind myself to you forever. Just this one thing, that's all I want."

"Very well," the other person said. "You realize, of course, that if you fail to bring the dagger to us within a fairly reasonable time, we will have to assume you are trying to cheat us. In that case, Mr. Van Alan, you will never learn who killed Michael Scott. Period."

"I understand," Morgan said. He didn't like the idea of giving this Lodge anything it valued. Once he had the identity of Michael's killer, he would come back to the Lodge and take the dagger away from them again. He started to say something more, but before he could speak he felt a crushing lurch, and the floor gave way beneath him.

PART FOUR

Humans yield to Evil for simple reasons. They sell their souls to the devil for revenge, sex, wealth, notoriety, power.

In stories about pacts with the Devil, the signer usually gets off the hook by some bit of cleverness. That isn't the way it works. What the people who tell the stories forget is that it isn't the exchange of services that damns the signer. It is when the mortal first accepts the exchange. Whether the contract is ever fulfilled or not is irrelevant.

Not everybody who signs a pact with the Devil winds up damned, of course. There are those rare exceptions where the demonic minion is especially stupid, and those are the ones people remember and elaborate into stories.

There are also the cases where a mortal has the moral courage and strength to turn completely away from the Tukhanox, and in so doing immolate him- or herself and escape with their souls though their life is lost.

Immortality is promised, but never given. Eventually, all mortals under the influence of Evil die and, simply by virtue of their being evil, are assumed into the network of Intelligence which is Evil. They are damned.

Some of them, however, while they live, have the potential and desire to be of further service to the Force of Death. They are taught magic, and have popularly been called "witches,"

131

though not all "witches" are evil. Their objective is simply power.

They go under many names: The Agents of the Tukhanox, the Court of the Cold Throne, the Followers of Fryga. Most commonly, they are called the Servants of Death.

Many work alone, but in isolation are rather ineffectual. They achieve most in deed and satisfaction when they band together in Lodges.

Chapter Seventeen

✤ ✤ ✤

MORGAN FELL to the ground, shocked, stunned.
His stomach heaved. He knelt on his hands and
knees among low weedy plants. He felt nau-
seous; but he didn't actually throw up. He held
his forehead, which was cold and sweaty. He
gulped a couple of times but didn't vomit. When
he was sure he was going to be all right, he
stood up to look around. Phoebus was nowhere
in sight.

Gradually the scale of the place penetrated
his still-dazed mind. He was in a forest, but the
trees were gigantic. The nearest one was maybe
thirty feet away and as big around as half a city
block. The trunk went up and up and up, three
hundred feet before the first of the huge limbs
branched from it.

He looked around at the plants growing near
him on the ground. They were no bigger than
what he was used to back home, and seemed
very grasslike. "Phoebus," he called. There was
no answer.

He saw a flat place he could clear of the
grasslike plants and weeds and prepare a spell
that would enable him to find the dagger. There
was no sense in wasting time. He inscribed a
large cross on the patch of bare ground. In the
corners he scribbled Hebrew and Raen char-
acters. He started the spell, one hand in the
Space position, the other in Form, and chanted
a rather long incantation.

When he finished he stood still for a long moment, feeling the thrill of the spell, feeling the folds and lines in space that pointed to the location of the dagger. It was here, but about two hundred miles away.

He stood, put both hands in the Space position, with thumb, first, and little fingers out, second and ring fingers folded in across the palms. He held his arms out to the sides, palms up. He chanted, *"Shehraeraengie."* He felt the thrill begin, but it was different this time. It started in his shoulders first, then worked down through his spine, building in intensity to a peak. And then he was up.

It was just an inch or so, but he was in the air. He'd never been very good at this, though he loved the sensation once he got going. It wasn't the flying but the looking down that frightened him and made him feel clumsy. It was six months since he'd flown last.

He felt the power course through him, a wave of pleasure from his head down through his shoulders and spine. It was the force of this power that kept him aloft, for he still had weight.

He put his arms down—he'd held them outstretched all this time for balance—looked up at the tree limbs far overhead, and felt the power flow through his body. He "pushed" and went up, up, faster, higher, going into it with a rush, like a swimmer diving into cold water.

He stopped short of a huge limb just over his head. It was maybe fifteen feet in diameter, its bark reddish green and smooth but rippled into waves. He reached one hand up and touched the limb. It was as if he was hanging there, held by the palm of his hand against the bark of the tree. Now came the part that always frightened him. He looked down.

Three hundred feet or so below him was the ground. He felt his stomach go tight. His bladder wanted to cut loose, but he kept control of himself. He hung there, feeling the fear, feeling the power, the exhilaration, waiting for the fear to go away, waiting for the excitement to die down.

After a while he began to feel better. Slowly he lowered himself until he could no longer touch the branch overhead. So much for pretending to be dangling from it. He was just there, in the air, supported by his will alone, balanced on the thrust of the power of flight. In spite of his fear, he held his position perfectly well.

His teacher had taught him a maneuver designed to help him get the worst over with. Morgan had done it under supervision several times, and it worked. But now he was going to have to do it alone. As it always did, the thought of it frightened him silly.

He bent over backward, pushing with the power of flight, which made him curve out and down in a huge arc until his feet were up over his head. Turning upside down backward was the worst part, because it disoriented him, but now he could sense his position accurately again. Then, still pushing, he shot straight down toward the ground, far faster than a fall. He watched as the ground rushed up to meet him. He waited until the last minute, then arched upward, pushing as hard as he could, turning up in a tight arc until he was upright, six inches off the ground. He stopped dead still.

He panted. He was all over damp with sweat, and breathless. And he was exhilarated by the flight as well as the magic.

He rose up into the air and started off, flying halfway between the branches and the ground, a hundred fifty feet up or so. He moved off toward the east as fast as he could, flying free, following the trace of the dagger.

Now that his initial fear was overcome, he felt good. Though he seldom had the courage to get himself started without prodding from his teacher, he had to admit that flying was one of the greatest pleasures a magician had.

He watched the landscape slip by below him. From his position it was easy to lose track of the scale of the forest. Only occasionally, when he passed over animals browsing on the verdure below, would his true altitude become obvious.

It was a mature forest. The trees were well spaced, and all the weaker specimens had long since been shaded out. There were exceptions, two or three varieties that, like the dogwood or holly or redbud back on Earth, were much smaller than their neighbors, and that seemed to prefer the protection of the lower stories. They were layered and spreading, and none was more than two hundred feet tall.

As he passed by one of these, Morgan saw that its leaves were no bigger than those on trees back on Earth. As far as he could tell, the same was true of the larger trees. The growth on the forest floor, all creepers, shrub, or grasslike plants, also seemed of a normal size.

His exhilaration increased as he flew along. Now that he was getting used to it, it was hard to believe that he had ever been afraid of flying. But he knew from past experience that once he spent any amount of time on the ground again his acrophobia would come back with renewed force.

He flew over a place where one of the huge trees had fallen. Its gigantic trunk was half sunk into the soft soil of the forest floor. The swath it had torn in falling, perhaps two or three years ago, was phenomenal, but already its neighbors were growing into the clear spaces overhead, where for now the blue sky above was visible.

After a couple of hours he went down to take a rest. Flying was faster than walking, but took a lot of energy. He landed near a bush that was covered with small, purple berries. A simple spell to warn against poisons told him they were fit to eat. He gathered them and ate them as quickly as he could.

He was interrupted by the appearance of an animal, a mantislike creature of some kind, taller than he, reddish brown in color. It stalked through the undergrowth on four long, thin legs, with two more forelegs held up as if in prayer, with very mantislike claws. It was not an insect, however, since it was covered with fur, had four eyes, and a mouth like a wolf.

It was still some fifty feet off when it made a sudden move into a clump of reedlike plants. It came up with an animal that looked like an insane cross between a rabbit and a pelican, with long ears, large hind legs, and pouched beak, and four front limbs folded up against its chest like wings. It was as big as a turkey. It screeched until the mantis-creature bit through its throat. The blood was bright red. The mantis-wolf looked over at Morgan and commenced to eat where it stood, apparently not minding his presence at all.

"I think it's time to move on," Morgan said to himself. He cast the Flight spell and was up in the air at once, without even a thought for his fear of heights.

He was enjoying the experience as he flew on. He regretted his timidity about heights that had kept him from flying more often. The power rushing through his body exhilarated him, as did the sense of freedom, and the speed and motion. It wa—

The invisible strands had him before he knew what was happening. His body recoiled from the sudden stop, swinging backward, then forward again, then hanging still.

Then he noticed the globules of glue on the strands, even as he managed to wrap a few more around himself in his effort to get free. That could mean only one thing. This was a spiderweb.

The sudden awareness of his predicament made him freeze. Now he could feel the faint tremors running through the web. Somewhere, not too far away, was the spider.

He forced himself to be calm. He let himself hang, putting his full weight on the strands holding him, and started to disentangle one hand. The glue on the web seemed to be about as tacky as adhesive tape. It peeled off if he was slow and careful about it. It stuck especially well to his clothes, but not so well to his skin, where perspiration got under the glue and loosened it.

Though the glue was not that sticky, the strands of the web were incredibly strong. Thick as hundred-pound test monofilament line, they resisted his efforts to break them. He couldn't get to his pocketknife, tangled up as he was, so he had to just pull himself free, strand by strand.

He felt a tremor in the web and looked up.

Its body was about as big as his own. Its legs spanned maybe eight feet. It was brown and russet, with odd points along its abdomen. It had ten legs instead of eight, and three segments to its body instead of two. But for all that, it was still a spider in his book.

He ceased his struggles. If he was still, the spider might take longer coming to investigate.

He felt his stomach knotting. Here he was, so tangled he could hardly move. The spider was not more than forty feet from him, upward and to his left, no longer partially concealed by a low loop of leafy vine.

The only spell sure to be effective that he knew one hundred percent was the flame thrower. But he didn't know it well enough to do it in his head with any degree of certainty. Under the circumstances, his anxiety and fear were certain to ruin his concentration.

The spider took a step or two and slid five feet nearer.

The more Morgan thought about the flame-thrower spell, the more he thought it worth a try. Anything was worth a try as opposed to just hanging here waiting to become a spider's lunch.

With that spell, the direction the fire went depended in part on where the magician was looking, and in part on where his or her hand was pointing. In Morgan's present case, neither hand was pointing at the spider. Still, if he let off one charge it might frighten the monster and at the same time burn through some of the strands holding him.

The spider moved again. Now it was less than thirty feet away. It had seven eyes, three on each side of its face and one in the middle. Its mandibles were partially open, gaping sideways. Each one sported two fangs, like ice picks.

One of the front legs reached out tentatively to test the web where the force of Morgan's impact had torn it. The clawed foot touched the strands, then plucked them, sending Morgan jiggling. From the resonance of his shaking, the spider would know Morgan's position and weight. Morgan remained as quiet as he could, not giving in to the urge to thrash around and entangle himself more. Maybe the spider would think he was just a piece of debris.

He stayed motionless, but he put his left hand, which was nearer the spider, into the Fire position. Now to trace the sigil. He didn't trust his visualization under these circumstances. It didn't have to be large, just precise. As gently as he could, he moved his hand through the lines of the sigil and chanted the incantation.

A gout of flame a hundred feet long streaked out from his hand, most of it wasting on empty air, the flaming material falling to the ground below. But some of the web had been burned. When those strands let go he was jerked up and to the right, away from the spider, which recoiled but did not retreat. Morgan started to cast the spell again.

The spider was distracted. Morgan twisted around so that his left hand was pointing at the monster and finished the chant. The flame roared out, burning away the web and enveloping the spider, which fell, legs curled, to the ground a hundred fifty feet below, where it splattered.

That left Morgan swinging, suspended by only two strands now. His arms and legs were hopelessly tangled and twisted in the fibers.

Then he realized his flight spell was no longer working. The strands above him lowered a foot with a jerk. He felt panic rise up in him as his acrophobia came on full-force. He dropped another foot.

He tried to hold himself still, but the web above him was giving away, and dropped him another six inches. He was covered with a mass of sticky webs, which hindered him as he worked his hand into his pocket, found the knife, pulled it out, and opened it with his teeth. He was grateful he habitually kept his knife sharp.

He cut away the strands holding his legs. He swung away to the right, then dropped another five feet.

He couldn't think. It was nearly a hundred fifty feet to the ground, and he was going to fall. He could feel it, see the forest floor rushing up to meet him—

He wrapped some loose webbing around his chest, stretching it from an undamaged part of the web, hoping it would hold while he cut his arms free.

He worked carefully, so as not to dislodge himself any farther. At last he had his left arm untangled. Bits of web still dangled from his coat sleeve, but he could move his hands.

Then his right arm was freed. He assumed the position for the Flight spell. And glory, it worked! He rose up into the air as the power flooded through him.

Quickly he cut off the rest of the web and flew down to the ground as fast as he could.

He stood a moment, shivering with relief at his escape, then methodically divested himself of the remnants of the spider's web. He looked over to the carcass a dozen feet away to his left, saw the broken body, and shuddered. Then he let the power flow through him again, and he went up, away from the shreds of the great spiderweb.

Chapter Eighteen
❖ ❖ ❖

AROUND THE MIDDLE of the afternoon—it was hard to tell for sure with the sky completely screened by the foliage of the giant trees—he flew over what looked like another good berry patch and went down.

After eating his fill he flew on without incident for a couple of hours. Then, out of the upper reaches of the forest, a hawklike bird with four wings dived at him and nearly took off a part of his face as it whistled by. He saved himself only by flipping over on his back so that the bird's talons missed him by inches.

The bird was very angry for some reason and attacked him several more times, but he put up an anti-animal shield that kept it from getting any closer than ten feet. It screeched its frustration, still trying to get to him. He flew on, and after a while it dropped behind.

The light in the forest began to fade as night came on. He started to look for a place to spend it. He didn't want to fly through the dark. He didn't really know what kind of a place he was looking for, so he kept on flying until he came to a clearing in the woods, half a mile across or more. The ground here was thickly grown with low plant life, nothing more than twenty feet tall. He could see that the forest roof was about a thousand feet above the ground.

But what caught his attention, in the warm light of the setting sun behind him, was the tree growing at the opposite edge of the clearing, dwarfing all the rest. Its trunk rose, straight and limbless, clear of the tops of the other trees. Only then did its branches spread out, the lowest one at a thousand feet, the top of the tree at least another thousand feet higher.

He flew around the edge of the clearing, staying just inside the margin of the forest, keeping the giant tree in sight. As he rose higher into the branches, he could see that the canopy of the forest was roughly divided into layers, with a whole ecology of its own. It was richly populated with dozens of kinds of animals, hundreds of species of birds, huge metallic and iridescent insects. There were parasitic plants, epiphytic vines, symbiotic bushes growing on the middle

limbs, dangling below the branches, bridging
the trees. Every species of plant seemed to sport
its own flower, even the trees, many of them
over a foot across, all brilliantly colored and
bizarrely shaped.

He came around the edge of the clearing, still
a hundred feet from the uppermost branches of
the forest, and neared the trunk of the great
tree. It was like approaching a cliff.

The bark of the tree was deeply fissured, cut
up into rough diamond-shaped plates by diag-
onal cracks. Each plate was thirty to forty feet
across, the separating cracks about a hundred
feet or so long and up to ten feet deep and five
or six feet wide.

There were ample signs that some kind of animal lived in the fissures, using them as a highway up and down the tree. There were
pathways worn into the tough material of the
bark, just inside the cracks, zigzagging back and
forth up the tree. Here and there a hole had
been bored through from one fissure to another, to get past a dead end or constricted
place. In other places huge chunks of bark had
been wedged into a crack to form a kind of
bridge. In the steeper parts rough steps had
been gouged out of the bark path to make
climbing easier.

Morgan began to suspect that the path was
an artifact of intelligent people, rather than of
animals.

He flew upward, just a few feet from the
trunk of the great tree. At last he rose above
the top of the forest, a green sea of foliage,
golden-lit by the last rays of the setting sun.
Above him now were the first of the lower

branches of the super giant. It was well over twenty feet in diameter, flattened on the top. It would provide a perfectly safe place to rest for the night.

He continued to rise, past another great branch twice as big as the first, and stopped suddenly when he saw the three furry people standing on top of it, looking down at him as if expecting him.

Morgan hung in midair, startled and surprised and trying not to show it. The three furry people stood about fifteen feet from the edge of the limb, stiff and wide-eyed, staring back. They wore long loincloths of red and purple and gold cloth, but otherwise were naked except for their short fur, light brown and unmarked. They each had six limbs, like all the other animal life here except the spider. Two limbs were legs, two were arms, and the middle pair could function as either, judging from their postures.

They were not cute in spite of their soft fur, long bushy squirrellike tails, and flat humanlike faces. Their noses were small and black, like a cat's; their eyes, though large and liquid, were like a horse's; their large round ears were set too high on the sides of their heads; and their human-looking lips concealed imperfectly their large, strong, but nonrodent teeth. In fact, they were rather ugly.

They all carried what looked like short spears, with narrow barbed heads, attached to light lines that were coiled at their belts— harpoons. They must have been the ones who made the trails in the bark, Morgan thought. The three tree-dwellers looking down at him were totally inhuman, but patently intelligent.

Morgan moved slowly upward toward the three tree-dwellers until he was level with the edge of the limb but still just beyond its curving edge. Then he moved sideways, away from the trunk of the tree, circling a bit, and so came to rest on the limb a few yards from them.

When he was over the flat part of the limb, he settled down onto it but kept his Flight spell in full operation. He started to raise his empty hands as a gesture of friendliness, but the three harpoons came up as he did so. On a sudden inspiration, he crossed his arms and stuck his hands under his armpits. The harpoons went down. The three tree-dwellers visibly relaxed.

"I apologize for my intrusion," he said. He bowed slightly but kept his hands clasped under his arms. "I'm sorry I frightened you. I have been sent here to find a dagger. Can you understand me?"

"Yes," the leader said slowly, "I can understand you." He—or she—wore no marks to distinguish him or her from the other two. His or her leadership was apparent solely from his or her attitude. "You are *se* of whom it has been spoken. Will you come with us?"

He couldn't understand how these people could have heard of him; nor did he believe it was going to be as easy as it seemed. He didn't ask any questions, but followed the tree-dwellers to the main trunk of the tree, where they went up one of the paths cut into the deeply fissured bark. Morgan frequently had to use his hands to help him climb the steeper parts. The tree-dwellers, however, went to four legs when the situation required, which still left them with two arms free.

After about half an hour of climbing, just as the sun was finally going down behind the horizon of trees, they came to a platform built out on a branch. It was not large, but it was solidly built—a permanent structure instead of a temporary camp. As they stepped onto the platform, lights started to wink on here and there among the leaves above and around them. There was a whole city here up in the branches of the tree.

Morgan was winded from the climb, but the tree-dwellers seemed unaffected. They walked on two legs here instead of four. Morgan was hard-pressed to keep up.

He was led from the platform, by means of a bridge, to another platform higher up. And so the climb continued, by bridges, stairs, ramps, higher and higher, from platform to platform. Most of these were fairly large, enclosed with walls and a roof, and with a balcony around all four sides. The construction reminded Morgan of Japanese paper houses, though the style was completely different.

These people were masters of the bridge in all its forms, both rigid and flexible. Many of the platforms were solidly anchored to the branches, but as many others were suspended between branches, by arches, beams, or cables. It was a three-dimensional city, half suspended in midair.

He saw few other tree-dwellers as they climbed. He suspected he was being taken by back ways.

At last they came to a railed walkway along a branch and followed it out to a building somewhat separated from the others. Here they

stopped on a railed porch while the leader
opened a sliding panel set into the wall. Then
they escorted him inside.

The space inside the building was divided into
rooms by partitions made of what looked like
paper stretched over lath frames. This first
room was only about ten feet wide by fifteen
feet deep, with a low desk at the far end, behind
which another tree-dweller knelt on four folded
legs. The walls of the room were painted with
bright pictures. There were portraits, land-
scapes, scenes of daily life, still lives, all separated from each other by painted borders.
There were no chairs.

"Here is the Sorcerer," the leader said to the
tree-dweller behind the desk. This other one
looked him over slowly. Morgan was unable to
read the changes of expression on the so alien
yet so humanlike furry face.

"*Se*'s with the finance committee right now,"
the one behind the desk said at last. He or she
was evidently a secretary of some kind. The
pronoun "*se*" didn't clear up the matter of gender any. "Still," the secretary went on, "I've
been instructed to send *hem* on in."

"Working awfully late, isn't *se?*" the guide
asked.

"Next season's budget," the secretary said,
still watching Morgan closely. He—or she—rose
from the desk and went out through a sliding
door at one side of the room. Morgan stood, trying to reconcile the prosaic dialogue of the tree-
dwellers with the rest of the situation. After a
moment the secretary came back.

"Will you come with me, please," the secretary said from the doorway. Morgan crossed the room to it. The three guards remained behind.

They entered another room, the walls of which were decorated with abstract designs. There were three or four low tables near the walls, but no people. From there they went into still another room, this one with another low desk, a table in the corner, and a cabinet that looked like it might conceal a bar beside the desk. There was nobody here either.

The secretary indicated that Morgan should sit on the flat cushions in front of the desk and then left.

Morgan looked around at the paintings on the walls. These were pictures of the forest and the great tree, repeated several times. They were stylized, each picture done differently, and all different from those Morgan had seen in the other two rooms. As before, the painting was done directly on the paper of the walls.

There were several lamps, as in the other rooms. Each consisted of a small pot of oil, a burning wick, and a piece of stone on a wire that hung in the flame of the lamp. This stone, like the mantle of a Coleman lamp, glowed white hot and provided all the light. There was no glass chimney, only a polished metal disk behind the flame to reflect the light into the room.

He was left alone for only a moment. Another door behind the desk slid open, and another tree-dweller entered. This one was older than the others. The fur was yellowed; the flesh was sagging like that of an out-of-shape athlete. Morgan started to rise, but the tree-dweller waved him back to his seat. He/she squatted down behind the low desk and looked at him silently for a long moment. Morgan wished that he could read the expression on his/her face. The tree-dweller could be showing abject fear or great mirth and Morgan couldn't tell the difference.

"You are the Sorcerer," the old tree-dweller said, "who's coming has been foretold."

"I'm sorry," Morgan said. "I don't know that."

"Nonetheless, you are *se*. You fly, you have only four limbs, and you seek a dagger."

"Yes, that is true. Do you know where the dagger is?"

The tree-dweller stared at him for a long moment, his/her fingers drumming a rhythm on the top of the desk. Morgan noticed the structure of the hand for the first time. There were six fingers, and a thumb on either side of the palm.

"It is in the *roxeth place*," he/she said at last, "where it has been kept since before our recorded history. I will take you there now."

The tree-dweller stood on two legs, a little taller than Morgan, and led him out through the door by which he/she had entered. The secretary was waiting for them there, and accompanied them as they went through another office, where there were six desks but only one worker left. They paused a moment while the old tree-dweller asked that worker to prepare the *roxeth place*.

This, when they got to it, turned out to be a rather large open-air theater, with low circular platforms surrounding a round stage, sort of like a planetarium theater but without the seats. Lanterns hung all around the perimeter and over the central stage area. Morgan estimated that maybe five hundred of the tree-dwellers could sit there at once.

Two other tree-dwellers met them, and escorted them up to the center stage. On a low table stood an elaborately carved box. The old tree-dweller opened it and took out a dagger.

It had the same straight, thin blade as the mark in the door of the mausoleum, but the large round pommel was missing. It was a ceremonial tool, not a weapon. It had a black hilt and handle, made of some bonelike substance. The only flaw was the missing pommel piece. The prongs that had held it were bent out of shape.

Morgan held out his hand, and the old tree-dweller hesitantly gave him the dagger. It had no edge, was not intended to cut anything. The only reason Morgan knew this was the dagger he was looking for and not some other was that his location spell indicated as much.

"When will you begin?" the old tree-dweller asked.

"I'm sorry, I don't understand."

"You have come to release the power of the dagger. We have waited a long time for this."

"No . . . ," Morgan said warily, "I have come to take the dagger away."

"But no, you cannot do that. This is our dagger, our heritage, our sign that we are the chosen of all the *penarsh*. You are *se*, who's coming has been foretold. You will invest the dagger with your *teva* and release its power."

Morgan looked at the two tree-dwellers. "I think there has been some misunderstanding," he said. "I am not the person you think I am."

"But you must be," the secretary said. "You have all the attributes.

"You are mistaken. I have come to take the dagger back to my world, where it belongs."

As he spoke, a score of tree-dwellers appeared around the perimeter of the theater, all bearing harpoons.

"If you are not the *shama*," the old tree-dweller said, "then you must give the dagger back." He reached for it, but Morgan stepped away from him. The secretary made a grab for the dagger. Morgan knocked him down.

And then harpoons were in the air, arcing toward him. He raced through the same spell that had protected him from Weiss's bullet, orange sparks showering around him, and the harpoons bounced harmlessly off the Matter shield.

"I'm sorry," he said, then levitated straight up into the air, through the foliage overhead.

He went up through the branches as quickly as he could, guided in the darkness by the lights of the structures suspended from and between the limbs. He was close to the trunk of the great tree, within a couple hundred yards or so, where the population was densest. There was enough artificial light for him to be able to avoid natural or artificial obstructions if he didn't fly too fast.

Three times he was attacked by harpoon-wielding tree-dwellers. But his shield still held, and he was not hurt. He thought he should feel guilty about depriving this people of their "heritage," but pushed the feeling out of his mind.

At last he rose above the city with its lights and milling people. Now he had to proceed through the night-dark branches more slowly.

Flying was more difficult this far from the ground, and that slowed him further. And he was tired from his long day's flight, and the climb up the tree. That slowed him still more.

He swerved to miss a branch. It was much smaller than the ones he'd passed below, only about five feet in diameter.

Then he caught a glimpse of purple sky off to the side. He rose higher through the branches, at last nearing the top. All at once he was above the tree. He settled down onto a branch to rest a moment. The purple-black sky was powdered with stars. A glow near the horizon hinted at an as yet unseen moon.

Morgan softly chanted the spell for Night Vision, cursing himself for not having thought of it before. As he said the words, his eyes adapted to the starlight so that he was seeing as well as in daylight.

And then there was a blinding flash of light. His eyes were dazzled, and he clutched for the tree limb to keep from falling.

. . . and found himself in the strange dark parlor of Michael's dream, with its square, modern furniture. It still had a dreamlike quality to it, but this time it was real, and he was awake.

Chapter Nineteen

✥ ✥ ✥

THE DOZEN OR SO people in cloaks, and in hoods this time, stood around the edges of the dark room. They were real too. He was going to be put through an ordeal.

He stepped uncertainly into the center of the room. The people around him began a soft, measured, polite applause.

"Well done," a man said, stepping forward. The voice was oddly modulated, as if to disguise it. Though there was more light here than there had been in the place Morgan had just left, the man's face was totally obscured by the shadow of his hood. He stood in front of Morgan for a moment.

"You have the dagger," the man went on. The deadly applause stopped. The man reached out his hand. Morgan took the dagger from his coat pocket and handed it to him.

"And now will you tell me who killed Michael Scott?" Morgan asked.

"Right after your initiation," the man said.

"Now wait a minute," Morgan said, "that was not a part of the bargain. A service for a service, that was what you said."

"That may be what you were told, but I can't help that. You don't think we'd give you anything if we couldn't be sure you wouldn't use it against us, do you, Mr. Van Alan? No, you will have to sign." He stepped to one side to reveal behind him a brazier glowing hotly. It shed remarkably little light into the room. There were other beings around it, whom Morgan could not clearly see at first. Five of them, he counted, then started as his eyes adjusted to the dim light and the scene before him.

These five beings were demidemons, of a low order compared to others of their kind, but terrible enough in the human world. They would not be here at the service of mere mortals unless someone of great power, such as a Grand Master, was directly involved.

The demons were like huge caterpillars, though they only looked that way when they chose to make themselves visible to mortal eyes. The forward parts of their long pulpy bodies were raised up as high as a man's head. Great webby wings hung from their backs. Their four armlike appendages were doing something to the brazier, and to something in it.

Hard, chitinous faces turned his way, multifaceted eyes stared at him. The fear and the loathing Morgan felt knotting his stomach was caused by their psychic auras, which were intended to make him feel just the way he was feeling. It didn't help him to know that the demons really had no corporeal bodies, that their appearance was just an illusion. He was terrified.

"We have all gone through this little ritual," the man with the oddly modulated voice said as two of the demons came toward Morgan. They gripped his arms with four clawlike hands each and held him securely. His skin crawled at their touch.

"It will hurt," the man said, "but only for a while." Two more demons came to him and dropped down to hold his legs. They might be insubstantial psychic beings, but the bodies they now wore were all too solid, made real by the magic at their disposal. And all too strong.

The fifth demon came up now and opened Morgan's jacket and spread the collar of his shirt wide and pulled it down halfway off his left shoulder. The mandibles of its mouth clicked as the demon worked. Morgan suspected what was coming and tried to brace himself.

"Very well, then," the man said triumphantly. "With this initiation we receive you into the Court of the Cold Throne. All hail to the Crown of Death!"

"All hail to the Crown of Death!" the other members of the coven cried.

Morgan didn't say anything.

Then the fifth demon returned to the brazier. As Morgan had feared, it pulled out red-hot glowing pincers. Sweat broke out all over his body. He had to fight to retain control of his sphincter.

The demon came toward him, its webby wings pulsing, its insect eyes glittering in the glow of the hot instrument it held. It reached out with the pincers. Morgan could feel the heat even before they touched the fold of flesh under his left arm. Then the pincers bit, the pain scorched through his whole body, and his nose filled with the smoke of his own burning flesh.

Then it was over. Gasping and sobbing, held standing by the sixteen strong arms of the four demidemons, he fought to recover himself, to think clearly again. He wanted to curse the people around him, who were all applauding again, but he dared not do so. The Servants were easily offended, and took harsh retribution. What they had done to him they thought of as an honor, not a punishment.

As his strength returned, the man who was leader of this coven came up to him, now holding a large, green-bound book, and a pen. He touched the nib to Morgan's breast. Morgan looked down, saw that he was bleeding. He did not examine the blackened, torn wound, but looked up quickly. The pen filled with his blood. The demons who had held his legs let go to prepare a bandage. The other two holding his arms let go as well, and Morgan swayed a moment before he found his balance. Then the man gave him the pen and held up the book, open toward the back.

On the right-hand page was a contract. Morgan read it.

I hereby swear fealty to Fryga Tukhanox, the Crown of Death, to do her bidding and her work, in all ways required of me.

He was surprised by the feminine pronoun. He noted grimly that there was no clause listing the benefits accruing to the signer.

His hand, holding the pen, shook not just with pain but with the knowledge that this was the real test. Everything that had gone before was just preliminary. But he could not back out now. If he refused to sign, the Servants would kill him. But if he did sign, his soul would be damned the moment he died, and that was worse than death itself.

Unless he didn't use his real name.

If the Servants found him out, using a false name would be taken as the worst kind of in-

sult and his death would not be pretty or quick.
But he had to take the chance. He raised the
bloody pen and scrawled across the bottom of
the page the same name by which these people
knew him: *Lester Van Alan.*

They didn't jump him. There was no earth-
quake. He didn't feel his soul wrenched from
his body. He had just passed the test.

It seemed anticlimactic. The man handed the
book, still open, to another member of the
Lodge, who took it away somewhere. The demidemons applied the bandage to his wounded
armpit. Then all five of the monstrous creatures
went back to the brazier. As Morgan buttoned
his shirt with numb and shaking fingers, demidemons and brazier all shrank to a point and
were gone.

"Welcome to the club," the man said sardon-
ically, extending his hand.

Morgan shook the hand, though he didn't
want to. He was too much at their mercy to
antagonize them now. "When do I learn the
identity of Michael Scott's killer?" he asked.
The pain in his left armpit was terrible.

"Right now, if you wish," the man said. "You
understand, of course, that while we will not
hinder you in attempting vengeance, we will
not aid you either. And your victim may wish
to defend himself."

"I understand," Morgan said simply. He
wished the man would hurry up. He was going
to get sick.

"Very well," the man said. "Dana Kirkpatrick killed Michael Scott." He threw back his
hood, and Morgan stared into the laughing eyes

of Nick Jones. He had not noticed before that they were an amber gold in color.

Then suddenly he was standing in the middle of a grubby public men's room somewhere.

Chapter Twenty
✣ ✣ ✣

THIS FINAL TRANSITION, on top of everything else, took all his remaining strength away. Since he was right in front of the stalls, he entered the nearest one and sat down, then turned around, knelt in front of the stool, and threw up.

The pain in his armpit kept him from thinking coherently. He needed a chance to collect himself, organize his thoughts. Jones's claim that Dana had killed his brother, and the implication she was a Servant, upset him even more.

He spat, wiped his mouth with a tissue, and got shakily to his feet. He had regained just enough composure to wonder what had happened to Phoebus. The cat had not been with him since he'd been transported to the miniature universe. He spoke his familiar's name quietly, but there was no answer.

He left the stall and washed his hands at the sink, thankful he had gotten away from the Servants with nothing more than a torn armpit and a falsely signed contract. But here was not the best place to think things through. He left the men's room and found himself in a tavern. How appropriate, he thought wryly.

He went to an empty stool and ordered a scotch on the rocks. While waiting for his drink to come he took out a small cigar and lit it, this time with a match.

The drink came, and Morgan took a long pull. When he put the glass down he saw a familiar face reflected in the mirror. Gary Weiss was sitting beside him.

"Take it easy," Weiss said. "I'm not going to jump you." He waved the bartender over.

"How kind of you," Morgan said sarcastically. "I've been jumped enough already today."

"Run into somebody tougher than you are?"

"Several times," Morgan said as Weiss ordered a beer. "A guy named Nick Jones, for one, the Marshall of the Lodge, and somebody else who's the Lodge Master."

"You're really getting around." The bartender brought the beer. Weiss looked as if he was trying to make up his mind about something. "I talked to Dana today," he said at last. "She confirmed your story about Michael having been missing for six weeks before you came."

"Well, that's progress," Morgan said, not sure just how much Dana had admitted about her own involvement with magic.

"She also said you seemed pretty damned intent on finding Michael's killer."

"I am that," Morgan said, thinking about what Jones had told him.

"So what did you find out?"

"You're not going to like this, Weiss. The Marshall of the Lodge told me it was Dana who killed Michael."

The other man turned to look at him with an expression of mingled dismay, disbelief, and anger. "You damn well better be joking." His voice was a harsh hiss.

"That's what he told *me*," Morgan said. "I don't like it either, because before that they suggested it was another Servant who'd killed Michael."

"So which is she—ah, no, no, you don't mean that Dana's a Servant?"

"That's the implication, and I just hope it's a lie."

"Of course it's a lie," Weiss said. "What else could it be? Dana's no magician." He stared at his reflection in the mirror for a long moment, and then, hesitantly, his eyes turned to look into Morgan's image. "Is she?"

"You'll have to ask her that yourself."

"But Jesus!" Weiss cried. "Even if she's—"

"Keep quiet!" Morgan hissed.

"Even if she's a magician," Weiss said more softly, "I can't believe she's a Servant. Hell, I've known her ever since she came here, three years ago."

"I don't believe so either," Morgan said, "but she could have killed Michael."

"Why, for God's sake?"

"Because she hated the Servants as much as any good magician does, and she had reason to believe Michael had been tricked into signing a contract with the Tukhanox."

"So she killed him, just to reduce the power of the Lodge in Harborbeach."

"She could have. At least, that's what Nick Jones wants me to believe."

"You seem to be on awfully good terms with

these bastards," Weiss said, a new note of suspicion coming into his voice.

"That's what I want *them* to believe," Morgan said softly. He stared at Weiss until the other was forced to turn away.

"Just how deeply into this are you?" Weiss asked after draining his beer and ordering another.

"A lot deeper than I like," Morgan admitted. "I've put my life on the line in order to get to the bottom of this."

"And your soul?"

"That too."

"Jesus." Weiss drank his beer, refusing to meet Morgan's eyes. "Hell, maybe it's not too late, maybe you can just go back to California and forget this all happened."

"It's not that simple," Morgan said. "And besides, what about Michael?"

"But if he signed a contract, his soul is damned. What can you do about that?"

"I've seen the book," Morgan told him. "If I can get to it, I can destroy Michael's contract. God knows how he's suffering now, but with the contract destroyed, that would end and he could pass on in peace."

Weiss was looking at him again. "You signed a contract, too," he said.

"With a false name."

"Jesus, Van Alan, you think *I'm* crazy. They've *got* you now. The Servants will be *watching* you, if you don't take vengeance . . ."

"That's exactly my problem," Morgan said. "I don't want vengeance from Dana, even if she did kill Michael. From her position, she was doing exactly the right thing, and I might have had to kill him myself, in time—"

"If you—touch her—I will—come—and—*get* you."

"So then help me!" Morgan pleaded. "What can I do that will satisfy the Lodge, and get Dana off the hook at the same time? Because if I don't kill her, they will, and blame it on me."

"You are so *stupid*," Weiss almost shouted, then became aware that the other patrons were watching and listening. "You've been set up," he said more quietly but no less intensely. "*Dana's* been set up. If she were a Servant, they'd kill her themselves."

"Unless that's exactly what they're doing, only using me as a tool."

"Jesus! You kill her, I kill you, and the Servants win. You don't kill her, they kill you and her, and the Servants win."

"And in any event," Morgan said, "Michael goes unavenged." He called the bartender over, ordered a double, and left him a big tip to keep him placated.

"When was the last time you talked to *your* teacher?" Weiss asked.

"About a month ago."

"So call him for help."

"I've tried. He seems to be out of touch at the moment."

"You know other magicians? You've tried calling them?"

"Everybody's out of town," Morgan said dryly.

"Jesus." Weiss finished his beer and ordered another. "So what the hell are you going to do?"

"I don't know," Morgan admitted. "Right

now, the fact that I forged the contract might mean they can't actually bind me to it. But if I kill Dana, then they'll have me for sure."

"Not unless I get to you first."

"Gary, if I have to kill Dana, I'd much rather you took me out than that they did."

Weiss looked at him for a long moment. "It's that way, huh?"

"She's given me no encouragement," Morgan said.

"Fat lot of good that does *me*." He called the bartender over for another beer. "Look, Lester, did this Nick Jones say anything about witnessing the killing?"

"Dana's? No. In fact, he said the Servants would not help either of us, in any way whatsoever. Which makes sense, considering."

"So all they want is a body, right?"

"I don't think they'd believe I'd killed her without one."

"But suppose you could put her soul away someplace, give the Lodge her body, and then, when it was safe, bring her back."

"To a rotting corpse?"

"Hell, no, to a new body, or a soulless infant, or anything."

"I kind of like the body she's got."

"Goddammit, so do I, but that's something that can be taken care of later."

"What the hell do you have in mind?"

"Come on, Van Alan, have you never heard of the Retreat of Lost Souls?"

"Ah-h . . ."

"So you're not so smart after all. Think about it."

"That's a bit over my head," Morgan said reluctantly.

"You got any better ideas? Look, Van Alan, you're in a perfect position to do these bastard Servants some real damage—if they trust you. And if you *don't* send her there, *they'll* kill her, and she'll be lost forever."

"Can you help?"

"No." He turned away. "You were right about me. Dammit, I don't *like* being this way. All I know about the Retreat is that it's there, a place where a magician's soul can go or be sent if they're killed or die prematurely. And that you can be reincarnated from there in one way or another."

"Or at least be fully prepared for true death," Morgan added.

"That too. And sometimes contact other living magicians."

"I think I may have something in my grimoire."

"Make it work," Weiss grated. He finished his beer but waved the bartender away. "And then take the Lodge for all it's worth."

"And what will you do?" Morgan asked.

"I don't know. Whatever I can." He got up from his stool and walked out of the bar.

Morgan finished his own drink and left the bar a few minutes later. He was somewhere in downtown Harborbeach. His car was a mile or so away, in front of Nick Jones's house. Walking back to get it would give him more time to think about Weiss's idea. He went to a corner, got himself oriented, and started up the street toward the residential part of town where Jones lived.

He stopped once at a pay phone and tried calling his teacher and fellow magicians again. Again, nobody seemed to be home. He'd upset the balance too much; even the physical systems of the mundane world would no longer work for him.

It was his desire for vengeance for Michael's death that was at fault, he knew. It was small consolation that vengeance was a perfect cover motive for what he was about to do. It was just the kind of thing the Servants understood. Besides, it was what he really wanted anyway, even if he didn't like to admit it.

But it was the desire for revenge that was shutting him off not only from his fellow magicians, but from contact with the Dreamer. It wasn't the Dreamer's doing, but an effect of the laws of balance that prevented Morgan from communing with his patron.

The walk to Jones's house took about an hour. He got in his car, drove back to the hotel parking lot, and walked into the shabby lobby. He climbed the rickety stairs to the seventh floor and went down the crooked corridor to his room.

He was half hoping Phoebus would be waiting for him there, but the cat did not answer his call. He could have gotten lost somewhere in one of the astral zones Morgan had been sent to. Or, as it apparently was with the Dreamer, his familiar could have been cut off from him by his dealings with the Servants and desire for revenge.

He didn't like that thought, but he was now too tired to do more than worry about it. He needed to get some rest, and hoped it would be enough to replenish at least some of his magical energy. He undressed and crawled into bed. He was asleep almost instantly.

When he awoke it was dark. He got out his grimoire and found the spells that would send a person's self to the Retreat of Lost Souls. Those he had recorded were not the most sophisticated, and were intended to be used on someone who was not yet dead but on the verge of dying. The casting of the spell would finish the separation of soul from body, in effect killing the body while preserving the personality.

He dressed, trying not to think about what would happen, to Dana or to him, if the casting failed. Then, in the dark, he performed the complicated ritual that opened a magical aperture between his hotel and Dana's bedroom. The fiery ring of the portal formed, but the thrill of magic gave him no pleasure. Through the ring he could see, in the darkness on the other side, a bed with a sleeping form. A simple spell identified it absolutely as Dana.

He was not surprised at how frightened he was. If he made a mistake, Dana would be unrecoverable. But if he did not present the Lodge with a body, the Servants would more than likely do the job for him, and then either attack him or shut him out, and he would have no chance to discover who had really killed Michael, or why, or what the stone and the dagger had to do with anything. Had it been only his own life at risk, he would have felt the risk was justified, even though he would be damned for murder.

But if he went ahead with this insane plan, the worst that could happen to Dana was that she would be just dead, not damned. And at best, her soul would be preserved, and he could bring her back to life later, when he had the chance.

He stared at Dana for a long time as she lay there in the darkened room. Then he gathered his courage and resolve and cast the Refuge spell. It gave him no pleasure at all. Dana's eyes opened, her heart stopped, her last breath escaped with a sigh, her eyes glazed over, and she was still.

PART FIVE

Worldwide there are hundreds of Lodges of Servants. Large cities may have several. They are by no means organized; their basic greed and philosophy prevent that. They vary in size from about four or five people, to perhaps as many as twenty or so. They vary in strength and effectiveness, depending on internal organization, degree of magical ability, and presence or absence of a demonic mentor.

Within the Lodge "system" there is a hierarchy. Highest is a Grand Master, who is a member of one Lodge but directs the activities of several others. Below that is the Master, the leader of a Lodge. Even a Grand Master's Lodge has a Master. Larger Lodges may also have a Marshall, a second-in-command.

Below that are the Initiates, the magicians of the Lodge, and below that are the Novices, those who have no magic yet, or who are temporarily invested with certain forms of limited power.

People who have simply sold their souls for mundane things are not members of a Lodge. They are only victims. Some of these people take their pittance, thinking they have gotten something in exchange for their souls, and never learn more. From their ranks, Lodge members can sometimes be recruited.

The Servants are cautious and secretive. They are few in number, and while they will hesitate at nothing to achieve their ends, they have learned the folly of exposing themselves to their fellow humans.

If the outside world ever believes that a person can truly do magic, either the magician is persecuted and martyred, as being too dangerous to be allowed to live, or people try to capture and enslave them, which usually results in an early death. This happens whether the magician is a Servant or not. Greed and fear on the part of the rest of the community brings down his or her destruction. Those with the power of magic work in secrecy, for their lives' sake.

Chapter Twenty-one
✦ ✦ ✦

STILL STARING AT the now dead form on the dark bed, he let the fiery ring of the portal close. There was no way of knowing whether his spell had been successful until he had the chance to try to bring her back. He resisted a panic-driven impulse to start searching through his grimoire for the proper spells, and instead lay down on his bed, fully clothed.

He tried to relax, but images of Dana, the dagger, Gary Weiss, and Nick Jones kept intruding on his consciousness. He could understand his concern for Dana. Though he'd met her only twice, something emotional had clicked within him. Morgan had fallen in love once or twice before, and thought he could recognize the symptoms again.

The dagger, too, was easy to understand. He felt guilty about taking it from the tree-dwellers, and even more so about giving it to the Lodge, the last people in the world who should have it.

Gary Weiss was an enigma. No matter how disturbed the man might be, he was still the only person in Harborbeach who might be of help. He could also be Morgan's most present danger, if his paranoia got the best of him. That very uncertainty was good cause for his image to keep repeating in Morgan's mind, now the raving enemy, now the potential friend.

But why should he think of Nick Jones? There was something about the man's eyes . . . When he'd revealed himself in the dark parlor, Jones's eyes had been golden-colored. What color had they been on his front porch—brown? Why did that matter?

His thoughts continued to spin, getting ever more confused until, in spite of his anxiety, he fell into a troubled sleep. In his dreams he tried to sort out his problems, to decide what to do first. The dagger and the stone seemed connected, but so did the dagger and Dana, the dagger and Michael, Dana and Weiss, Michael and the dark parlor, Michael and the mausoleum behind his house, the mausoleum and the dagger, then back around again, with a different set of relations and importances.

He woke with a splitting headache. It was still dark outside the window, but his watch read quarter to six. The remnants of his obsessive dreams clung to his thoughts, confusing them as he got to his feet and went to the bathroom. He got some aspirin from his toilet kit and took them with tap water that tasted like iron.

He undressed and took a shower, first hot to relax his aching muscles, then cold to help wake him up. By the time he was dressed again, only one thought remained—revenge, both for Michael's death, and for the position into which Morgan had been forced.

"The catacombs," he said to himself as he went down the rickety stairs to the dingy hotel lobby. Michael had been there, the door had once held the dagger, Michael's dying apparition had appeared there, the *tsedik* had attacked him there. He left the lobby and went to his car, sure that the catacombs held some key to this mystery. His stomach growled angrily as he started the Lotus's engine, so he drove over to the McDougal's emerald arches and ordered breakfast.

He almost ordered an extra sausage biscuit for Phoebus. His cat's mysterious absence was another worry, and perhaps more significant than the others. On the one hand, it implied that Morgan had gone horribly wrong somewhere, not just apparently but in fact. On the other hand, without his familiar, his own powers were diminished, his defenses drastically reduced. He ate his breakfast, alone and miserable, then drove to Michael's house.

He parked in the driveway again and went around to the back. The door was still open from the last time he'd been here, so he shut it before going on to the woods.

There was no trail through the trees. It took him almost half an hour of thrashing around before he found the clearing with the mausoleum. By then, his thoughts had focused and concentrated on the fact of his brother's death. The anger within him was cold and hard, and drove all other concerns from his mind.

The mausoleum looked no more inviting by daylight than it had at night. Now he could see that the marble structure was not all that old, just a couple of hundred years, perhaps, if he could judge by the weathering of the stone. It would have to have been built about the time this part of the country was just beginning to become populated by European settlers.

The eye over the bronze door was just as ominous, though, as if it had been carved yesterday. As he looked at it in the bright light of

morning he could see it had once been painted
yellow.

He went inside, making a small ghost light as
he did so. The mystical illumination of the mausoleum was not as much as he wanted. The urn
at the back was in its proper place. He moved
it aside and started down the stairs. Though he
wasn't being forced this time, his hair still stood
on end.

A few moments later he reached the first
tombs, where his thunderbolt had shattered the
door and destroyed the white *tsedik* that had
been lurking there to grab him. The door was
still broken open, the walls were still charred
black and scorched white. But the *tsedik* bodies
were all gone. Other *tsedik* had come and eaten
the dead ones. They ate any flesh they could get
their pallid tentacular hands on.

He descended to the second level, passed
through the second set of tombs, and on down
to the third level. There he followed the broad
corridor past the first intersection to where he'd
seen Michael's apparition.

The supernatural illumination then had been
very dim, but now, in the light of his signifi-
cantly brighter ghost light, he was able to see
that the massive stone walls of this passage had
once been painted. Though over the years the
color had mostly flaked off, there were still faint
traces of red and yellow pigment showing half-
obscured abstract designs, with an occasional
stylized animal figure peeping out from behind
some shape or other.

The paintings did not cover the whole wall of
the tunnel but were confined to an area about
eight feet long by six feet high. A thread of color

went along the wall for maybe twenty feet, leading to another ornamented and illustrated panel.

The artwork was of prehuman origin, and its interpretation would be of more than passing interest, but what Morgan wanted now was a connection between this place and Michael's murderer. After only a few cursory glances at the decorated walls, Morgan turned his attention back to the footprints Michael had left here just before his death.

Michael's prints were overlayed by his own and Phoebus's, and by the marks of the *tsedik*. But just about twenty feet from where Morgan had seen his brother's apparition, a little farther along the wide corridor, there was another set. These footprints had come from somewhere farther on; their maker had stood and shuffled here for a while, then had gone back. And they had been made by a man's shoes, not a woman's. As Morgan had suspected and believed, Jones had lied about Dana being his brother's killer. Whoever these prints belonged to, they would lead Morgan somewhere.

Though the maker of these tracks had undoubtedly left a psychic trace like Michael's, Morgan was not attuned to it, and could not follow it. He had to watch the floor of the corridor closely as he followed the doubled line of prints. The dust was not very thick and there were occasional marks of bare feet with tentacular toes, footprints of the *tsedik*. They overlay and underlay the shoe marks, obscuring them, sometimes for several yards at a stretch.

The corridor continued straight past a side passage on the left, then began to curve gently to the right. He passed more passages on right and left, narrow and dark, and still the corridor curved. Another broad corridor joined on the left, another narrow passage joined on the right, and then a broader connection on the right, by which time Morgan had the feeling he'd turned one hundred and eighty degrees. The paintings on the walls still occurred every twenty feet or so, on both sides of the corridor. And then the floor gave way underneath him.

In the dimness of his ghost light he could see, as he fell, dozens of white hands with ten-inch tentacles instead of fingers, reaching for him. Then the *tsedik* had him, their cold hands all over his body. Their bulging eyes were close to his, the tendrils around their mouths, eyebrows, and ears weaving and wriggling in the dimness.

He kicked and fought as they started to drag him along this lower passage, but there were too many of them. He formulated a Light spell in his mind, and saw just the beginning of the resulting radiance, and the *tsedik* starting to cringe from it, when something struck him above and behind his right ear, and for him, all the lights went out.

Chapter Twenty-two

✣ ✣ ✣

CONSCIOUSNESS CAME BACK to him slowly. He was lying facedown on a wet, muddy floor, in total darkness. His arms were tied behind his back at wrists and elbows; his legs were tied at knees and ankles.

He tried to roll over, but his head throbbed so badly he just lay there, breathing short, rapid breaths, concentrating on the pain in his head, trying to make it go away. After a while it did.

Now he could think of other things, such as how to get himself free. He hadn't fallen into the *tsedik*'s hands accidentally; it had been a trap. The *tsedik* had merely done what they had been commanded to do.

He twisted his hands around but couldn't reach any of the knots. The cords were slender, but he couldn't break them when he tried. He would have to use magic, if he could.

There was a spell that would allow him to quadruple his strength for about thirty or forty seconds. It was a long, involved one, which required complicated hand positions, and the tracing of sigils and waving of arms. Just what he couldn't do at the moment. He would have to try to do it all in his head.

He had nothing to lose by trying but time and energy. Someone was bound to come for him eventually, so the sooner he went to work the better. He was fairly well off as far as magical energy was concerned, but if the spell didn't

work on the first couple of tries, he'd have to
save whatever energy he had left for later.

He calmed himself, withdrew into himself in
much the same way yogis did. He imagined
himself standing, with his arms free. He visualized the positions his hands had to take until,
in his mind, he could feel them that way. He
imagined himself making the proper gestures
with his arms, and subvocalized the incantation. He felt the Lattice tremble and energy
drain from him, but that was all. The spell
hadn't worked.

He was encouraged nonetheless. The tremble
in the Lattice told him he had done the spell
correctly, in all its essentials. If he'd made an
error he would have felt nothing.

He rested a moment, then tried again. This
time he went more slowly, concentrating his attention until he almost believed he was physically performing the spell. This time he felt the
strength and exhilaration pour through his
body.

He broke his bonds with a wrench, ripped the
cords from his legs, and stood up gasping. He
had to lean against the wall for a moment, an
earthen wall. The spell passed, and he sat down
heavily, drained both physically and magically.

He rested a while, to recover himself as much
as he could. Then he made a ghost light, just
the faintest glimmer, so he could see where he
was.

He was in a cell carved out of soft earth with
an arched roof that somehow didn't collapse of
its own weight. There was a massive wooden
door set into one wall, just a yard or so from
where he sat. Still trembling from his exertion,

he got back to his feet, went to the door, and pulled it open. On the other side was a white *tsedik*, brandishing a crude knife.

Morgan staggered back into the cell, frantically casting a light spell, using all the gestures and sigils and chants, not daring to trust himself with a mere visualization. The *tsedik*, all its tentacles waving, lurched in after him.

Then the light came. The creature squeaked in pain and tried to cover its sensitive eyes. Morgan kicked it in the groin as hard as he could. It was not as hard as he would have liked, but the *tsedik* doubled up, dropping the knife. Morgan scooped the crude blade up from the muddy floor and slashed at the monster's throat. Brilliant green blood spurted. The *tsedik* collapsed to the floor and died bubbling.

Morgan let the bright light go out and waited until his eyes had readjusted to the dimness. The spell had drained his magic energy too quickly, and the brilliance would alert any other *tsedik* who might be nearby.

It took him longer to recover himself this time, but when he could stand without trembling he could see again, in the near darkness of the ghost light. He left the cell, cautiously entering the narrow passage beyond. It stretched away to right and left, the ends obscured in deeper darkness.

Just on general principles, he went up the tunnel to the right. After forty feet or so the passage started to slope down. Worse, he detected a rank odor, the concentrated scent of the *tsedik*. This was certainly not the way he wanted to go. He turned and went back. He passed the cell and continued on in the other direction.

This way, too, started to slope down after a while, but there was no bad smell here, so he kept going. A little later the tunnel started to climb a bit. After a few turns he caught a whiff of fresh air.

He threw the knife down and started running. Around another bend he saw a faint glimmer of light up ahead. Another turn and he could see the opening, not far away at all. He ran panting up to it and looked out through the narrow vertical crack from the side of a sandy cliff. It was afternoon out there. Below him was a beach; beyond that lay what he assumed was Lake Michigan. He glanced back into the tunnel, but nobody was following him. He stepped through the opening—

—into a twisted place where everything was stretched and bent. They had been playing with him. He'd thrown the knife away too soon.

Streaks of color moved around him. His own shape was distorted. There was a grating sound near his ear, which oddly enough was a voice.

"You cheated," it said, "but you can't get away with it." They were Servants, and they had found him out.

"Look who's talking," Morgan responded weakly, trying to see who was addressing him. The streaks and smears of color moved. Though everything was bent and twisted, he thought he could distinguish the features of Nick Jones.

Chapter Twenty-three
✣ ✣ ✣

SOMETHING STRUCK HIM painfully on the left arm. He sidled away, only to be snared in what felt like a giant rosebush. He traced the sigil and chanted the incantation for the repulsion spell—it took less than a second—and the tangle of thorns went away.

Morgan felt a pain like a hot wire strike his back, and a fist hit him above the left eye. Jones was obviously not alone. Morgan repulsed again, but the respite was only momentary. Something hit him in the thigh, and he felt blood welling from the deep wound.

They weren't just going to shove him around, they meant to do him real damage. If Morgan could see his attackers, his long years of marine training would be more than enough to defend him. But Jones and his companions seemed in no way hindered by the visual distortions Morgan was suffering.

But neither were they using magic on him, Morgan realized, as nails tore at his face and a foot kicked his knee from the other side. He lashed out with a kick of his own, and swung at the smears of color hovering near. He struck nothing, and heard distorted voices laughing at him.

He put his hand in the Mind position and started to trace the sigil and chant the syllables for the Fear spell. He wanted to stop their attack until he could neutralize the spell they'd put on him, so he could find out who they were,

and disable them without killing them. But
something icy sharp grabbed his hand and
ruined the casting.

In a fit of frustration he worked an electric
shock spell in his mind, as quickly as he could,
and struck out blindly at the twisty colors. He
heard a satisfying yelp as he connected with
somebody. But other somebodies renewed their
attacks, striking him from behind with hot,
cold, sharp, dull, all painful and disorienting.

Quickly, twisting and turning to avoid whoever was trying to grab him, before they could
use an anti-magic spell, he worked through the
complicated procedure for the Great Thunderbolt. He was hit and jostled, but he completed
the spell. Four bolts of lightning crackled from
his weaving hands. There were screams and
smoke, and the distortions rectified. He was in
the strange dark parlor where he'd been initiated. Afternoon sunlight came in through the
now undraped windows.

His lightning strikes had make a shambles of
the room. Furniture was overturned, lamps
broken. One couch was smashed and smolder-
ing. There was a great scar on one wall, showing lath sticking through the plaster. If any
people had been hit, they had been taken away
instantly.

There was no sign of Jones. Morgan was alone
with an old couple, a man and a woman who
looked to be in their seventies or eighties. They
cowered and cried by the big front picture window, which was cracked from top to bottom.
Morgan had heard their voices before. They had
been the ones who had explained the trap in
Michael's dream.

His anger was quick and cold. He started to say something, then his eyes focused beyond them, through the window to the house across the street. It was Michael's house. These old people were Michael's neighbors.

When he didn't immediately move to strike them, the old people stopped whimpering, though they continued to clutch at each other and cower from him. Morgan stared at them, struggling to contain his anger and disgust. He understood now why they had struck him physically, instead of using well-practiced spells. These two people weren't Initiates, they were just Novices, granted small power for limited purposes.

But they were the people who had set Michael up, who had laid the trap, who had done the deeds that had caught Michael in a snare of obligation.

In spite of himself he felt rage well up inside, an overwhelming anger at what these people had done to his brother. He stepped forward and struck the old man on the face, knocking him sideways across the room. The old woman screeched. Morgan grabbed her by the shoulders and shook her so hard her head rattled against the cracked pane of the picture window.

"How do you know I cheated," Morgan snarled, still shaking the woman. "You told me you'd identify Michael's killer if I brought you the dagger." His anger was too strong. It felt so good to let it ride. "Well, how about it? I brought you the dagger. Who killed Michael Scott?"

The old woman didn't answer him. "Was it Jones?" he demanded.

"The Ma—" she started to say, but choked off and didn't finish.

"The Master, the Marshall . . . Come on, which was it? Was it Jones?"

He was holding her throat so tight she couldn't speak. She shook her head frantically.

"All right, then," he grated harshly between clenched teeth. "Whoever it was, it wasn't Dana Kirkpatrick, was it?" She shook her head again, her hands tearing at his. He eased up his stranglehold slightly. "Where is the dagger?" He shook the woman even harder, so that her head rattled against the glass, threatening to knock it from the frame.

"Leave her alone!" the old man cried, struggling to his hands and knees. Blood ran down his face. Morgan glared at him. He hadn't been aware of hitting him so hard.

"You suckered me," Morgan yelled at the man, and threw the old woman into the middle of the room, where she fell in a heap. It seemed to take practically no effort at all. Morgan strode to where the old man crouched, knocked him down again with his knee, and trod heavily on the fragile old hand. The man screamed as bones broke.

"Where's the dagger?" Morgan demanded again. The rush of power through him was intoxicating. The old man pointed, with his other hand, to the bookshelf at the side of the room.

Morgan went there and threw books on the floor until he found a box behind a set of the works of Mark Twain. Inside was the dagger.

"You can tell Jones," he snarled at the old

people lying on the floor, "that I'm not through with him. I'll find who killed Michael and make them pay."

"But you've got the dagger now," the old man protested weakly, holding his crushed hand to his chest.

"So what, you didn't uphold your end of the bargain after I gave it to you, so the deal's off. You want your dagger back, give me Michael's killer."

The anger went out of him suddenly, all in a rush. He was no longer exhilarated by his power over these pathetic old people. In place of that was a sense of self-revulsion at the enormity of what he had done to them.

But the power had felt so good. It had been a joy to vent his anger without restraint.

He looked around the shattered room, sickened. Evil was so sweetly easy. Even now, he could kill these people, punish them for what they had done to Michael, and what they'd tried to do to Dana, and for cheating him. It took an effort, but he let the moment pass.

Yet he had enjoyed it. The thought of that pleasure terrified him. With a curse he strode toward the front door, lurching past the old man, and left the house, covered with mud and blood. His car was still parked in Michael's driveway across the street. As least he had the dagger now. He would bring Dana back, just as soon as he could.

Chapter Twenty-four
✜ ✜ ✜

EMOTIONS TORMENTED HIM as he drove back to his hotel. He would think of what the Servants had done to his brother, and his rage would rise, blindingly. Then he would think of how near he had come to damning himself had he yielded to the power offered him, and terror would chill him numb.

He had difficulty driving, and once had to stop the car on a residential street, to just sit and shake for a long moment. He fought to bring his anger and fear under control. He was dismayed that he could have been so overwhelmed by his anger in the first place. He was appalled by his violence, his brutal treatment of the old couple. He tried to justify himself on the grounds that they had done him severe damage. He was bleeding all over the seat of his car.

But he had done much more than was necessary merely to defend himself. It was true that the old couple had set the trap for Michael, and had most certainly been at least partially responsible for Michael's death. But somehow Morgan couldn't seem to bring himself to use that to justify what he'd done to them.

In his mind's ear he heard the old man's finger bones crunching under his foot, and he winced. He had really damaged those old people. It would take him a long time to sort through his memories of the episode, examining how he'd felt about it. It wouldn't be easy to come to terms with it and himself.

When he could drive safely again, he went on. By the time he pulled into the hotel parking lot, he was more or less in control of himself.

His back stuck to the seat of the car when he got out. Shoppers on the street stared at him. As discreetly as possible he cast a few spells, while leaning against his car, which would at least stop the flow of blood from his back and leg. As he contemplated his wounds, he began to feel less bad about what he'd done to the old couple. He'd been bruised, burned, scratched, kicked, and stabbed. His leg hurt abominably. The wound felt as if it went all the way to the bone.

He limped across the parking lot to the hotel. He shed mud with every step, even if his bleeding had stopped. He was stiffening up badly. He entered the lobby, where the clerk stared at him in surprise. Morgan just glared back and hurried past to the stairs. It took him a long time to climb all the way up to his floor.

"Phoebus," he called out tentatively as he entered his shabby room. The cat did not come. He was still cut off from his familiar. His recent violence certainly hadn't helped the situation any.

He needed a shower, and healing spells, and lots of rest. He started peeling off his clothes. They were so badly muddied and bloodied and torn there was no sense trying to do anything with them other than throw them away. He got into the shower, turned the water on hot, and while the mud and blood sluiced off him, worked slowly through the spells that would promote the healing of his wounds.

By the time he was through he was exhausted, physically and magically. He stepped out of the shower and dried himself off. He wanted to go to bed, but he got dressed instead, in the last of his clean clothes. He put the dagger in his jacket pocket.

He took out one of his little cigars and tried to light it with a snap of his fingers. His magic was so drained he had to use matches. If his enemies came for him now he would be helpless to defend himself.

He needed more than a little rest, but instead of going to sleep he sat in his chair, smoking, trying to figure out what to do next.

Vengeance for Michael's recruitment and murder would have to wait. That, after all, had been only part of a larger plot, involving not only the dagger but the stone Michael had been recruited to get. Learning how they all fitted together was far more important than the identity of the individual specifically responsible for Michael's death.

Morgan needed help, and his first thought went futilely to Dana. He forced himself to put her out of his mind. Gary Weiss, he was sure, was not under the Lodge's influence, but he didn't feel he could trust the paranoid's reactions when Weiss learned that Morgan had actually followed through on his half-mad idea of sending Dana to the Retreat of Lost Souls. After he brought Dana back, then he would go to Weiss for help.

There was Jerry Pickard, but his ignorance of Logan O'Reilley, and the fact that he'd done nothing to disband the Lodge, did not instill any trust in Morgan. The man could be just stupid, but on the other hand he could be an unwitting tool of the Lodge. The other magicians Morgan had talked to, Dona Beloin and Edmund Berg-holm, did not seem promising either, though he did not dismiss them completely.

Once again his thoughts came back to Dana, the only person in Harborbeach about whom he had no doubts. The only problem was that he was too depleted to go through the exhausting spells of reincarnation right now. She might hate him for what he had done to her, but he hoped, when he was able to bring her back, that she would understand his actions and agree to help him. He had no doubt she'd make a good ally. The Lodge had wanted her dead, which could only mean she had been a menace to them. But there was nothing he could do for her right now.

There was no sense even trying to contact the Dreamer, even had he had the energy, considering how badly he'd violated the laws of balance. As far as the other magicians he knew were concerned, the ones out of town, he had no reason to believe he would be any more successful in trying to call them now than he had been before. That left him still and completely on his own.

There was only one trail he could possibly follow, and that was the footprints left by Michael's killer in the catacombs. Vengeance could wait, yes, but finding where those footprints led would give him something useful to do while recovering his magical energy. That is, if the prints hadn't been erased by now.

The afternoon was wearing on. He needed rest, but he wanted knowledge more. He took the dagger out of his pocket and looked at it. He felt it, tried to draw from it the essence of itself.

There was something special about this dagger. Else why had it been hidden away in that astral world, and why did the Servants want it so badly?

It was a charmed thing. That much he could tell just from the feel of it, though it had not been apparent in the world of the tree-people. Spells had been put into it, by one or more powerful magicians who had wanted to save themselves the trouble of casting them whenever they were needed.

He held it. His cigar slowly burned down. He concentrated on perceiving the dagger. At last he began to be able to feel something of the nature of the charm within it.

It was alive, in a strange sort of way. There was sentience, a metallic mind of sorts. He'd read of that kind of magical object. Few were known to exist, and those were supposed to be safely in the hands of high-order magicians. Yet here was one such. It was inactive now, but it could be awakened. That knowledge was the first key to unlocking its secrets.

He tried to put his mind into it.

A magician, no matter how powerful or skilled, could not put his or her mind into an object that had no mind or capacity for one. Into a computer, yes, or an animal, or a demon if one was not fastidious. But not into a chair, or an automobile, or a plant.

But this dagger had been provided with a mind of sorts, an artificial, mechanical, alien mind.

For a long time its very strangeness defeated his efforts to get into it, but at last he began to feel out its form. He sensed its properties, found its point of access. Then he was in. The dagger spoke to him.

It did not speak in words, but in concepts. He had no idea what kind of spells the dagger contained, only that they were very powerful and very old. And that there was some connection between this dagger and the stone the Servants had wanted Michael to get for them, not just a casual relation, but a profound one.

Part of the purpose of the dagger had been to store power and magic, so that it could be used by its owner without the expenditure of personal energy. He could not pursue the details of that mechanism now; it would take intensive study, when he was rested. Later, he thought, after he brought Dana back—and after he did just one more thing.

Chapter Twenty-five

❖ ❖ ❖

HE HAD AN early supper in a small restaurant not far from the hotel, taking his time, restoring his strength. He was still tired when he got back to his room, but he had regained some magical energy and wanted to try that one thing before bringing Dana back to the real world.

He lay down on the bed, relaxed, and performed the spell that projected his astral self from his body. Though an astral form appeared, to astral eyes, to be dressed as the living body had been dressed, that was illusion.

He felt for the dagger in his "pocket," but of course it wasn't really there. It was still with his real body, lying on the bed.

But he could feel, in his deep unconscious, the spells the dagger had contained. Though now was not the time to learn what they were or how to use them, he felt among them until he found something that was like a psychometric trace spell.

Being in an astral form did not hinder him, or help him. He examined the ancient knowledge, couched in archaic terms and forms. Comparing it with the psychometric spells he knew, he soon had the spell mastered.

The old woman had tried to tell him who had killed Michael. "The Ma—" was all she had said. It could have been "Marshall," but that wasn't right. That left "Master." So then, Morgan wanted the Master of the Lodge. He wanted to know who that person was anyway, if he was going to destroy the Lodge. He thought about the old woman. He thought about Michael. He thought about the concept of the Master of the Lodge. He felt a sense of direction. The dagger's spell would guide him.

He passed out through the wall of the hotel and floated away over the city, north to the wealthy residential neighborhood on the bluff overlooking the lake, until he came to Pickard's house. There he stopped.

Could that be right? Could Pickard, whom Dana had recommended, be the Master of the Lodge? The subtle resonances of the dagger indicated that he was. Or it could be his wife, but Morgan didn't believe that. He drifted toward the house, floating inches above the lawn.

He became aware of a pressure, pushing him away from the house. It was gentle at first, but grew stronger as he neared. At last, ten feet from the house, he could go no farther.

He'd never encountered anything like this before. No matter how hard he pushed forward, he could get no nearer. He relaxed, and his astral form was gently pushed back until he came to the street.

He could not go in this way, at least not in his astral form. That meant he would have to go back to the catacombs. He didn't want to confront Pickard tonight, only to find a way in and confirm his suspicions.

He rose up over the city and drifted away southward, not moving quickly but very easily and comfortably. It was coming on toward evening, but that didn't hinder him. He saw Michael's house, saw the woods behind it, and the clearing with the mausoleum. He floated down, through the still-open bronze door, under the single eye carved in the stone, and down underground.

He needed no ghost light this time. His astral vision let him see everything perfectly clearly, even in utter darkness. Black on black it was, but sharp and clear. He floated through the first tomb, through the second, into the wide corridor, past where he'd seen Michael's apparition, around the curve, to where he'd fallen through the floor. There he paused a moment.

The hole in the floor was still there. It did not extend all the way across the passage. It was just big enough to allow a man to fall through, no more. He could sense easily that it had been created by magic. The *tsedik* had known exactly where he was.

He felt eyes on him. He looked around, but the corridor appeared empty. No one could see him in his astral form, except another astral form, and then Morgan should be able to see that person too. The only possibility left was a demidemon.

He felt the hairs rise on the back of his neck and arms. One of the things could be next to him right now. Unless it assumed its avatar, Morgan would never see it, no matter how well it saw him.

But his enemies could not have anticipated him again. The watcher must be a sentry posted here, just in case.

He could flee or fight. He had recovered enough magical energy, so he put both hands in the Fire position. With them both he traced the twisting loop of the sigil. He chanted, *"Ngehrah-ngehtsah, Diengahshah."* Hundred-foot-long gouts of flame roared up the passage in both directions.

The rivers of flame would burn for half a minute, their heavy black smoke filling the tunnels, their magical light casting shadows even from such beings as demidemons. He started repeating the spell, still thrilling from the first successful casting, and looked both ways up and down the corridor, and saw a demonic shadow against the wall, only feet from him.

As the demon shape darted up the passage away from him, he let go with two more flames, enveloping the space where the demon itself should be. There was a scream. The demidemon was caught by the fire, and was consumed.

The fires crackled and hissed. A little way from Morgan a peculiar eddy caused the flames to swirl and twist where the demon burned. The sensation of being watched was gone.

He passed over the hole in the floor, carefully avoiding the still-burning fire. Mundane fire could not damage him in his astral form, but this fire could. He found the footprints beyond the reach of the flames, and followed them.

He passed four side tunnels, then came to where his corridor teed into another just as broad, running straight to right and left. He suspected the right branch eventually intersected the corridor he had just left on the other side of the great curving U, perhaps at the first intersection after coming down from the second tomb. Rather the long way around, he thought. Pickard must have had a reason.

The footprints turned left, so that was the way Morgan went. He passed a narrow passage on the right. Then there were no more passages until he came into a large room with a door in each of the other three walls. The door opposite the corridor had been opened; the other two were closed.

He passed through the open door into a narrower hallway. The walls were lined with niches, each one holding a body, long since mummified and shriveled. Even so, Morgan could tell that most were not human. He did not linger to puzzle out what they were.

At the end of this hall was another door, beyond that another room. On the far side were stairs going farther down. There was also a corridor to the right, but the footprints went down, so Morgan went down too.

At the bottom of the stairs was a narrow passageway. Like the one above, this one was lined with niches, each holding an ancient body. He did not pause to investigate but followed the footprints as the passageway turned, branched, and was crossed and intersected by other passages. He followed it, west a bit at first, toward the lake, then north. Toward Pickard's house.

At last, after several miles of the labyrinth, a new-cut stairway climbed upward toward the surface. Morgan felt himself swell with exultation. If it was Pickard's house at the top of the stairs, from this direction it did not repulse his astral form.

He dared not prepare any spells. The tension in the Lattice would give him away to anybody who might be above. All he wanted to do now, anyway, was find out where the stairs led. But he kept himself ready to cast the Fire spell again, though he wasn't sure he had the energy to complete it.

He floated up the stairs to a door at the top. He opened it and stepped through into a perfectly normal cellar. Except for a caterpillar-bodied demidemon with a silver knife in each of its four hands.

Morgan started the Fire spell, started to duck back through the door, and got confused. The demidemon struck at him, and one of the silver blades passed through the cord that connected him with his corporeal body. As the astral cord parted, a shock passed through him. His physical self at the other end died. The demidemon laughed its insect laugh. Morgan faded, faded, and was gone. . . .

PART SIX

The universe consists of several fields of energy, superimposed on each other. Intelligence perceives the consequences of that superimposition as matter, energy, position, relation, and so on.

Science knows of electromagnetism, gravity, the strong and weak force, and suspects the existence of some others that they try to relate to these. Besides these there is another field, which magicians call the Lattice. It is comparable to electromagnetism, a spectrum of energy that penetrates the whole cosmos.

Magic is simply the manipulation of the Lattice, as radio technology is the manipulation of electromagnetism. Traditions indicate that the study of magic might go as far back as the days of the Cro-Magnon people. In spite of this, very little is really understood about what the Lattice is, or how magic affects it.

A magician can attune himself or herself with the vibrations of the Lattice. It is a complex field, existing on many levels at the same time. With sufficient skill, one can ascend through the levels, serially, from the phase that is nearest to the real world all the way to the phase that is the source of the Lattice itself, and even into the blackness beyond.

Most things exist in many layers of the Lattice at the same time. It is this that enables magic to be performed on them. There are some things that exist in only one phase, and they are imperceptible to the mundane world. Still, they can be manipulated by means of the proper spells, and they in turn can have effects on other things, or other parts of the Lattice.

Each phase of the Lattice, each frequency, is a set of relations. Each has certain characteristics, which magicians have sorted out over the years. White is pure Chaos, all potential. Black, on the other end, is Entropy, total lack of potential. In between are the twenty-one colors. When one goes traveling in the Lattice, after white, magenta is the first.

Chapter Twenty-six
✛ ✛ ✛

THERE WAS A light shining in his eyes, so he opened them. He was sitting in a comfortable chair, in a large and sparsely furnished room, looking out through a huge latticed window. Beyond the glass was the blackness of space, with points of stars pricking out brightly everywhere. Right in the middle of the window was a great full Earth, shining white and blue and brown.

He just sat for a timeless moment, his mind blank, not wondering, not caring, not thinking at all, just perceiving. He didn't feel drunk, or confused, or dopey, just empty. After a while he regained some sense of self, enough to know that he shouldn't be here, that he shouldn't be anywhere. He had died.

At least, he thought he had. That was what happened when one's astral cord was severed. But this wasn't heaven. It certainly wasn't hell. So either he was alive after all, or else . . .

It had to be the Retreat of Lost Souls, built by magic, maintained by magic, and accessible only by magic. It did not spin, nor did it orbit the Earth. It hung, always in the same place, in front of the Earth so that the reflected light of the sun always shone in the great windows. No satellite would ever collide with it; no radar could ever detect it. From the back it wasn't there at all.

He sat staring out the huge window at the blue and white Earth. Africa was no longer visible on the right. Time had passed. For him, that probably didn't matter anymore because, since he had not prepared for his own return, without someone down on Earth to bring him back there was no way he could be reincarnated. He could send messages, perhaps, but it would be only a short while before he would begin to lose interest in the mundane world and want to take the final step to true death.

He looked down at himself. He seemed physical enough, though what he was and felt was only a psychic analog, apparently dressed as he had been when he'd gone in his astral form down into the catacombs.

He remembered nothing of the transition. One very seldom did, though messages occasionally got back to living magicians on Earth from those who made it to this limbo. Though his body no longer lived, he was not yet truly dead. There was still one more step to take. Despite all the mediums and séances, no word ever got back from that *final* stage. Nobody knew anything about what lay beyond true death.

He wouldn't have to worry about the Lodge anymore, or try to verify that Pickard was his brother's killer. The Lodge had won; the fight was over. So much for avenging Michael's death. So much, too, for the stone, and the Lodge's plot.

The question that presented itself foremost in his mind was, how had he gotten here? He had not cast the spell for himself, so somebody else must have cast it for him. The *meloy* he had called up to rescue him from the endless plain would certainly never have brought him here. And the Servants had no access to the Retreat whatsoever, even supposing they might want to save him for some reason. His teacher didn't even know where he was, and he had been cut off from the Dreamer for days.

He heard someone moving behind him. Turning to look over the back of his chair, he saw Dana standing in an open doorway. His spell to send her here had been successful.

"It worked," he said, half to himself. He felt a tremendous sense of relief, and at the same time a sudden thrum of guilt, for having taken advantage of her in the first place. After all, now that he was here too, his plan to bring her back was foiled.

The guilt became overwhelming. He turned away from her, afraid of her justified anger.

He felt a touch on his shoulder. "I'm sorry," he said.

"I know," she answered softly. "I knew that before it happened. The portal you opened into my bedroom woke me up. At first I thought it was a Servant, but then I recognized that it was you. I figured out what you were up to just as you cast the spell. By then, there was nothing I could do to stop you. I was rather surprised to find myself up here."

He forced himself to look at her. "I'm glad it worked," he said.

"Why did you do it?"

"To cover myself. To convince the Lodge I was on their side. I'd learned that a Lodge member had killed Michael, and they told me you had killed him, and what was I to do?"

"You didn't believe them, did you?"

"No, but I had put myself in the position where I had to pretend that I did. I told them

I'd do something for them if they gave me the name of Michael's killer."

"Oh, Lester."

"I know. The service I did for them backfired, as it turned out. Anyway, I got something for them that they wanted, and they told me it was you who had killed Michael. But the thing was, now that I had the information, even though I didn't believe it, I had to act on it, or they would think—know that I was not what I seemed." He told her about his conversation with Gary Weiss. "That's why I sent you here," he finished. "I was going to bring you back, just as soon as I had identified the Lodge Master, who was the one I think really killed Michael."

"Good intentions, and all."

"Yes."

"So what did you do for them?"

"There was a dagger, hidden away in an astral realm, where they couldn't get to it. I brought it back. But when I learned that they had lied to me, I took it away from them again."

"And just when were you going to return me to the living world?"

"As soon as I had identified the Lodge Master. I didn't want to tackle him alone. I figured, if the Lodge wanted you dead, you must have done something to upset them, and we could work together."

"Yes, we could have done that. I discovered the Lodge some time ago. No names, no identities, just the fact that they were active in Harborbeach. I'm not strong enough to fight them, even their rawest Initiates. I could have dealt with their Novices, but that wouldn't have done any good. What I was after was the identity of their Master, and of as many of the Initiates as I could discover. I hadn't had much luck, but I did learn that there was a Grand Master here."

"I was afraid of that. It would certainly explain their facility in shifting me around from one astral realm to another."

"It would. *Did* you identify the Lodge Master?"

"Jerry Pickard." He watched Dana's jaw drop. "And a man named Nick Jones is the Marshall. It's a big Lodge down there, Dana. If that's the home Lodge of a Grand Master, it's even bigger than I thought."

"Oh, God, and I sent you to Pickard myself." Now it was her turn to turn away, embarrassed.

"The worst part is," Morgan went on, "that now that I'm here, I can't bring either of us back to life."

"Then it's all over. The Lodge has won."

"It seems that way. But I'm not ready to give up yet. We can still do some good up here, while we have the time, before we take the last step to true death."

"I don't know how much good we can do."

"We're not helpless, Dana. Tremendously restricted, yes, but we can at least spy on the Lodge, pass on a message to other magicians we can trust."

"I guess I'm just feeling sorry for myself. I feel like I've been made a complete fool of."

"Don't sell yourself short. You upset the Servants enough to make them go to great lengths to remove you. Their plot against you is a bit convoluted, but then, aren't all their plots? It's all part of their game, I guess."

"I guess so. It's just . . . after working on this for two years, to have missed that Pickard was the Lodge Master really makes me feel stupid."

"Poor consolation, but you're not alone. They weren't fooled when I sent you here; they knew I'd cheated. And I misjudged both my own ability and theirs. I should have just kept low, not gone after them until I'd rested and brought you back. But dammit, they'd cheated Michael, hooked him, forced him into a contract, then killed him, and then tried to foist the blame off on you. I was angry. I wasn't thinking straight."

"You know," Dana said, "you're a lot like Michael, in a way. We weren't at all close, but I've known him for several years. And Morgan, he was hard, he was very hard. There was something tragic about him."

"I know," Morgan said. "I still think that the reason they killed him was that they were afraid of him. He'd discovered he'd been cheated and put in a bind. It would have been like him to have played their game until he found their weak spot, and then destroyed them from within. I have no idea what he intended to do, but he was that kind of person. He was just up against something bigger than he was. For the first time in his life. And the last time. Like we were."

"But you say there's more that we can do. Like what?"

"I haven't figured that all out yet. Conditions are different up here. Feel the Lattice—it has a different tension. But the Retreat wasn't created just so a dead magician could rest his soul before passing on."

"You're right," she said. She went over to

stand in front of the window. Stars shone everywhere. Over her right shoulder Morgan could see the moon. "I guess I'm just feeling depressed," she said.

"You should be. You don't wake up dead every day."

"I guess that's as good a reason as any to feel bad." She turned back to face him. "We've got to accept what's done."

"Can you accept it?" Morgan asked. He got out of his chair and went to stand beside her.

"It's not easy," she admitted. "For a while there, I really hated you. But that passed. And I do regret being unable to finish spying out the Lodge. That will pass too. But there's no question we have to send a message back to somebody alive on Earth," she said.

"Yes, we do," he agreed, looking down at her.

"There's more to be done," she went on. "But now that we know Pickard is our enemy, he can be attended to by people down there. Maybe they can even find out who the Grand Master is."

"There's another thing," Morgan said slowly. "The hardest part is that I was falling in love with you."

"I kind of figured that out the second time we met."

"Was I that obvious?"

"No, not at all. I was paying special attention, because I was falling in love with you, too."

Chapter Twenty-seven
✢ ✢ ✢

"Oh" was all Morgan could think of to say. There was nothing either of them could do about it now. Mundane love had no place in the Retreat of Lost Souls. "I wish I had it all to do over again," he said at last.

"Could you really have done any different?"

"I'd like to think I could. I made a lot of mistakes. The worst was probably not taking you into my confidence as soon as I knew the Lodge wanted you dead."

"Well, yes, though working with the Servants does not inspire one to trust. As I should well know, since I didn't trust you enough to tell you I had been investigating the Lodge for over two years. Perhaps if I'd said something, when you asked me to help you . . ."

"At first I thought you were just afraid of the Lodge, but later I began to wonder if you might not have been under their influence somehow."

"I don't think I ever was, at least not in the way you were toward the end there. But who's to say that they weren't manipulating me in some more subtle way?"

"All the more reason for us to not just give up until we've done whatever we can from up here. We'll have plenty of time to get over our regrets for missed opportunities later, as we reconcile ourselves to true death. I'm not exactly sure just how everything works up here, but I think we should start making plans right away."

"Yes, we should. Time works differently here, I've found out, but we can't waste what we have. The longer we wait, the more strongly we will want to take the last step and pass on. I've been here only a little while, but already the affairs of the mundane world are beginning to lose their significance for me. But I'd like to contact Cindy, in a dream, and try to reassure her. Finding my body must have been horrible for her."

"I hadn't even thought of that. Goddamn. All right, we can try, but there's no guarantee your message will get through to her. After all, she's not a magician. And even if you do reach her, she might not interpret the message properly."

"I know. Will you help me?"

"Of course. It will be good practice for trying to contact other magicians who can put our information to good use."

"Yes. Then how about you? Is there anybody you want to reassure?"

"I have some friends back in California, but I'd better just leave them alone. I don't want to confuse them, or initiate any false belief in 'spirits.'"

"No family at all?"

"None . . . now."

Dana looked at him for a long moment. "I think I'm beginning to understand," she said. "You don't really look anything like him, but Michael was your brother, wasn't he?"

"Yes. My real name is Morgan Scott."

"Any other secrets you want to tell me about?"

"Plenty. Such as the whole rest of my life, as

if it mattered now. But aside from the false name, I told you no lies."

"But not very much of the truth, either, although I'm guilty of that as well. Did you learn why they killed your brother?"

"No, I didn't. I learned very little, disappointingly little considering the price we have to pay for it. They wanted Michael to get a stone, but what kind of stone, and from where, I have no idea. They wanted me to get a dagger, which I did, and it's connected somehow." He told her about his brief analysis of the magical weapon.

"Aside from that," he finished, "and the fact that Jerry Pickard is the Master of the Lodge, and that a guy named Nick Jones is the Marshall, I'm as much in the dark as before."

"You uncovered an awful lot more than I did during the last two years," Dana said. "Now we know that we're not dealing with just your run-of-the-mill coven, but with a large and powerful Lodge, headed by a Grand Master, and possibly with demonic support. We know that at least one Servant is passing himself off as a valid magician, and that implies there may be more. We know that whatever this stone and dagger might be, they are the nexus of a plot the Servants have spent over six years developing. And we know that there has to be some kind of schism within the Lodge."

"How do you figure that?"

"Because why else would Pickard, the Lodge Master, kill your brother when he was being specifically recruited to get this mysterious stone? If the Grand Master just wanted Michael dead, he wouldn't have spent six years setting it up. So it looks to me like Pickard and the Grand Master are at odds for some reason."

"But if Pickard fouled up the Grand Master's plans that badly, why wasn't he punished?"

"Maybe Pickard made it look like O'Reilley had done it."

"That might explain why O'Reilley's soul was bottled, but it doesn't feel right to me somehow. And another thing, if it's the stone they want, why didn't they send me after that, instead of after the dagger?"

"Maybe the dagger is necessary to get the stone? And Michael was killed before he could get it for them."

"We're just speculating here," Morgan said. "There's still too much we don't know."

"That's true. But what we *do* know we have to pass on. Whatever that stone is, it's something that will give the Lodge a lot of power, more power than even the dagger will, if your evaluation of it is correct. And power, after all, is what the Lodge is really interested in, whatever their more subtle motives."

"And now the dagger is right where they can get it," Morgan said. "I think we'd better get in touch with Gary Weiss, and have him take it away somewhere."

"Can we trust him?"

"We'll have to. But let's try to take care of Cindy first. I've not studied anything like this, and I'll need the practice. You'll have to tell me what you want me to do."

"It's not hard. Let's sit over there where we can be comfortable."

They went to a pair of elaborately carved chairs with a low table between them and sat down. Dana reached over and took Morgan's hand. Then, with their hands resting on the table, they relaxed, and gathered their energies.

"Any time you're ready," Morgan said. A huge red-and-black-striped cat jumped up on the table from somewhere behind them.

Chapter Twenty-eight
✤ ✤ ✤

"Damn!" Morgan yelped, letting go of Dana's hand. She recoiled from the animal, nearly knocking her chair over. The cat sat itself calmly, like an Egyptian statue, looking from one to the other.

"Good God!" Dana said, "is that Phoebus?" Her voice was an octave higher than normal.

"Phoebus," Morgan said, reaching out to scratch the cat behind both ears, "how did you find me?"

"There was nowhere else to look," Phoebus said, accepting the attention for a moment and then turning to look at Dana.

"B-b-but," Dana stammered, "is it talking?"

"Sure sounds like it," Morgan said with a chuckle just barely short of hysteria. "But Phoebus," he went on, "you were cut off from me. How did you manage to get to me?"

"You died," the cat answered, turning back to his master. "You give up too easily."

"Cats can't come to the Retreat," Dana protested. "Morgan, what is it?"

"A *vendra*," Morgan said, "and aside from the Lattice, they can go pretty much where they want to go." He reached out and took the cat off the table, cradling him in his arms. Phoebus purred loudly.

"Morgan," Dana said, reaching out a tentative hand to stroke the red and black fur, "what is a *vendra?*" Phoebus purred even more loudly.

"Oh, well, a *vendra* is any of a number of species of being that are half animal, half dragon. They share some of the qualities of both kinds of life." Dana just stared blankly at him for a moment.

"But dragons . . . they're not corporeal," she protested.

"The cross-breeding that produced Phoebus's line," Morgan explained, "and the other varieties of *vendra*, took place a very long time ago. These days they reproduce just as mundane cats do, or as humans do."

"I see," Dana said uncertainly. "I guess, ah, he's a rather useful familiar, isn't he?"

"He is that," Morgan said, "though 'familiar' isn't really the right term. He's more like an assistant." Phoebus just kept on purring.

"But if you can come back to me," Morgan said to the cat in his arms, "then that changes everything. We may not have to pass on, after all," he told Dana.

"You mean, go back to our old bodies?"

"No, we've both been dead too long for that. Our old bodies are no good anymore. I mean reincarnation."

"Well, yes, I suppose so. There are infants whose souls have died just before birth. We could replace those lost souls."

"I don't mean that either. We don't have time for a protracted childhood. Pickard and the Lodge will have accomplished their ends and God knows what else more before we were old enough to be able to do anything about it. I mean new bodies."

"But we've made no arrangements. It takes an awful lot of preparation."

"That may be, but we've got Phoebus to help us. Besides, magic is different up here in the Retreat."

"We'll have to destroy our old bodies, then," Dana said.

"Yes. Were we found?" he asked Phoebus.

"Dana was," Phoebus said, climbing out of Morgan's arms and back onto the table. "Your body has not been discovered yet."

"How many people know about Dana?"

"Only Cindy Vann. She's not told anybody. She needs help."

"Then let's do that now," Dana pleaded, giving Phoebus a scritch.

They recomposed themselves in their chairs, but this time they each laid a hand on Phoebus's back. Morgan felt the Lattice around him. He didn't actually cast a spell. But by manipulating the Lattice directly he became aware of Dana, a thin blue flame beside him. This was her true spiritual form. Phoebus was like a blazing coal between them.

It's like this, Dana thought at him. She showed him the trick of how to look down at the world.

It was not like looking through a telescope, or seeing the room in a television, but Morgan could see Cindy, lying in her bed, staring sightlessly at the ceiling. He could feel her anguish and dismay. Michael's death, and Dana's death, coming so close together, had locked her out of her own mind. He could feel Dana's intense surge of compassion.

How do we do this? he asked her.

I don't know, she said.

Let me, Phoebus suggested. They let him reach out with a filament of his more divine nature. He touched Cindy's mind, and she fell asleep.

She has forgotten, Phoebus said.

They shifted their viewpoint to Dana's room. It was not like moving, or astrally floating; they were just there. Dana's body lay on the bed.

Black magic, Morgan thought to the others. *An entropic spell of disintegration*. Without hands or voice, he could not perform the spell the way he had been taught. But his spirit did not need those outward gestures. He touched the Lattice. Dana's body dissolved like dry ice and was gone.

They shifted again, this time to Morgan's room at the House of Aaron. He had not been discovered. Morgan grimly dissolved his own corpse, and they returned their consciousnesses to the Retreat of Lost Souls.

"At least that's done," Dana said. There were tears in her eyes. Morgan wasn't feeling any too cheerful himself. He stroked Phoebus's fur. "Thanks for your help," he said.

"Before we go on," Dana said, "let's decide what we're going to do when we get there. We may not have time to plan later."

"I think straightforward action is best," Morgan said. "Jerry Pickard is our biggest threat, at least who we know and can identify."

"Are you sure you're not just seeking revenge for Michael's death?"

"Of course I am, but that's really beside the point. First, Pickard is the Lodge Master, and if we can neutralize him, we'll hamper the rest of the Lodge as well."

"Until this Nick Jones takes over, or unless the Grand Master steps in."

"True, but then, Pickard has also been passing as an honest magician. With all his contacts, he can pervert every other magician's understanding of what's really going on. And aside from the Grand Master, Pickard will know more than any other Lodge member what this stone business is all about. So I suggest we get to him first."

"I think we should get the dagger first," Dana said. "I don't like the idea of that thing being around where the Lodge can get their hands on it."

"You're right. I'd forgotten about that. I'd hate to destroy it, but unless we can put it somewhere safe, we might have to."

"You can't destroy it," Phoebus said. "You'll have to assimilate it."

"What do you mean?" Morgan asked.

"It means taking the dagger's essence into yours, so that you and the dagger are one thing and not two."

"That's very powerful magic. I may have some notes on that in my grimoire, and the dagger itself may be of some help, but I'm not sure."

"I can help you," Dana said.

"You'll have to," Phoebus said. "It will take two people to assimilate this dagger, to share its power and its magic. Unless you have somebody else in mind, that means the two of you."

". . . Oh," Morgan said.

"What does that mean?" Dana asked.

"It means we'll have to blend with each other, become bond partners."

". . . Oh," Dana said. She averted her eyes. Blending was a sharing of self more intimate than sex. And it was permanent—unlike marriage, there was no possibility of divorce. "I'm not sure I'm ready for this."

"I'm not either," Morgan admitted, "but do we have any choice?"

"It depends," Phoebus said, "on how much of a risk you want to take that the Servants won't steal it from you."

"I think that's our answer," Dana said. "We'll have a *little* time to get used to the idea."

"But first," Morgan said, "we have to return to Earth and get new bodies."

"New bodies will be the easy part," Phoebus told them. "I can create them for you when I take your souls back to earth."

"Will they be like our old bodies?" Dana asked.

"Enough so you won't know the difference."

"Nobody will even know we've died," Morgan said.

"Except the Servants," Dana said. "But they won't know we're alive again. It will be quite a surprise when they find out."

"I'm looking forward to it," Morgan said grimly.

"The hard part," Phoebus said, "will be putting your souls into your new bodies, the actual reincarnation."

"I have every faith in you," Morgan said. "But I think we have to decide one more thing before we go down." He turned to Dana. "What are we going to do with Pickard, once we get to him?"

"I hadn't thought about that. You don't suppose he or Jones would just surrender, do you?"

"That's not very likely. If we could assemble a tribunal of superior magicians, we could strip them of their powers and render them helpless. But I haven't been able to contact anybody during the last few days, let alone a possible tribunal. Are you still in touch with your teacher?"

"I am. I'll call him right after we . . . assimilate the dagger."

"Good. As far as I know, there're no satisfactory ways of keeping a fully powered magician prisoner. At least, none that are at our disposal, and most of those are less pleasant than simple death. And if we have to kill Pickard, we certainly won't learn much about the stone afterward."

"Then that's what we'll do," Dana said.

"Okay. Now for our reincarnation."

Chapter Twenty-nine
✤ ✤ ✤

MORGAN SAT FOR a moment, thinking over the problem. It was a complex procedure, involving the yellow magic of Life, the purple of Spirit, violet Mind, deep olive Function, and the white magic of Potential. The relationships were intricate, but the Retreat of Lost Souls had been provided, in part, for just this kind of thing.

"I need help," he said.

"Take hold of my fur," Phoebus told them, "just behind my shoulder blades, with both hands." They did so. "Don't worry about hurting me. Just don't let go for anything."

"Are you ready?" Morgan asked Dana. Even with Phoebus's help, there was a good chance of failure.

"Yes." She sounded frightened. "Let's do it."

He felt again for the Lattice, found it, and manipulated it in the complex and intricate patterns called for by the procedure of reincarnation. He and Dana were blue flames in a crystalline space, with the blazing coal of the dragon cat between them. Phoebus started his own magic, peculiar to *vendra*.

Then Phoebus stretched upward and forward. Morgan felt himself being pulled along, Dana beside him, out beyond the facets of the Retreat, into the deeps of space, accelerating faster and faster, the *vendra* a blaze of fire, himself just a wisp of light, down toward the Earth, and down, and down . . .

Morgan became confused as the rate of their

217

motion increased. He couldn't see, he couldn't hear, he felt covered with a prickly velvet. He hung on to Phoebus's fur as tightly as he could, but he didn't really have fingers. After a moment he could no longer tell if Dana was still with him.

He felt like a flag on a moderately breezy day. He felt the light of the sun, the light of the Earth on him, saw it though he had no eyes. He heard a rushing sound, though he had no ears, a sound that was almost melodic, distant and in unfamiliar modes. His thoughts became numb. After a while, all he could think was, Hang on, hang on, hang on . . .

He didn't feel as though he was falling until the last moment. Then suddenly a sense of up and down returned and he opened his eyes. He saw a flash of blue water off to the side, and green grass and sand a few feet below him. He fell to the ground and rolled to a stop, resting on top of a bluff overlooking the lake.

Morgan sprawled a moment, then sat up on the grass. Dana was a few feet from him, shaken but recovering. Phoebus was lying on his side, between them, panting heavily. Morgan felt alive, breathless, dizzy. The sky overhead was deep blue, the sun just setting brilliantly into the lake.

He looked over to where Dana was lying, gazing up at the sky. Phoebus, in making them new bodies, had provided them with clothes, as well. "Are you all right?" he called to her.

"Yes, I'm fine," she answered. She sounded surprised. "How about you?"

"A bit disoriented, but otherwise perfect. Phoebus, are you okay?"

"Give me a minute," the cat said. "Making bodies is hard work."

Morgan climbed unsteadily to his feet. He couldn't stand, and went down on one knee, momentarily overcome by dizziness. Dana rolled over onto her stomach, then sat up.

"It takes a minute," she said. When she stood she didn't stagger.

Morgan finally got his balance and stood facing her. He thought he'd never seen anyone looking so beautiful.

"I think we're awfully lucky," she said, looking up at him. "Not everybody gets a second chance."

"We may die again in this second chance."

"I know. We should be careful not to waste what time we've got."

Morgan wanted to reach out and touch her, to take her in his arms, but this was not the time—or the place.

She must have seen the confusion on his face, because she reached out and touched his arm. "At least we'll be working together now," she said.

"I just hope we both survive this mess. Then maybe we can start off on the right foot."

"We can't wait for that. We have to assimilate the dagger."

"I'd rather court you on my own time."

"Me too, but I think we'll have to give that up."

He nodded silently. Then, seemingly without any transition, he was kissing her, gently, briefly, and she was kissing him back. The thrill of successful magic was nothing by comparison.

He stepped away after just a moment. "We should do the thing with the dagger," he said, trying not to sound too husky.

"Yes," she agreed, "we should."

"It's still back at the House of Aaron."

"I'll portal us there." She cast a spy spell, like a portal but very small, one way, permitting vision only.

"This will take a couple of minutes," she said. She looked as if she was staring at nothing. Morgan couldn't see her side of the spy at all.

"We could walk back," he suggested.

"Don't be silly," Phoebus said.

"It's seven miles," Dana said. "Just wait a minute. I think I've got it." She was silent for a moment, moving her hands to shift the position of the other end of the spy. "Yes, here we are." She worked another spell. A fiery ring opened in front of them. Phoebus jumped up onto Morgan's shoulder, and they stepped through into Morgan's room. Phoebus dropped down onto a chair.

Morgan looked at the bed where he'd lain when sending his astral form off to explore the catacombs. The body was gone, leaving his clothes lying empty, an oddly macabre reminder of his former self. He went over to the bed, took the dagger from his jacket pocket, and handed it to Dana.

"I can feel the magic," she said, turning it over and over. "But I can't tell what kind of magic it is."

"I haven't figured it all out either," Morgan said.

Dana held out the dagger to him. "You're going to be the primary," she said. "You should hold it during the assimilation."

"All right," he said, and took it from her. Phoebus sat in the chair watching them.

Morgan held the weapon by the hilt, point down. Dana placed her hand over his. Then they took each other's free hands and concentrated on the dagger.

Assimilation did not require the casting of a spell, though it involved magic. What they were trying to do was to adjust reality slightly so the dagger would cease to have any existence apart from their idea of it. There would be no physical dagger at all anymore. It would be only a concept shared by them, though its previous existence would not in any way be altered.

When the assimilation was done, Morgan and Dana would have all the spells the dagger contained, though they might not understand them. They would also have, for a while, the power that was stored in the dagger. But once assimilated, that power would no longer be self-renewing. It would eventually be used up.

There was another consequence, and a price. Morgan and Dana would be married in a sense beyond the experience of normal people. The dagger, shared by them, would form a bond between them that neither one could ever break. Each would always have access to the other. Only when one died would the other be free—if, indeed, either could survive the death of the other.

Morgan held the dagger firmly, felt Dana's hand squeeze his. Through their other hands he felt the circle close. He cleared his thoughts, put aside fear and doubt and infatuation, and concentrated on the dagger.

He tried to see it as it truly was, an artifact of the mind. He tried to believe that there was really no dagger, just a complex set of ideas. With a start that made his heart stop and his breath catch and his skin feel on fire, he realized it was true.

The idea of the dagger exploded in his mind, and through it, and with it came the person of Dana, her soul and his for a moment superimposed.

He stared at her, surprised at the power of the dagger, ashamed of his self so exposed, in love for her self equally exposed to him. For a long moment there was nothing he could do but look at her looking back at him, though vision was superfluous. The complex of thoughts, perceptions, understandings was overwhelming. The intimacy was agonizing, ecstatic, numbing. He was consumed, renewed. He/she/they were on fire.

Then, simultaneously, they let go of each other's hands and just stood facing each other. The dagger was gone. The imperishable bond remained.

In time he was able to bring his attention away from the bond a little bit, then some more. Dana did the same. The bond remained, but little by little they withdrew from it. With an infinite regret but with an equal hope, they put aside their ecstasy and their shame, disentangled themselves from each other, and became individuals once again.

"My God," Dana whispered. "I never dreamed it would be like that."

"It's going to take more than a minute to get used to," Morgan agreed. He cleared his throat.

"And the dagger, what was *in* it?"

"More than I realized," Morgan said, trying to make himself calm. "There were some spells in it that I didn't even know were possible."

"Just because we have the power doesn't mean we know how to use it."

"I think that's fairly clear. We'll have to be very careful."

"That's putting it mildly." She shook herself, rubbed her face with her hands, trying to regain some composure.

"As soon as you feel up to it," Morgan said, not feeling up to it himself, "we'd better get started." Phoebus jumped from the chair onto his shoulder. "We have surprise on our side right now. Let's not waste it."

"I agree. I'll call my teacher, and have him assemble a tribunal."

Dana raised her hands and started working a different kind of portal spell, one that permitted long-distance communication. But no threads of fire flowed from her fingers as she formed the sigils.

"It's not working at all," she said anxiously.

"Try something else," Morgan suggested.

"All right." She hesitated a moment, then went through the ritual for flight. This time the sparks were there, and she rose several inches into the air.

"So it's not me or magic," she said as she settled back down to the floor.

"I should have thought of it before," Phoebus said. "Morgan has been cut off from the Dreamer and the other magicians because of

what he's done here. Now that you're bonded
with him, you're cut off too. Calling the tribunal
should have been the first thing, before you assimilated the dagger. I misled you. I'm sorry."

"So even a *vendra* can make mistakes," Morgan said. "And without a tribunal, we have no
way of holding Pickard."

"Does that mean we'll have to kill him?" Dana
asked unhappily.

"Unless you think we can just talk him into
telling us what we want and abandoning his
project."

"Morgan, I've never hurt anybody in my life."

"I'm sorry, Dana. I'll try any alternative you
suggest."

"And besides, I don't know any martial magic.
What will I do when we confront him?"

"Fake it. When we find him, put your hands
in the Fire position, and do anything that's fire
magic. But don't actually cast a spell. Pretend
you're waiting for me to get into place before
you attack. He may not realize you won't be
able to do him any harm, and you'll distract
him, divide his attention. That will give me a
chance to talk to him. If he thinks he's overpow-
ered, he may tell us something before he finds
out he's not really in that much danger."

"But if he tries to fight anyway?"

"I'll be ready for him. I was a marine for six
years, Dana, and martial magic is my spe-
cialty."

"All right. I guess there's no sense in putting
it off any longer."

"I'm afraid not. My car's downstairs."

"No," she said, "we'll do this the easy way."
Then she worked the spell for the portal. This

time her magic was not hampered, and the ring of fire opened. Without further hesitation, they stepped through it into Pickard's backyard. Phoebus remained visible on Morgan's shoulder.

They were in danger now, but they had to trust in the poorly understood power of the dagger to see them through. They walked up to the back door of Pickard's house and entered without knocking.

They surprised Mrs. Pickard working in the kitchen. Quickly, before she could cry out, Morgan worked a spell that put her to sleep. Then they went through into the living room.

The room was empty, but Jerry Pickard was at home. They could feel him on the other side of the study door. Again, without knocking, they entered. Pickard looked up. The expression of surprise on his face made Morgan want to laugh.

"Greetings, Lodge Master," Morgan said.

"You're dead," was all Pickard could say. "Both of you."

"We were," Dana said, "but no more." She moved away from Morgan around to the side of the room.

"How did you do it?" Pickard asked. "It was the dagger, wasn't it?" His face was frightened as he looked from one to the other. Phoebus, on Morgan's shoulder, stared back at him.

"That, and a little help from my friend here," Morgan said, reaching up to scritch Phoebus under the chin. "Now it's time for you to tell me who really killed Michael Scott. Was it you?"

"No, I . . ."

"Come on, Pickard, it was you or Jones, and I have reason to believe Jones didn't do it. Another member of your Lodge, perhaps?"

Pickard was sweating. "Yes, another member." He raised his hand, and it trailed bright yellow sparks. Phoebus growled. Morgan could feel the Lattice tremble and tense as his familiar canceled the half-completed spell.

"Who was it, Pickard? And what about this stone you wanted Michael to get? And what does the dagger have to do with it?" He moved closer to the desk, while Dana closed in from the side.

"You leave me alone," Pickard said. "You cheated."

"Don't talk about cheating, Pickard. You set me on Dana, made me think she was a Lodge member, that she had killed Michael. But I followed your footprints, down in the catacombs. You were the one who was with Michael when he died down there. The trail leads right back to you. You killed him, didn't you?"

"No, I . . ." He choked on the denial. And then there was a shimmer in the air as the Lattice of magical relatedness became manifest. Pickard slipped into it, and out of the real world.

Chapter Thirty

❖ ❖ ❖

MORGAN DIDN'T HESITATE or pause to check with
Dana. As soon as he saw what Pickard was doing, he shifted himself into the first, white phase
of the Lattice. He had to trust she could take
care of herself and would do what she thought
best. If he needed her, or she needed him, they
could communicate with each other by means
of their bond. As far as Phoebus was concerned,
the cat could be of no help to them.

The study was the same, but the colors were
all brighter now, purer, and pastel. There was
a shimmer and a sparkle in the air, as if it were
an effervescent fluid of some kind, which in this
case it was. An eddy persisted where Pickard
had been, but he had not remained here in the
white. Morgan penetrated into a deeper layer
of the Lattice.

There were magenta tints to everything now,
in this second layer that was the phase of the
Astral. This was not the astral zones themselves; nor were things in their astral forms
here. Rather, this frequency of the Lattice had
been found to have more of an effect on things
and relations of the Astral than on any other
condition or quality.

The optical distortions were stronger now.
The walls and edges of the furniture were defi-
nitely rippling. One's perceptions in the Lattice
were altered, though much of that was a matter
of intellectual interpretation. On this level, the
books on the shelves were swelling and con-

tracting rhythmically, or appeared to be doing so.

Morgan realized that he had lost track of Dana. But he could just see Pickard, sliding across the web of the Lattice instead of going deeper into it. He followed.

Though his location in the real world was the same, the analog here was altered. The room was larger now, dingier. The windows were cracked. There were mounted animal heads hung on the walls. But where was Pickard? There, moving toward the door, with strange, rippling, sliding movements. Morgan intercepted him. Pickard shifted again.

Now a bright shade of lavender became dominant. This was the frequency of Fire. There was a pulse in everything in addition to the shimmer, ripple, and sparkle. Morgan felt a twist of the Lattice closing around his throat, a spell in its true form, not disguised by mundane perceptions. He waved it off. There was the eddy of Pickard's passage. Morgan followed. The light became pale blue, the phase of Air.

It was hard to see the walls of the room now. Space was distorted. Vision passed through matter as if it were glass. Morgan could see the molecules making up Pickard's desk better than he could see the desk itself. But Pickard had made another lateral shift.

The room, if that was what it was, was even larger, with pillars in the corners and steps down to some green lawn. Morgan moved to follow Pickard, who was translating across the room—not walking, but moving in a kind of magical glide. Then Pickard shifted again, Mor-

gan followed, and the pale-green radiance of
Water washed over them, in constant motion.

The ground was round, the sky was high, and
Pickard was over there. Morgan followed into
pale-yellow laces that drifted across his sight.
They swelled on the left and shrank on the right.
This was the phase of Deity. Morgan reached
out a tremble that should have been a hand.
Pickard tried to translate away but got con-
fused by the light.

Pale orange sparks of Earth surrounded
them. A lateral shift made amber rainbows of
the ovalness. Morgan closed, sent a tremor
along the Lattice, but Pickard stopped it before
it reached him and parted two strands back at
Morgan in return. With a fist of pale Earth gold,
Morgan closed the spreading gap, and followed
his quarry into the pink of Light.

Nebulous. Lateral shifts were hopeless now.
Only an experienced explorer could make sense
of this cloudy light-streaked environment.
Where was Pickard? A shade ahead. Morgan became purple in the phase of Spirit.

All he could perceive was color now. Morgan
had never been beyond lavender before, but
Pickard was going into the violet frequency of
Mind, where the first strains of music were
heard. They thrilled along Morgan's consciousness. For a moment he was distracted; then a
tinkling caught his eye and he went blue after
Pickard, into the Animal phase.

Where was Dana? he wondered as he trem-
bled along the web of sound. He was linked to
her, but that was no help at the moment. The
bond between them was a whole new set of perceptions that he had as yet had no time to sort

out or even begin to understand. Being in the Lattice so distorted his perceptions and sensations that he had difficulty recognizing himself, let alone an unfamiliar addition to himself. All he could do was follow and trust. The notes went the green of Plants, and he could feel other presences in the music.

A yellow node of Life now. Then the orange of elemental Matter. Then red, which was Energy. Then the deep purple of Space, and they were going out the other side of the spiral. He had to hurry; Pickard was still ahead of him. Things went ultraviolet as they entered Time itself. The foundations of the cosmos creaked under his fleeing. Deep indigo next, which was the magic of Sex, followed by a grating olive drab, the realm of pure Function. Where was Pickard? There, still ahead. Morgan convulsed, but the quarry slipped away into ochre, the frequency of pure Form.

The end was near. Morgan didn't wait but went into Mineral brown right on Pickard's tips. That left only crimson lake, the source of Magic. And Pickard was there. And Morgan was there. But so was another echo. Dana was there, between Pickard and the blackness of Entropy and escape.

"Leave me alone," Pickard screamed. They reached for him, and he shifted dimensions on them, sliding back down the spectrum.

"Morgan," Dana called. He could just barely distinguish her from the ripples in the color. "Grab hold of me." He fibriled a wave at her, and felt the connection. Then Dana started to follow Pickard.

Morgan could just barely detect the faint

traces of Pickard's passage, but he could make out no details of direction. Dana, however, was already moving through the colors, and moving laterally to them at the same time.

"Get your spells ready," Dana said, "but make them one-handed if you can. If you let go of me, you might be momentarily stranded, in spite of our bond."

They were backtracking now, from red through orange to yellow and green. Morgan had lost track of just where Dana was taking them. She had made certain unusual twists in her route through the Lattice. Morgan had felt several times the strange resonance of the Lattice as she made small dimensional shifts.

He prepared the Explosive Fireball. It was kind of overkill, but he didn't want to take any chances. He put his hand in the Fire position, traced the sigil, and chanted the incantation. But in his mind he held back the last bit of intention. He concentrated on holding the spell at this all but completed stage, and waited.

They traveled laterally through the Lattice, so fast Morgan could barely make out the environment. What he could see was fascinating. Their route took them in a long slant closer to reality. Around them trees were dying, it seemed, and moonlight flickered, faded, brightened. Distant buildings rose and fell, then were obscured by more trees.

He saw a shadow up ahead, racing before them. It was not Pickard but the wake of his passage. Dana was gaining. Morgan held his spell in readiness.

The Lattice was pale green now. There were stone hives dotting the horizon. The Lattice turned pale blue, then lavender. They were in an apple orchard. They were almost out of the Lattice, a few feet above the now almost normal-seeming ground.

There was Pickard. He saw them, and turned to defend himself. Dana stopped. Morgan let go her shoulder, according to her unspoken request, and faced Pickard alone. Dana disappeared, and a moment later reappeared on the other side of Pickard, a magenta cast to her image. She was between Pickard and escape.

Morgan held his Fireball spell ready, stepped to the side a bit so that Dana was no longer in the line of fire. At the same time, using all the gestures and chants, he cast an anti-magic shield spell.

For once his guess was good. Just as the shield went up, Pickard's black entropic spell struck and dissipated, like a shower of black confetti.

"Give it up, Pickard," Morgan called. His voice sounded like a distorted guitar. Around them, the trees of the orchard rippled and sparked.

"I will not," Pickard called back. "You don't understand. It wasn't me. I've worked too hard for this. Give me the dagger, I'll tell you everything."

"It's too late for that," Morgan said. "It's been assimilated."

"You fool!" Pickard called, his face distorted by hate and anger as much as by the effects of the Lattice. "You've just signed your death warrant. There's no other way to get the stone."

"What is the stone, Pickard?" He moved again to keep Pickard from being directly between him and Dana. "There's a Grand Master involved in this, isn't there?"

"You know too much already. I'm not telling you anything. I've almost won Ghebr's favor. I'm not going to give up now."

"Ghebr?" Morgan asked, surprised at the name. He'd heard it before, read it in certain dark texts. "I don't want to kill you," he said.

"Do you think you can, you weakling? You're stalling." He turned on Dana.

Morgan was almost too late. Pickard's hands swept the air, leaving a wake of ultraviolet sparks as he prepared to blast Dana with a spell. She lurched backward to avoid it, and Morgan loosed the Fireball he'd held in his mind for so long.

From his pointing hand a blob of flame sped, the size of a softball. It roared as it arched and struck Pickard on the side. It exploded with a blinding flash, a numbing roar, knocking Morgan to his knees, throwing Dana to the ground. Eerie flames, mingled with the ultraviolet of Pickard's disrupted Time spell, rippled in the Lattice, dancing in a way fire never danced in the real world. After a moment or two, the fire died and was gone. No trace of Pickard remained.

Dana got to her feet and came over to Morgan, her image color changing from magenta to lavender as she came. Her eyes were very large. Morgan reached out to take her hand—she was trembling. He could feel the distress in her mind, held in check now, but threatening to overwhelm her at any moment.

"God," she murmured, "I wish there had been some other way."

"So do I. Maybe later we'll find that there

was. Hindsight always knows better. But when he struck at you, I didn't have any other choice. We did what we had to do."

"That name he spoke, Ghebr. That means something to you, doesn't it?"

"That's the name of one of the more powerful demons on Earth. Pickard wouldn't have had any contact with him, but the Grand Master might. I think Pickard was trying to overthrow the Grand Master, or something. He kept on trying to say he hadn't killed Michael. Maybe he didn't. We don't know the truth yet."

"But with Pickard dead, the Lodge will be handicapped for a while, won't it?"

"It should be, but there's still Jones to deal with. He was the Marshall; he'll be ready to step right into Pickard's place. And if the Grand Master is personally involved, that will make things a lot easier for them—and a lot harder for us."

"I wish we could have talked to him some more," Dana said, "learned more about the stone."

"The stone is at the core of all this business. It must be Ghebr, not just the Lodge, who wants it. With Pickard dead, maybe we'll have a breathing space until we can learn more."

"I sure hope so," Dana said, sounding tired. She looked around as if expecting to see the ashes of Pickard's body, but there were none.

"Well, there's still Jones to talk to, and two other Novices. But I think we need a rest first."

Dana looked up at him, and he kissed her. It felt odd, because while there was a pleasurable sharing of affection, there was also the awareness of the other's fatigue and dismay and anxiety. At the same time, Morgan felt as if his lips were filled with Novocaine, and that hers were vibrating.

"Sometimes the Lattice can sure take the fun out of things," he said.

Chapter Thirty-one
✢ ✢ ✢

THEY CLUNG TO each other for a moment, for mutual support and reassurance. Then, reluctantly, they pulled apart.

"We've got to find our way home now," Dana said tiredly. "Hang on."

She took his hand again. Once more they shifted laterally, changing their position relative to reality while remaining in the lavender phase of the Lattice.

They left the orchard and were now inside a building. As they continued to move across the layers of reality, the walls around them changed from wood to stone and the room grew larger. It became divided by partitions, the spaces thus made became smaller, the ceiling went up, the walls moved out, furnishings appeared, shifted their positions around the room, changed their style, their function, their form. Then they were standing in Pickard's living room.

All colors returned to normal. It was very early morning. The sun was just barely up, shining redly through the eastern windows. Phoebus was not with them.

"We'd better get out of here," Morgan whispered. "We don't know where Mrs. Pickard is, or even if she's awake yet."

"She won't hear you," a soft male voice said, coming from the study behind them. They jerked around and saw a man standing in the shadowed doorway of Pickard's study.

"Who are you?" Morgan asked. The man stepped forward out of the shadows. Morgan could hear Dana gasp, even before he recognized who it was. He felt as if he'd been hit hard in the stomach.

"Michael!" His heart leaped with sudden joy. "You're alive!" Then a terrible suspicion swallowed his happiness. "But I thought you were killed."

"Just biding my time," Michael said, "until the right moment, which is now." He came closer. His eyes were golden, not blue. "Pickard is dead," Michael said. "You've committed a murder, Brother Morgan. Now you will have to do what we want you to."

"But Michael, how did you escape?"

"He didn't escape, Morgan," Dana said. "He's the Grand Master."

"No," Morgan said, "that's not true. Michael, what's happening?"

"It is true," Michael said. He laughed. "The Lodge belongs to me."

Michael seemed to be receding from him, but it was only Morgan, staggering backward. He made himself stop and stand still. "Oh, my God, Michael. Why?"

"Power, Morgan. The same reason you became a magician. But while you and these other magicians study in secret, afraid to exercise your power for your own benefit, I've been doing exactly what I want, securing my position, laying my plans. It's not so difficult to understand."

Morgan stared uncomprehendingly at his brother. "Knowledge," he said. "That's what I'm after, not power. My God, Michael, there's so much to know, the whole spectrum of magic to discover, the—"

"Nonsense. Don't delude yourself. You can't tell me you haven't sneakily taken advantage of what you know. I used to wonder how you managed to rise so quickly in the marines, especially considering your record beforehand. And afterwards, everything went so easily for you. How could you be so successful, so happy, when I had all the talent, all the brains? When you came to the miniature universe, it was me you were talking to, not Jones, not Pickard. 'Lester Van Alan' indeed."

"But this whole masquerade . . . ?"

"Miss Kirkpatrick was too close." He looked at her briefly. "I had to drop out of sight. And Pickard was causing problems. What better opportunity to get rid of all my enemies? And at the same time, finally get a hook into you."

"I can't stand this," Morgan said. He looked at Dana, saw her shocked, drawn face. "Let's get out of here," he told her.

"Just a moment," Michael said as they started to turn toward the door. "We have more to talk about."

"Not as far as I'm concerned," Morgan answered. He took Dana's arm, felt her own fear and concern, and took another step toward the door.

"I think you'd better listen to me, Morgan," Michael said. "Your name is on a contract."

"It's not my real name," Morgan said loudly.

"You could have written gobbledygook," Michael said, "and you'd still be bound. Your hand held the pen, the pen wrote on the page. The name you used doesn't matter; it's what it represents that counts. Especially now that you've committed a murder.

"Understand that when you signed the contract, you *were*, in effect, Lester Van Alan—just as you sometimes were back in Los Angeles. Yes, I know about that, Little Brother. You still owe us, Morgan. You owe us, and you will pay what is due."

"Owe you for what? For the identity of your killer?"

"For that, for the dagger, for O'Reilley's death. The agreement was made. Now it is time for you to uphold your end."

"That doesn't make any sense."

"Sure it does," Michael said, "when you look at it from our point of view." He came across the room and stood directly in front of them. He smiled pleasantly enough, but it made a chill run up Morgan's back. Michael's golden eyes— they should have been blue—smiled into his own.

"And you will see things from our point of view—eventually," Michael said, not threatening, just stating fact. Then he walked around them, out the front door, and out of the house.

Chapter Thirty-two

✛ ✛ ✛

MORGAN STOOD STARING at the closed door for a long moment. He jumped when he felt a hand on his arm, but it was only Dana.

"I'm sorry," she said. What more was there to say?

"Phoe—" He cleared his throat. "Phoebus."

The cat materialized on a coffee table. His hackles were up, and his tail was huge.

"There's something terrible there," Phoebus said. His voice sounded like a tomcat Siamese.

"What do you mean?" Morgan asked.

"I don't know, but I don't like it." He jumped from the table into Morgan's arms, and climbed up onto his shoulder.

"Let's get back to my hotel," Morgan said. "We need to rest and figure out what to do next." He was numb. He couldn't think. All he wanted to do was go to sleep, shut the image of his brother's golden eyes out of his mind.

"All right," Dana said. She was on the verge of tears. She tried to open a portal from Pickard's living room to Morgan's room at the House of Aaron, but flubbed it.

"Dammit," she snapped, stamping a foot. She was frustrated, and frightened by the implications of Michael's appearance and conversation. What was supposed to have been a moment of victory had turned into a crisis of helplessness and despair. Morgan put his arm around her, to calm and reassure her, but he was too shocked and unhappy himself to help her black mood much.

She cast the spell again, more carefully this time, and opened the portal. They stepped through into Morgan's room. Phoebus jumped down onto a chair, Dana went into the bathroom, and Morgan opened a dresser drawer and took out a bottle of scotch. He poured out two drinks, then flung himself into another chair and lit a cigar.

Dana came out of the bathroom after a moment. Morgan handed one drink to her, sat back in his chair, and took a long pull of his own. Dana went to the other chair, picked Phoebus up, and sat down with the cat curled up in her lap. She sipped her drink more sedately.

Morgan wanted to cry. "I killed the wrong man," he said. "Hell, there was no *right* man, there was no murder, until I killed Pickard."

"You killed him to defend me," Dana said.

"That doesn't matter. You heard Michael. You know the kind of twisted logic they use. I don't know what the problem was between Pickard and Michael, but it didn't involve me at all. Michael just made it seem that way, so he could suck me into his trap.

"My own brother is the one I have to stop." He felt as if he couldn't breathe. "That stone he wants . . . my God, it's so important to him that he'd damn me to get it."

"You're not damned yet, Morgan," Dana said, trying to keep from crying.

"Not yet, but I've committed murder in their eyes, and now my soul is in terrible danger. Michael knew it and he set me up on purpose. All for the stone. I can't let him get the stone if it's *that* important to the Lodge. But—but . . ."

He became aware that the thin wailing he was hearing was himself, and he stopped. He threw back the rest of his drink, and without getting up from his chair, used his magic to fill his glass again. Anesthesia was what he wanted. He took a long pull and choked.

"He sounded so envious of you," Dana said. He couldn't look at her. It was as if Michael's shame was his own.

"I don't understand it," he said. "I always looked up to him, though he was only a year older. I was a wild kid, and he kept me from getting into more trouble than I did. I always envied *him* his calm, his strength, his level-headedness."

"You know, Morgan, the people who come under the influence of the Force of Evil are unbalanced. If not at first, eventually. I don't think Michael held anything against you until he discovered you were a magician, in the miniature universe. And then he just went over the edge."

"I wish I could believe that. We always got on so well together. We were such good friends . . ." He couldn't finish. He gulped more scotch. "Now what am I going to do?"

"Can we just go away?" Dana suggested.

"We could try. I don't think it would do any good. Michael wants that damned stone. He's set me up so he can make me get it, or so he thinks. My God, what can the thing be? Anything that important to a Lodge, and to a Grand Master, can only mean evil for the rest of the world."

"And there really is a demon involved too, if we understood Pickard correctly."

"I know. A stone, a Grand Master, a demon. And the dagger, which now, thank God, is out of their hands forever, except inasmuch as they can use it through us, and you can bet that they will try."

"What about your contract? Do you think he can invoke it?"

"I don't know. I can see arguments either way. We'll find out all too soon. And if Michael's a Grand Master of the Lodge, he must have signed a contract long ago. I'd guess about the time he got the gun shop. God, and I never even guessed . . . I can't think about it. Right now I'm tired. I want to rest for a little while. Sort things out."

"How much time do you think they'll give us?"

"Not much. Maybe none."

"Michael isn't bothering us now," Dana said. She put her half-empty glass down, put Phoebus down off her lap, and came over to where Morgan was sitting. "Let's take advantage of the pause while we can." She sat down in his lap and put her arms around his neck.

He kissed her once, softly, feeling the bond between them, sharing her feelings and thoughts as she shared his. His arousal was instant and total, and was made all the more poignant by his awareness that she was equally aroused.

He looked over at Phoebus.

"Don't worry," the cat said. "I'll be here when you want me." He jumped off the chair and faded away as he walked toward the bathroom.

Morgan was not a large or a strong man, but he had no lack of strength when he stood with Dana in his arms and carried her over to the bed. Together they lay down, side by side, and took off each other's clothes, not hurrying, doing it right. The bond between them augmented every sensation and feeling. They did not fool around. When they were both naked, they made love. Then they slept.

PART SEVEN

The world's magicians, perhaps fewer than a thousand at any one time, have learned their magic from great teachers, and are the recipients of a tradition older than history.

In early historic times, in Egypt and China, magicians began a worldwide process of separating themselves from organized religion and scholasticism. They have a tradition of independence, individuality, and personal freedom. They pass their knowledge on in a one-to-one basis. At some time in his or her career, a magician looks for a young person with the right potential, who can be taught the art of magic, and who can be trusted to carry on the tradition.

A magician's studies and job leave him or her little spare time, which was why they are so frequently reclusive, asocial, and solitary. Not because they like living that way, but because if they are going to be magicians, they have little choice.

Freedom is their watchword, and self-discipline their only law. They are strict individualists, nonconformists, who nonetheless exist within a loose framework of cooperation and mutual assistance, a band of free companions.

Magicians agree on only one thing, at least outwardly, and that is their policy toward the Lodges of Servants. Magicians might be diametrically opposed in matters of philosophy, attitude, and practice, but they are in complete

agreement as to their desire to hinder the Tukhanox at every opportunity. Were they able to
cooperate more, they might be more effective
in thwarting the Servants of Death. But the
Tukhanox, through its agents, takes advantage
of their differences and magnifies them to keep
them divided.

Chapter Thirty-three
❖ ❖ ❖

HE SEEMED TO BE floating on the surface of a great sea, under a clear blue sky. The water was so clear he could see far deeper into it than would have been possible on a real ocean. He felt something stir and became distantly aware of Dana, lying beside him on the bed. He rolled over on his stomach and stared down into the depths of the ocean. His head was under water, but it didn't seem to hinder his breathing any.

The ocean was filled with fish. There were large ones, small ones; schools and individuals. There were long fish, broad fish; gray ones, iridescent ones. They swam, each according to its nature, some as if on an urgent mission, some as if idling the day away. Some were of one color, some had streaks of complementary or contrasting colors. Some had huge gaping mouths. Some had elaborately fringed fins and tails.

Everywhere he looked there were fish swimming in this sea, this ocean almost as clear as air Then he noticed that he wasn't just lying still on the surface of this ocean. He was moving as if caught in some kind of current that was slowly taking him toward some unknown destination.

He rolled over on his back to stare up into the cloudless sky. There was nothing to see there. There was no land anywhere visible on the ever-so-distant horizon. After a moment he rolled facedown again, to watch the fish.

He was passing over a shallows now, a kind
of reef only twenty feet below the surface.

There was a sunken boat on the reef, with a
single mast and no deck. It was canted over on
one side, its mast broken, the sail torn away.
There was a drowned man in the boat. The current paused here so he could watch the
drowned man and see what he was doing.

The drowned man was very busy with a
bucket, trying to bail out his sunken boat. He'd
swing the bucket along the bottom as if to scoop
up the water there, then he'd swing the bucket
over the side and turn it upside down, as if to
empty it. He did this for a long time, then put
down his bucket, rocked the boat until it
righted on its keel and canted over the other
way. Then the man picked up his bucket again
and started to bail once more.

Once in a while the drowned man would look
up at the surface of the sea, longingly, as if he
desperately wanted to get up to the air. But
rather than swim he just bailed and bailed,
hopelessly, endlessly.

The current caught Morgan again and carried
him away from the sunken boat on the reef, out
over deeper water.

There were sea weeds here, long filaments,
short branches, tangled masses, all olive green
or brown or muddy red. There were corals
growing from the bottom, maybe fifty feet below. There were sponges, more fishes, and
strange creatures that, had they been washed
up on shore or seen on the surface, might have
been called sea monsters. They were long creatures with fins and spines and frills. Some had
cock's combs, some had a row of points along

the back, some had flippers or feet. They all had long necks and tails.

Sea monsters they might have been, but in their own element, brightly colored and graceful, they were anything but monstrous. Bizarre, but not frightening. Now and then one would swim up toward the surface but go back down again before reaching it.

He drifted on. Ahead was a sunken house, moss-grown and crumbling. Four drowned people moved around it, two men and two women. They bumped into great corals as if they couldn't see them. They collided with fish as if they weren't there. They tried to do the normal things people would do, tending a garden, hanging out wash. But there was no garden, and the wash was tangled in sea weeds.

The current took Morgan on. The seabed below fell away in deep gulleys and steep ravines. Bare rock showed through the deposits of silt and mud. Farther on, the floor leveled again, now a hundred feet lower. The underwater plain beyond the slope was dotted with ruins, broken buildings, crumbling towers, castles, shops, and houses. Fishes swam in and out of the windows and sea weeds grew from the rooftops.

Slowly Morgan became aware that this was all a dream, that he was asleep, that in truth he was lying in bed with Dana beside him, and that he should be waking up now. But he was so comfortable lying there, and so fascinated by the content of the dream, that he tried to sleep a little longer, and to think what the dream meant.

As in most dreams the sea and the things it

contained were symbolic or allegorical. The sea itself was often a symbol for the unconscious mind, a well-understood Jungian archetype.

Morgan started to pursue the meanings of what he'd seen. The details of the dream became preternaturally sharp. He could feel the wind evaporating the water on his back and the small ripples splashing over him and wetting him again. But he knew it was a dream, gone lucid now. There was no mistaking that knowledge.

He tried to wake up, as he drifted over a place of tropical corals and tiny fish. He couldn't wake. Maybe his enemies had come to him in his sleep and put a spell on him.

He tried to feel his waking body through the stimuli of the waves and the ocean air, but he could not. The dream was too real, the water too wet and warm, the air too chill. He knew he was dreaming, but he might not be in his bed. If he had been magicked in some way, he could as easily be in a real ocean as in his own room.

But why couldn't he wake up? Usually, lucid dreams were the most fragile. If he couldn't wake, he had to be enchanted. So instead of trying to wake up, he concentrated instead on sleep . . .

The images around him grew vague. He lost his lucidity. Away from the ocean now. Lying on—his side, not his face. He felt the surface on which he lay. It was not a bed. Stimulate the brain—no, stimulate the muscles. Not the dream limb but the ghost limb that was his real arm. There, there it was, a real arm. Now, move it.

He woke. He was lying on a sandy plain.

Overhead was a too-blue sky, with only a point source of light instead of a sun. He smelled smoke. He sat up and looked around. A hundred yards away was the burning ruin he'd seen once before. Beyond, the infinitely far horizon.

Chapter Thirty-four

✣ ✣ ✣

WHY SHOULD HE have been sent back to this place, he wondered, when he'd gotten away so easily the first time? He performed the spell that had called the *meloy* to him. There was no response. He composed himself and tried it again. Still nothing. He made himself relax, cleared his mind, performed the spell a third time. Still no response.

He thought he might still be thickheaded from the strange dream he'd been put into. He went over in memory his three attempts to call the *meloy*, and realized they hadn't just been misses. He should have been able to feel the Lattice tremble when he took the position, traced the sigils, chanted the incantation, even if the spell had gone wrong.

But this time there had been nothing, as when he had been in the miniature universe. It was as though there had been no magic to work with.

He felt for the Lattice. There was nothing to feel. He put his hand into the Magic position, traced the broken triangle of the sigil, chanted, *"Kehdae-tsehshah Hlaerae-dehtsah."*

It was the most basic spell and should have put him in tune with the Lattice, causing the bright colors and shifting ripples that meant he was in contact with the white phase. The desert was unchanged. His perception was unchanged. The spell hadn't worked at all.

That should have been impossible. If he had been hit with an anti-magic shell, even that couldn't cut him off from the Lattice. It would just prevent him from having any effect on it. A self-repeating, dispel-magic curse would still let him feel his spells' failing to have effect. It was, instead, as if all the laws of magic had been canceled, the Lattice destroyed.

And it hadn't been done, for if the Lattice were destroyed, the rest of the universe would be a simple soup of constant energy, an even distribution of all mass and matter. The Lattice held the universe together. If the universe were destroyed, the Lattice would be the last thing to go.

There were places, he knew now, where the Lattice didn't reach, or had no effect, or was so simplified that it came to the same thing— places on the very edge of reality. But this plain wasn't one of those places. When he'd been here before, there had been plenty of magic. And Morgan didn't know of any way that one kind of reality could be made into another kind.

He felt his stomach clench with anxiety. He was stuck here. He thought he understood why. Michael had probably tried to invoke his contract, to force him to get the mysterious stone they wanted. For some reason, the invocation had not worked. He had dreamed the ocean instead.

When the invocation had failed, they had sent him here. The only reason he could think of was to get him out of the way for a while. And why would they do that, he wondered, unless it was so they could get to Dana? The thought terrified him.

He'd have to get himself out of this mess before he could do anything about her. It didn't help any that the bond between them was not functioning anymore. It was a magical bond, and since there was no magic here, there would be no bond either. Nor could he expect any help from Phoebus.

He looked around at the horizon once more, then turned back to the building. It was made of stone, three stories tall, with a stone-walled garden or courtyard to the right. He was facing the front door, a hundred yards away. There was a gate in the wall to the right of that. The smoke of the fire was coming from behind the building, from some back part he couldn't see from here. Thick clouds of black smoke rose vertically into the all-but-still air.

The building had no right to be here. Neither had it any right to have been burning for so long. It had been put here for a purpose, but that could have nothing to do with Morgan personally. Still, he thought, somewhere inside it might be a clue to the mystery of this place, and of his presence here.

He walked across the gritty sand toward the building. There were no other footprints but his, as if occasional winds blew across this plain, wiping out all marks.

The front door of the building was made of wood, vertical slabs bolted to three cross pieces. It was ajar, so he pushed it the rest of the way open and stepped into what looked like some kind of common room.

There were tables and chairs, a counter across the room, and behind it a stair going up the far wall. There was a wide doorway into another room on the left, benches along the near and side walls, another door at the back of the room under the stairs.

The place was old. The wooden furniture had dried and shrunk in the desiccating air. There was the thinnest film of dust everywhere. If strong winds blew here, there would be more dust than that, drifts of it.

He went into the room on the left, a dining room. Some of the tables were even set with plates and utensils. There were two more doors toward the back. He went through the one on the left, into what could only have been a tavern. Behind the bar were two more doors, one on the right in the far corner, one in the middle of the far wall.

He went around the end of the bar. On the shelves below its warped and cracked surface were bottles, once sealed with corks that had all dried and shrunk. Some corks had fallen into the bottles, which were now empty, though some had thick stains on their bottoms.

He went through the back door and into what had once been a private parlor. Here was where the master of this inn had lived. There was another flight of stairs going up, and two more doors. The one on the right was open. Beyond it, Morgan could see the courtyard and the fire.

He went out into the courtyard and stared at the ruins of what appeared to be a washhouse and a kitchen. The flames were low, burning dark orange against the black smoke. How long had this place been burning? he wondered. There were no footprints in the courtyard.

He reentered the building, went back the way he had come to the first main room. There he went behind the counter to the stairs going up to the second floor. At the top the stairs doubled back and went up another flight, but Morgan went past into the hall that ran from one side of the building to the other. He went to a door directly across from the landing and opened it. Beyond was a bedroom, with two chairs, a wardrobe, a trunk, a table by the head of the bed, and a little dust.

There were no clues for him here. The place was empty; it hadn't been disturbed for ages, and may never have served its purpose here. It was just a good place for his enemies to dump him for a while. Morgan left the desolate bedroom and went back down the stairs.

And saw on the wall opposite the foot of the stairs a dingy mirror. It was covered with a thin but nearly opaque film of dust. There was something about it that set alarm bells ringing in the back of his head.

Gingerly, fearful that it might be some kind of soul-stealing trap, Morgan approached the dark glass. He could just barely make out his shadowy reflection in it. If this were a soul trap, even that much would have caught him already, so it wasn't that.

He rubbed away some of the grime with his hand. Now, at least, he could see his own face.

He felt his hair standing on end. Behind him, in the mirror, he could see the stairs, a portion of the main room, the counter. There was nothing odd there. He returned his attention to his own face.

It was gently twisting and rippling, as if seen through disturbed water, as if felt through Novocaine. It was not a quality of the glass. The rest of the room looked perfectly normal and still. Only his face was affected, and it looked just like other reflections he'd seen before—where?—in dreams!

He was still dreaming. The awakening on the plain had been false. He had to wake up, now. The Servants had put him here so they could get to Dana. He'd already lost too much time, wandering around in this inner dream. He closed his eyes, leaned against the mirror, and sent his thoughts inward. He tried to feel where he really was, how his limbs were positioned.

He felt himself rotate until he was lying on his face. He moved his arms and legs until they corresponded with the position of his real body. Then he woke, and this time he could feel the Lattice, and knew he was truly awake at last.

He was still on the bed in his room in the House of Aaron. Dana was gone.

Chapter Thirty-five

✠ ✠ ✠

HE SPRANG FROM the bed, naked. He looked everywhere, like a madman—in the bathroom, the closet, under the bed, even out in the hall—though his nakedness brought him back in a hurry.

He closed the door and looked around the room again. Her clothes were lying where he'd dropped them on the floor, by the bed, mingled with his own. She hadn't just walked off, she'd been taken.

With that thought he got a definite impression of golden eyes mocking him, and silent laughter somewhere out of hearing. He tried to trace the image back, but the sensation faded quickly and was gone.

He looked into his own mind for his bond with Dana. It was still there, but it was blocked. He was still tied to her, she was still alive, but he couldn't reach her.

He sat down weakly on the edge of the bed, all his strength gone. Golden eyes.

"Phoebus," he called.

"Yeow," the cat answered, materializing on the dresser. "Where's Dana?"

"Michael has her," Morgan said, his voice breaking. He told the cat about the dreams.

Phoebus's eyes widened, his fur bristled, and he looked around the room, his head jerking from side to side.

"Yes," Phoebus said. "At least, someone was here. I can't tell who." He went to the door, then, like a dog on a scent, followed an invisible trail across the room to the bed. "More than one," he said.

"They don't want her," Morgan said, "they just want to get at me. I can't stand thinking about it. Will they kill her? Are they punishing me for . . . No, they tried to invoke my contract, and they couldn't. They want to use her as a lever, that must be what it is."

He clenched his head with his hands, trying to think how he would go about finding her. Michael was a Grand Master, probably with demonic help, and therefore much stronger than he. It seemed hopeless.

"Control yourself," Phoebus said. "Think about it. You're still alive."

"Yes, yes, but did you see his eyes? Michael's eyes are blue. The eye carved over the mausoleum was once painted yellow. Isn't that Ghebr's sign? My God, Michael is being the demon's agent."

"Maybe you're overestimating the enemy," Phoebus said. "If Michael could manipulate you at a whim, why would he go to all the trouble of putting you away in strange dreams while he kidnapped Dana? The devil is devious, but he's also lazy. He'll go to no more trouble than he has to."

Morgan numbly pulled on his clothes. "I don't know where to start, except for that old couple who live across the street from Michael's house. They might know something. So help me, I'll beat them into a pulp, until they tell me where Dana is."

"Be careful, Morgan," Phoebus said, jumping

onto his shoulder. "You don't know if it will do any good, and it might do you harm."

Morgan ignored the warning. He left the room, went down to the lobby, out to the parking lot, and got into his car. Phoebus jumped down onto the seat beside him.

"I don't like this," the cat said as Morgan drove out onto the street. "You're getting all tangled up with hatred and vengeance again."

"So what do you expect me to do, just sit back and wait until they start sending her to me in pieces?"

"No, no. But look, don't go there until you've talked to Weiss. He may be able to help."

"Goddammit, this is my business."

"Failure to ask for help before is what got you—and Dana—into this mess!"

"All right, all right." He turned the car up a side street and headed for Weiss's house.

Weiss's car was just pulling into the driveway when they arrived. Morgan parked, left Phoebus on the seat, and met the other magician on his front porch.

"What do you want, Van Alan?" Weiss snapped as he put his key in the lock.

"I need your help," Morgan said, suddenly uncertain how to proceed.

"Sure you do," Weiss said. "Who are you going to kill this time?"

"Not anybody, if I can help it. The Grand Master of the Lodge has got Dana."

"I thought you were going to send her to the Retreat of Lost Souls."

"I did. Then she brought me up there when a demidemon cut my astral cord."

"And here you are. Isn't that nice."

"What the hell's the matter with you, Weiss? We *both* came back. The Grand Master got her just an hour or so ago when we—when our guard was down."

"If you were strong enough to reincarnate yourself and Dana into new bodies"—he punched Morgan's chest—"how come you weren't strong enough to keep this so-called Grand Master away from Dana later?"

"I was asleep," Morgan said, afraid to tell this man too much of the truth. "They stuck me into a false double dream, and then grabbed her. Besides, I had help with the reincarnation."

"Then what do you need me for?"

"Because it's not enough, dammit! I don't know how many there are, but this Lodge is big enough to have a Marshall besides a Master, *and* a Grand Master. Do you want to just *leave* Dana with those people?"

"Goddammit, I've just put in over ten hours at the paper, and I'm tired." He opened his door and stomped into his house, then stopped in midstride. His shoulders slumped, and he rubbed at his face with his hands. "I'm sorry," he said, his voice muffled. "I *am* tired. I get worse when I get tired." He dropped his hands, turned around, and faced Morgan. "What are you going to do?"

"I've got only one good lead, two Novices whom I've dealt with before."

"What about this Nick Jones, the Marshall?"

"I can't face him. He's too strong for me."

"And the Lodge Master?"

"That was a guy named Jerry Pickard. He's dead. Dana and I trapped him in the Lattice, and I killed him."

"With your name on a contract."

"A false name. I think they tried to invoke the contract, and it didn't work. And that's when they got Dana, so they could put a lever on me."

"What is she to you, that they could use her against you like that?"

Morgan closed his eyes and sighed, fearing Weiss's jealousy. "There was a dagger," he said, and told him about the magic weapon and how he and Dana had assimilated it together. Weiss's face went wooden as the implications of the joint assimilation sunk in.

"So you're bond-mates now," Weiss said stiffly when Morgan finished.

"It wasn't like we had much choice," Morgan said. "I'm sorry, Gary."

"Hell." He leaned against the doorjamb, his head on his upraised arm. "She couldn't see me for beans, anyway. Dammit."

"We've got to help her, Gary."

"I know." He straightened up, but wouldn't look Morgan in the eye. "What about this help you said you had with your reincarnation?"

"He's out in the car."

Weiss came out onto the porch and looked past Morgan at the Lotus parked at the curb. Phoebus was sitting on the roof of the car.

"That cat?"

"Phoebus is a *vendra*," Morgan explained. "Powerful in some ways, but limited in others. All right, Lester, what do you want me to do?"

"Meet me in front of Michael's place. These two Novices live right across the street from him."

"Pretty convenient for them, wasn't it? All right, I'll be over there in a couple minutes."

Morgan nodded, then went back to his car.

Phoebus was silent for a while as they drove toward Michael's house. "This is going to be tricky," he said at last, "in more ways than one."

"The thought did cross my mind," Morgan said dryly.

When he got to Michael's house, he parked in the street and sat waiting. After ten minutes Weiss drove up and parked behind him. Morgan got out, with Phoebus on his shoulder, and met the other man.

"You're going to have to call the shots," Weiss said. "I'm, ah, not as quick as I used to be."

"Just back me up, cover my rear, and play to my lead."

"What about the cat?"

"I'm going to hide in a 'pocket,'" Phoebus said. "Just call me when you need me."

"I'll do that," Morgan said. Phoebus cheshired and slipped into a dimensional adjunct of Morgan's being in the way that only a *vendra* could do. Then Morgan and Weiss crossed the street, walked up the curving drive of the Novice's house, and went up onto the porch. Morgan didn't knock, but just opened the door and walked in. Weiss, a bit uncertainly, followed him.

The old man was sitting on the living-room sofa, watching television. He looked up at their entrance, startled. Neither he nor the room, with its squarely modern furniture, showed any signs of the damage Morgan had wrought with his lightning bolts. Magic spells had healed and repaired everything.

"What is the meaning of this?" the old man quavered, rising angrily to his feet.

"We want to talk with you a bit," Morgan said, coming into the living room.

"You have no business barging into my house like this," the old man said.

"That's true," Morgan admitted, "but we're here, and you'll have to deal with us. Where's your wife?"

The old man started to turn away, but Weiss stepped up and pushed him down heavily onto the couch. The Novice twisted his hands around in the air as he started to cast a spell. His movements were clumsy and uncertain, as if it were a spell he'd been taught by rote. Weiss grinned derisively as he and Morgan took their time to cast an anti-magic spell. The old man painfully finished his casting, which disrupted in a blaze of pale-blue sparks, an air spell of some kind.

There were crimson lake sparks as well, a spell that affected magic itself. Morgan turned to see the old woman standing in the hall door, her hands contorted in a fashion he didn't recognize. She seemed totally nonplussed by the failure of her magic.

Weiss kept an eye on the man while Morgan went to the old woman, took her wrist, and pulled her into the room. She cried out in pain as he twisted her arm and made her sit down on the couch next to her husband.

"You leave us alone," the old lady cried, looking from Morgan to Weiss and back again.

"Why should I?" Morgan asked calmly, keeping his anxiety for Dana's welfare solidly under control. "Did you leave me alone? Did you leave Dana alone?"

"We were only doing what we had to do," the old man said. His wife rubbed her wrist.

"Then I hope you'll understand," Weiss said, "that we're just doing what we have to do."

"On whose authority?" the old woman asked.

"Our own."

"Bah," the man snorted. "You have no authority. How can anything that comes from yourself have any authority?" He didn't seem overly frightened. He and his wife just sat there, staring at the two intruders with crafty, angry eyes.

"Don't talk to me of authority," Morgan said softly. "What authority do *you* have, Mr. Who-ever-you-are?"

"Jurgen-Smith," the man said. "My name is Jurgen-Smith."

"Okay, Mr. Jurgen-Smith, let's get down to business. We want some information from you, and we mean to get it. It would be a lot easier on all of us if you just told us what we wanted to know without any fuss."

"We're not going to tell you anything," Jurgen-Smith said, with a sneer on his face. He sat back on the couch and crossed his arms over his chest. His wife looked uncertainly at him, then copied his position.

Morgan was not caught up in a momentary rage now. His anxiety for Dana's welfare was making him sick, not furious. He kept his face calm, and his voice low.

"I'll tell you what I could do," he said. "I could break all your fingers, then heal them magically. You'd be just like new, except for the memory of pain." He felt Weiss's eyes on him. "Then I could break them again, one at a time, and when I ran out of fingers, heal them again. I could do that over and over until you finally decided you'd had enough and started to tell me what I want to know."

"You wouldn't do thàt," the old lady sneered. "You're not angry enough. In a fit of temper, yes, when you're in a rage, yes, but not when you're so cold-blooded. And as for *this* one"—she glared at Weiss—"he couldn't do it at all. You're weak that way. All of you people are. Now, *I* could break fingers like that, and Harold could do it. But you can't, Mr. Van Alan. You can't do a thing to us."

"We'll find out, won't we," Morgan said, knowing he couldn't count on Weiss if it came down to that. At the same time he felt deflated, because if the Jurgen-Smiths had not been informed of his real name, then they probably didn't know anything worth torturing them for.

"We sure will, Van Alan," Jurgen-Smith said, with a smirk.

"Want me to hold him?" Weiss asked.

"Just keep Mrs. Jurgen-Smith from interfering," Morgan told him, and then hesitated.

"There was a book here the other day," he said, following another tack. "A green-bound book, full of contracts. You know the one I mean. Where is it?"

"It's gone," Jurgen-Smith said, shaking his head. "After you left here, it was taken away."

"Where to?"

"I have no idea," Jurgen-Smith said.

Morgan reached down and grabbed the old man's hand.

"I don't know, I tell you," Jurgen-Smith screamed, trying to pull away. "Leave me alone."

"Harold," the old lady said sharply, "wait until he breaks a finger before you start screaming."

"I'm sorry, Emily," Harold said, still trying to pull his hand from Morgan's grasp. "That's the hand he broke before."

Morgan let go Harold's hand, glanced at Weiss's sweaty but determined face, and turned his gaze to Emily Jurgen-Smith. She met his stare defiantly, until he began to grin. Then she looked away.

"How about you, Emily?" he asked. "Do you know where the book is?"

"No, I don't." She steadfastly refused to meet his gaze, and kept her arms crossed in front of her chest.

"Come on, Emily," Morgan said, as if talking to a child, "give it a try." He reached out as if he meant to grab her face.

"I don't know, I tell you," she cried, beating his hand away.

"Emily," Harold said sharply, "wait until he breaks your face before you start screaming."

"Shut up, Harold," she said, but Harold just chuckled.

"Very humorous," Morgan said dryly, beginning to feel on top of the situation at last. "Ignorance is always so amusing. And oddly enough, I believe you. You don't know anything. You're not important enough to be told."

"Oh, yeah?" Harold said, a nasty grin on his face. "You think I'm not important? You think you know everything? Well, Van Alan, let me tell you I know something you don't know."

"Harold," Emily snapped, "be still."

"We've got powerful friends," Harold said, ignoring her. There was an edge of triumph in his voice. "Friends we can call on any time we like."

"Don't you dare call him," Emily hissed, grabbing her husband's arm. But Harold was angry now; he would not be stopped. He put his hand into a strange position and traced a sigil with it, leaving a line of fire. The air between him and Morgan began to shimmer. Morgan and Weiss stepped back, both frightened, as a man appeared out of the shimmer.

Chapter Thirty-six

✣ ✣ ✣

"MICHAEL," WEISS SAID as the shimmer around Morgan's brother faded. The Jurgen-Smiths were both smiling broadly now, but Emily was still angry and frightened. "My God, Mike, where have you been?"

"How are you doing, Gary?" Michael asked. His eyes were golden and smiling. "I'm sorry to see you here, Morgan," he went on.

"These men were going to torture us," Harold said indignantly. Michael turned to look at the old couple. Weiss stepped up and pounded Michael on the shoulder.

"Goddamn," Weiss said, "you sure had us going for a while there."

"Sorry about that," Michael told him. "Things got a little complicated. Were you really going to hurt these people?"

"Dana's been kidnapped," Weiss said, "and Lester thought they might know where she was."

"Lester?" Michael asked, with no trace of sarcasm. He looked at Morgan, and Weiss's eyes followed his.

"Lester Van Alan," Weiss said uncertainly, looking from one brother to the other. "Didn't you grow up together?"

"We did, Gary," Morgan said, afraid of what kind of game Michael might be playing.

"Now, wait," Weiss interrupted Michael before he could say anything. "You called him 'Morgan.' "

"That's right," Morgan said, "that's my name. I'm Michael's brother."

"I'm afraid you've been misled," Michael said.

"Now just a goddamn minute here," Weiss protested, backing away from them. On the couch, the Jurgen-Smiths watched with confusion and growing fear. "You told me Michael was dead," Weiss accused Morgan.

"I thought he was. That's what he wanted me to believe."

"Sure," Weiss said, then turned to Michael. "Where the hell have you been for the last six, seven weeks?"

"In hiding from my enemies," Michael said, looking at Morgan. Again Weiss followed his gaze.

"Michael's the Grand Master," Morgan said.

"Oh, come *on!* Michael's *never* had anything to do with the Servants."

"You saw how he arrived just now, appearing out of thin air."

"That was the Jurgen-Smiths," Weiss yelled. He looked at the old couple sitting, frightened, on the couch. "You're in this together," he accused.

"*They're* in it together," Morgan said, trying not to shout.

"Your *brother*," Weiss said to Michael, "killed Dana."

"I know," Michael said.

"But she's alive again, dammit," Morgan said, "and Michael's got her."

"Oh, no," Weiss said, an angry smile distorting his face, "you're not going to sucker me again." His hands started moving in the preliminary gestures of a spell. Michael reached out and took his arm.

"I think you'd better go now," he said.

"But Michael—"

"I know. I'll talk to you later."

"Dammit, Weiss," Morgan started to say, but Weiss didn't let him finish.

"Shut up," Weiss yelled. "You shut up. Michael, what are we going to do?"

"Nothing right now, Gary. Let me deal with this."

"But he's dangerous," Weiss protested.

"Not to me, he's not."

"Then why were you 'hiding' from me?" Morgan snapped.

"You're not my only enemy," Michael said decisively.

"I can take him, Michael," Weiss said.

"No, leave him to me. He's my brother, after all."

Weiss looked at Michael uncertainly. "All right," he said. "But I'll be waiting, just in case you need help." Then he turned and walked out of the house.

"I suppose it had to come to this sooner or later," Michael said as the front door closed.

"How much of Gary's paranoia is real," Morgan asked, "and how much because of your manipulation?"

"Morgan, please. Gary's my best friend." His golden eyes seemed to almost glow. "But we'll talk about that later. Right now I must attend to the matter at hand." He turned back to the old couple, who were by now both totally confused and totally frightened.

"I wasn't expecting you to call," Michael told them, his voice softly menacing. "Under ordinary circumstances, I would pay no attention to such a summons at all."

"But you said—" Harold started to protest.

"Silence," Michael commanded without raising his voice in the least. The old man shrank back. "You have the right to call me in need. You may call me when policy is seriously in doubt. You may call me when you have performed a service. Why did you call me now?"

"Harold," Emily said, "I told you—" Her voice cut off, her face got red. Michael had done nothing that Morgan could see.

"You should have called Nick Jones, your new Lodge Master," Michael said quietly, "not me. You have lost your sense of proportion, and of propriety." He paused, but the old people did not dare say anything. Michael turned back to Morgan.

"I should make you leave now," he said, "as I did Gary. But you're my brother, and I will let you stay." He seemed perfectly calm, not at all angry, only a little sad. He turned back to the old people cowering on the couch.

"You have outlived your usefulness," he told them gently. The old faces went gray. "Come, my friends," he said, extending a hand to each. "It is time to go now."

The Jurgen-Smiths seemed frozen in their seats. Michael reached out and took them each by the shoulder. Faces white and numb, they stood, shivering, eyes wide, mouths slack.

"God!" Morgan gasped as he grasped the implications of the situation. These two people were already damned, but they were about to face the consequences for the first time. Michael was going to terminate their service to the Lodge.

One did not go to heaven when one finished serving the Crown of Death. One went to wherever Fryga Tukhanox wanted one to go, which, if the stories were true, were places that encouraged the Servants of the Tukhanox to prolong their usefulness and their lives as much as possible. To hell, in other words.

Michael's hold on the people did not loosen as he turned his head to look at Morgan.

"I see you are beginning to understand," he said.

"No," Morgan said, shaking his head. "No, I don't understand a thing."

"Yes, you do. These people have served the Tukhanox one hundred eighty-three years each." He turned back to the Jurgen-Smiths. He seemed to push them ever so gently. They could not scream; they could only squeak. A haze of black, shot with deep-red light, enveloped them. Slowly, like wax dripping, the flesh melted off their bones, and they were consumed in a lavender fire. It seemed to go on and on forever, their melting faces writhing, their arms jerking spasmodically. There was a smell of sulfur, of excrement, of charring raw meat. At last they rotated through another dimension, and were gone. Michael turned back to Morgan, his amber eyes blazing.

"You understand me very well, Brother Morgan," he said. The fire in his eyes died, and he was just a human being again. Morgan could only nod. Sweat dripped from his forehead and nose.

"You're a chess player," Michael said. "Devious, secretive, always planning at least two moves ahead. Almost always. I want you to know that I don't underestimate you.

"Pickard was treacherous. He wanted to get the stone for himself. He thought he could supplant me, promote his own cause. That was his mistake. The Jurgen-Smiths blundered when you slept in my bed, and when they fought you after you pretended to kill Dana, and that was their mistake. And look where it's got us. We have lost Jerry Pickard, Logan O'Reilley, Harold and Emily Jurgen-Smith. All we have left is you. Which is what I really wanted after all."

"You don't have me yet," Morgan protested weakly.

"Oh, but we do," Michael said. "Even though,

for some reason, your contract couldn't be invoked, we have something else up our sleeve."

"I understand that," Morgan said. "I've made mistakes. My judgment hasn't always been the best. But you can be sure I'll be playing a more careful game from now on."

"I'm sure you will, but time is on our side. Already you have been involved in the death of four people, one of whom you actually killed yourself. Inevitably you will come around to appreciate our way of thinking. You have already had a small taste of power. I am eagerly awaiting the day when you begin to think as we do. Then all this will have been worthwhile."

"Don't hold your breath," Morgan said. He was talking with false bravado, and he knew Michael knew it. "You haven't got me that well hooked yet."

"I think we have. Because you were right, I do have Dana. Take a look." He pointed over Morgan's shoulder. Morgan couldn't help but turn around.

The far wall of the room had opened up onto another place, a place of stone, where hairy, demonic serpent men with six arms each were preparing what looked like a torture rack. Between two of them, in a corner, stood Dana, naked, shivering. She saw Morgan, and her eyes went wild.

Morgan stood still, though he wanted to run to her. He kept himself steady and steeled his nerve. He tried to feel her through their bond, but she was still closed off from him. There was nothing he could do to rescue her. The demidemons, with their serpentine bodies and six arms each, would be much too strong for him, even if he could enter that stony place from here, which he probably couldn't. Any magic he could muster they could cancel without trouble, and deal out worse of their own.

"Have they hurt you?" Morgan asked her, struggling to keep his voice level.

"Not yet," she said, trembling.

"Okay," he said. He turned back to Michael. It was both easy and hard to do. He was reluctant to let Dana out of his sight, but while he looked at her he couldn't help but see the rack at the same time. Its construction had certain obscene implications that he didn't want to think about. The whole scene had been for his benefit, but Dana's torment would be just as real, if not as theatrical, as the scene implied.

"That's my trump card," Michael said. "If you perform a little service for me, I'll give her back to you." The implications of ownership and possession grated on Morgan's nerves.

"And if I don't?" Morgan asked, because he had to.

"Shall I describe to you," Michael said, "the operation of that racklike device my demons are preparing?"

"No, that won't be necessary. What do you want me to do?" He'd make sure Dana was safe first, and worry about the consequences of whatever Michael wanted later.

"There is a certain stone, as you well know," Michael said. "It is a red stone, like jasper, about this big around." He made a circle with his thumb and fingers, two inches across. "On it is carved an eye, very much like the one over the mausoleum behind my house. All I want you to do is get me that stone. Bring it to me, and I'll release Miss Kirkpatrick."

"I see. Just a stone. And where is this stone? On the moon? In a dragon's heart?"

"Come, come, please, nothing like that. This is not a test of your abilities. It is a true service, something needing doing that I can't do for myself. If the stone were just on the moon, it could be easily retrieved. It would take only a moment. If it were in a dragon's heart—an impossibility to begin with—it would be fruitless sending anyone after it. I don't want you dead, Morgan, and I already know what you are capable of accomplishing if you try. I just want the stone."

"But what do you need me for?"

"The stone is in a place where I can't go. I find that very frustrating. It's a bad place, yes, and dangerous to anyone who intrudes there. But that is coincidental, and has nothing to do with my exclusion from it.

"Pickard could have gotten the stone. He wanted to, though we had told him not to. But you have the dagger, Morgan. That is the key. That, and your natural ability.

"Come, Brother Morgan, if I didn't think you could get the stone for me, I wouldn't ask you to try. I'm not that wasteful. Or vindictive."

"Pickard said something about winning Ghebr's favor. Is that what this is all about?"

"That has something to do with it, yes. Come, Morgan, get me the stone. We have been wanting it for a long time. You're the first person who's come along who might be strong enough to get it. Not everyone could make use of the dagger. Will you try?"

"So *you* can win Ghebr's favor instead of Pickard," Morgan said bitterly. Michael's eyes flickered.

"Something like that."

"And this stone, it's the reason behind everything that's happened here so far, isn't it? That's what the Servants have been up to all this time."

"No. The stone, itself, is the cause of nothing. Our *desire* for it is the reason and the cause."

"And what good is this stone to you?"

"Much good, Morgan." Michael was becoming impatient. "Come on, will you get it for me? Will you try?"

"Are there other options?"

"If you refuse, you may watch my demi-demons put Miss Kirkpatrick on the rack. And I think I should warn you that not only are they hairy, they're also—"

"I'll get it," Morgan said hurriedly, before Michael could finish. "Where is it?"

Without warning or any sense of transition, he was standing on a high cliff overlooking a purple sea.

Chapter Thirty-seven

✢ ✢ ✢

THE CLIFF AT his feet was very steep. The surface, a creamy gray in color, was scalloped hollow, with sharp edges and points. Maybe two hundred fifty feet below where he stood was a pebble beach, sloping steeply into the purple water of the sea.

The ground on which he stood sloped gently down away from the edge of the cliff. It was covered with some kind of hummocky, knee-high herb like a round-leafed fern. Morgan followed the line of the cliff with his eyes, around to the left where a forest stood, several hundred yards away, dark green and dense.

The forest circled the whole promontory and cut it off from the rest of the land. There was nothing else here on these few open acres but Morgan, and a tower, to his right, sixty feet away, right on the edge of the cliff.

It was a round tower, built of massive flat slabs of rock like thick slates of a ruddy brown color, presenting an amazingly rough and irregular surface. It tapered from a broad base upward to a height of about eighty-five or ninety feet, then widened again and terminated in a short truncated cone with a round dome atop that. It was about one hundred thirty feet high, measuring from the landward side of the tower. The entrance was on the seaward side, right up against the cliff, with only a narrow ledge of land giving access.

It was not militarily defensible. The stones,

though heavy and dense, had been fitted together in flat, projecting courses, offering more than sufficient irregularity to make it eminently climbable. But it was impressive, even formidable, in a nonmilitary way. Michael's red stone would be there, of course, either at the very top or in the deepest dungeon.

The tower could serve little political function, since there was nobody around to impress. Perhaps, Morgan thought, it was purely symbolic, built to satisfy certain magical specifications, or perhaps religious ones.

Even as he started toward the tower, several beings came out of its great double door and along the ledge toward him. They were very like *tsedik*, with tentacular fingers and toes, tentacles around eyes, ears, and mouth, and with longer tentacles growing from the joints of arms and legs.

But these were gray instead of white, taller than the *tsedik* by about a foot, and more strongly built. And they were able to go abroad in the light. They were naked, like the *tsedik*, but they carried short spears with long tapering heads that glinted in the light of the very yellow sun overhead.

"Neow?" Phoebus asked, from some dimensional "pocket" of Morgan's being.

"No, not yet," Morgan said. There was no smell of sea salt, he realized, as the *tsedik*-like creatures ran toward him.

They had covered half the distance between him and the tower when he finally broke from his strange reverie. He cast a spell and a ball of fire sprang from his fingertips. It arched through the air and struck the first gray creature in the head, exploding with a shock that knocked the next three of them off their feet. Fire spread out in a twenty-foot radius.

The creatures were confused for a moment. Morgan cast another fireball into their midst, killing two more outright and burning several others. So much for the element of surprise.

The naked gray creatures turned and fled. Morgan sent two more fireballs after them to make sure they stayed fled. They ran down the slope toward the trees. He watched until they had all disappeared into the dark green undergrowth. It seemed too easy a victory.

He walked through the knee-high ferns to the tower, keeping an eye out for other gray creatures from the seaward door, or coming back from the forest. He was relieved to learn magic worked here.

When he reached the tower he could feel magic emanating from its rough stones. It had been built wholly by magic, and magic maintained it. He didn't know for sure, but he could guess, from the "flavor" of the magic in this tower, that it was the nature of the magic that was barring the Servants from this place, not anything inherently "good" about it. He looked up its rough face to the bulge overhead. The ruddy brown stones were only a skin, covering something else.

He walked around to the narrow ledge at the edge of the cliff, along it to the broad, double-leaved door. It was cast of bronze, verdigrised from exposure to the weather except where hands of one kind or another had polished the handles. He touched the bright metal gingerly.

There were no shocks or traps. He pushed, and the door swung slowly inward.

He stepped inside onto a balcony, with ramps curving down both sides of the inside wall. The ceiling was just a foot or so from his head; the floor was twenty feet below. The inside was in marked contrast with the rugged and jagged exterior.

It was a place of crystal and color. The ramps on either side of his balcony were brightly white, the walls iridescent like mother-of-pearl. There were great rectangular shapes on the ivory floor below, crystal prisms that captured the light and broke it into rainbows.

The sources of the light, hanging from the ceiling of pearly gray, were faceted crystals, each as big as his head, each shining with a diamondlike radiance. Directly across from him was another stairway, built of silver wire, leading up to another balcony halfway up the mother-of-pearl wall, where there was another door.

He started down the right-hand ramp. Huge, ponderous beasts, like some kind of a cross between a slug and an elephant, moved slowly across the floor below him, among the rectangular, crystalline prisms. They paid him no attention, but went on about their unguessable tasks as if he weren't there. They were dark, shiny grayed blues, greens, browns, with two supple trunklike appendages at one end with which they touched and fondled the prism-built objects.

He reached the floor. Still the beasts did not notice him. The only other door in this chamber was at the balcony at the top of the silver wire stair opposite the entrance.

He moved slowly between the prism-things, avoiding the elephant-slugs that tended them. He reached the silver stair on the far side of the chamber without incident or hindrance whatsoever.

He put a foot on the first wire step. The whole structure tinkled musically. He froze, but there was no response from the elephant-slugs. After a moment's pause to let his heartbeat return to normal, he climbed to the balcony. The silver wire stairway rang and sang the whole way.

He stepped onto the balcony and stood before the door a moment. The portal was made of milk glass, or something like it. He surveyed the chamber one more time, then grasped the handle and pulled. The door swung open easily.

Beyond was a small stone-walled room, ruddy brown like the outside of the tower, but polished smooth. There were two other doors, one on either side. He went to the one on the right first and listened. There was only silence.

From behind the door on the left came distant muffled sounds of heavy machinery thudding and clanking. And another sound, almost drowned out by the first, as of a man screaming in agony.

Beyond that door was the head of a flight of steps, curving gently downward, lit by frostily glowing domes set into the slanting ceiling. He descended past the level of the floor, twenty feet underground, to a landing.

There was another closed door on the inside of the curve of the tower. The sounds were louder here, thudding, clanking, hissing, heavy weights being dragged across a rough surface. He pushed the door open and stepped into a smoky dungeon with glowing furnaces providing the only light. Thick, man-shaped creatures worked here.

It was a forge. The troll-like beings were making weapons, armor, tools. The place reeked of magic as much as of smoke. But still, amid all the noise, he could hear a man's screams, coming from the far side of the chamber.

The two dozen or so workers here were all over eight feet tall, brown, leathery, thickly built. They were preoccupied with their tasks and did not notice his entrance. Morgan moved from shadow to shadow, keeping clear of their line of sight, working his way around to where the screams were coming from.

These beings, like the elephant-slugs on the floor above, paid him no mind. They went on about their business, hammering swords, casting hammers, shaping helmets, drawing wire that they twisted into cable. The heat was suffocating, the smoke choking, the light fiery red.

Morgan cast an atmospheric shield that let the air through to him but kept the smoke out, and another to keep the heat around him at a bearable level. He felt sure that with so much other magic going on here, his two little spells would never be noticed. Then he went toward the source of the screaming.

He found another stairway, recessed into the floor. He went down, twenty-five steps, and came out from the wall of a smaller, darker chamber, where only one fire was burning. It wasn't a bright fire, but it showed a ladderlike rack. Tied to it, naked and bleeding, was a man.

Demonic shapes moved around him, wielding red-hot instruments with which they twisted and tore at the man's flesh.

Morgan didn't know what was going on, but he knew that nobody deserved to have done to them what these lanky, deformed humanoids were doing to this man, no matter how great his crimes might have been. Good and evil were relative, but deliberately causing pain, simply for its own sake, was relatively evil everywhere. Besides, this man might be innocent of any wrongdoing.

The man's screams were unbearable. The shapes of his tormentors did not argue a benevolent purpose on their part. Morgan was determined to end the man's suffering, but he dared not kill the torturers outright. They might be as much victims as the man they worked over.

So instead he worked a light sleep spell. Nothing happened. He tried again. This time there was a collective sigh from tormentors and tormented alike. The humanoid shapes slid gently to the floor.

Morgan strode across the chamber, past the opening of a descending spiral stair in the center, to the rack where the man hung. His body, though bloody, was undamaged. The torturers were doing to him what Morgan had threatened to do to the Jurgen-Smiths, hurting him, then magically healing his wounds. There was no permanent damage, only endless agony.

The prisoner woke from his doze as Morgan untied his bonds. The man said nothing, but let Morgan finish freeing him. When he could stand on his own feet again, he held out a hand. Morgan took it.

"Thank you," the man said, not quite in English but perfectly understandable. "They've been at me for almost a year. My name is Tseraith. Who are you?"

"I'm Morgan Scott. I hope I've done the right thing by freeing you."

"Well," Tseraith said, a wry smile on his face, "*I* think you have." He didn't seem to be much the worse for his ordeal, and that bothered Morgan, but he couldn't judge this man by his own standards. "What brings you to Tower Venabile?" Tseraith asked.

"I'm looking for a certain stone, which is supposed to be here."

"Ah, the red stone with the single eye carved in it. Yes, I know it well. And what do you want with this stone?"

"To ransom a friend of mine who is being threatened with a torment similar to yours, only worse."

"I see," Tseraith said. "Well, since the stone is no longer mine to give or keep, I may as well help you get it. Would you consider that fair payment for the service you've rendered me?"

"I would indeed," Morgan said.

Chapter Thirty-eight

✢ ✢ ✢

TSERAITH WENT TO a box lying against the wall and took out some clothes lying in it.

"Quite dirty, I'm afraid. Haven't been cleaned since they were taken from me. Still, they will have to do for the moment." He shook them out and dressed. They were vaguely medieval in cut. He buckled on an empty scabbard. Around him on the floor, the demonic tormentors slept fitfully. "You'll have to show me how you did that," he said, gesturing at the humanoids and pulling on a pair of high-topped boots.

"Maybe not right here," Morgan said. "They could wake up at any moment. A loud noise will arouse them."

"I see," Tseraith said, lowering his voice to a whisper. "I wasn't aware the drug was so delicate."

"Not a drug. Magic. Surely you know about magic."

"Yes, I do, but I *didn't* know magic was so common or that it could do things like that. Well, anyway, let's get out of here and go somewhere where we can discuss your little problem."

Morgan let Tseraith lead him back to the stairs and up to the first floor. They crossed the landing, went through the other door, and up more stairs to a second floor. The stairs went higher, but Tseraith stopped here and ushered Morgan into a circular room with doors all around the wall.

The room was bright with enamels, intense pure colors with a glossy, hard finish. Each door was painted distinctively, in concentric patterns, checkers, and other geometrics, in two or three rainbow colors each. The furnishings were sparse but comfortable, clustered in the middle of the room on a woven rug in pastel shades. There was a red-painted bed with a blue coverlet, a huge green table with a couple of enameled chairs in red and yellow, some low stools in various colors, cabinets against the walls between the doors in shades of lavender and blue, an orange couch.

"Welcome to my normal abode," Tseraith said. "This is where I live when I'm not being shredded below." He pulled a cord hanging against the wall. A door enameled in a green and yellow checkerboard with black linings opened, and a being like the worker troll-types entered, slenderer than the ones down in the forge but just as brown and leathery.

"Clean clothes for me," Tseraith said. "Food and drink for two." The servant bowed and went out.

"What are they?" Morgan asked, indicating the retreating creature.

"Astral servants. You know about that?"

"Yes, but I've never seen one."

"Curious." Tseraith threw himself down on the orange couch and indicated that Morgan should take one of the red and yellow chairs from the table. "No hurry," he said. "The communications in this place are terrible. I should know."

The green-and-yellow-checkered door opened again. The servant entered, carrying a hanger on which hung clean clothes, tailored something like the popular conception of Robin Hood's attire, but more simply cut, bright yellow with blue ribbing. Two other servants followed, carrying covered trays.

Tseraith wigglcd a hand and was suddenly dressed in the new clothes. His old torn things now hung on the hanger. The first servant left; the other two set the table.

The smell of the food was delicious, and Morgan was ravenous, or he would have chafed at the delay. He wondered if heroes always ate so irregularly.

Tseraith sat down in the other chair at the table. "Dig in," he said, and followed his own advice. Morgan did as he was bid. The food, which consisted of something like white roast beef, yellow beans, a brownish-pink fruit like a slice of pineapple with no hole, and a very leafy salad, tasted every bit as good as it looked and smelled.

"You say you know the red stone I'm looking for," Morgan said when they were finished and were sitting back sipping wine from tall, slender, white-enameled goblets.

"I do," Tseraith answered. "It used to be mine, along with everything else in Tower Venabile, up until just a little short of a year ago, when Sarkoon breached my defenses, took over the tower, and cast me into the dungeons below."

"And why did he do that?" Morgan asked, reconciling himself to hearing at least a part of the story before being given the stone.

"Because he's greedy. I make the best swords in this part of the world, and he wanted the trade. He's offered to buy me out any number of times, but why would I want to sell? I enjoy the work, *and* the profits. So he decided to take me by force. I underestimated him, I'm afraid. He succeeded."

"I see. But the stone."

"Ah, yes, the stone, the red stone with the eye. I don't know its origin, other than it was not made on this world. Does that surprise you?"

"Not in the least," Morgan said dryly.

"Oh. Oh, well. Anyway, how the stone got here, I don't know, or when exactly, either. The earliest reference to it I could find was in a manuscript dating back some seven thousand years. But then, I'm no scholar.

"Anyway, about eleven generations back, the stone came into the possession of one of my ancestors. It has remained in my family ever since. So you can see why I might be reluctant to part with it. But, as I said, since it is no longer mine to give or keep, and since you did free me from my tormentors, and since I am disinclined to leave any heirs—legal ones at least—you may as well have it, especially since it will be for a worthy cause."

"I appreciate your help, Tseraith," Morgan said, with mingled feelings of impatience and fascination.

"Think nothing of it," Tseraith said. "The stone means nothing to me anyway. It's magical, that much I can tell, and it seems to be of considerable power. But I could never figure out what it was good for."

"I don't mean to seem in a rush, but—"

"Oh, by all means. I'm sorry to keep you waiting, but I've been a long time without a decent meal. A very long time indeed. When would you like to confront the villain?''

"Who? Sarkoon?"

"Yes," Tseraith said. "He has it with him in the chamber at the top of the tower."

"Any time. Are you ready?"

"I will be in a moment." He rapped the table sharply, and the servant entered.

"My sword," Tseraith commanded. Then something behind Morgan caught his eye, and his mouth fell open in surprise.

Morgan turned to see that the wall behind him was bulging out in a huge oval, six feet high and three feet across. As he watched, fascinated and not a little frightened, the bulge began to take on human features. Soon a giant face stared down at him and his now silent host.

"Ah, Tseraith," the face in the wall said. It retained the colors of the enameled wall, though the eyes were true eyes, liquid and moving. "I see you have been enjoying yourself."

"Sarkoon! How—?"

"As you can see," the face of Sarkoon said, "I have made a few alterations since I have taken over here. It comes in very handy in keeping an eye on things." The face's attention turned to Morgan. "And you, sir," Sarkoon said, "welcome, though I don't think you'll enjoy it. Very interesting, that exploding fire you used against the *kaltrosh*. I have never seen anything like it. It appears there are large areas of magic we here know nothing about. But then, I'll bet we know a few tricks that you would find most illuminating."

"I'm sure," Morgan said. His initial startlement passed. He felt calm and well in control of himself. "Perhaps, if you have the generosity and patience, we could all profitably spend a day or two comparing notes."

"We could," Sarkoon said, "but we won't. Sit down, Tseraith! No, Morganscot, the profit will be all mine, I'm afraid, and the loss all yours. I have ways to learn the things I want to know. Not crude ways like Tseraith has had the pleasure to experience. I know certain mind tricks, Morganscot, and with them I will pick you clean. After that, you can join Tseraith in the dungeon, and sing duets."

Tseraith leapt from his chair and flung his goblet at the face, but the goblet just bounced off, and the image laughed.

"Enough, Tseraith," the voice of Sarkoon said. "I will have my way." The eyes turned to the servants, who had stood waiting the whole time. "Take Tseraith below," Sarkoon said, "and return him to his keepers."

Tseraith threw a heavy platter at the troll-like servant, but the servant ducked and leaped upon its former master while several others came in from other doors.

Morgan cast an electric shock spell, which sent one of the brown creatures kicking and jiggling until it fell over. But the others were upon him. He started to put up the anti-animal shield, then remembered these were astral beings and wouldn't be affected by it. By then it was too late. Three of them had jumped on him. They bore him to the floor, where his head struck the flags—

Chapter Thirty-nine

✣ ✣ ✣

HE REGAINED CONSCIOUSNESS, dangling from a cross bar behind his shoulders, over which his arms had been twisted, and to which they were fastened by straps of some kind. His feet were several inches off the floor.

He was in a small round room under a stone dome pierced with many narrow windows. There were some cabinets up against the curving walls, a huge workbench all stained and scorched, a case of leather-bound books, and the head of a flight of spiral stairs going down from a circular hole in the middle of the floor. He was at the top of the tower.

He sensed movement behind him but could not twist his head far enough around to see.

"Patience, my friend," Sarkoon's voice came from behind him. "I'll be with you in a moment."

Morgan relaxed and let himself hang. His hands were strapped in such a way that he couldn't use his fingers to form positions or trace sigils. Still, he had done spells in his head before; he could do them again.

But for some reason his mind felt numb. The images of the spells didn't want to form. He felt panic grab him in the lower bowels.

His captor came around to stand in front of him, dressed much as Tseraith had been but in dark blue with pink piping. Morgan recognized Sarkoon's face even without the garish colors of the enameled wall to ornament it.

"By now," Sarkoon said, "you have undoubtedly felt the effects of one of my great secrets."

"A blank mind spell. Yes, I know."

"Hmmm. I am disappointed. I was hoping to present you with a spell with which you were unfamiliar."

"You did. That face in the wall."

"That? A little trick. But effective, yes? I wish I could have seen Tseraith's expression while it was forming."

"You would have enjoyed it," Morgan said. He tried to remember if there was a counter to the blank mind, but if there was, he couldn't think of it.

"I'm sure," Sarkoon was saying. "But Tseraith is back where he belongs. We must attend to you, now. Tell me, did you really hope to get the Eye in the Stone from Tseraith?"

"Is that what it's called? Yes, I did."

"How foolish."

"No, overoptimistic, perhaps."

"My, you're a cool one," Sarkoon said, not without some little admiration.

"It's the only way that pays," Morgan said.

"I took the liberty of giving you a cursory examination while you were unconscious," Sarkoon said, changing the subject.

"So?" Morgan asked, hoping to delay Sarkoon as long as possible.

"As a consequence, I know you're not from this world."

"So?" Morgan asked again. He was determined that Sarkoon would derive no satisfaction from this interview.

"So in spite of that," Sarkoon said, nettled, "you still respond to my magic." He calmed himself and smiled contentedly. "That, after all, is what really matters. But enough of this idle chatter. It's time we got down to business. You know magics that I don't know. That is an intolerable situation, which must be set to rights." He turned away and went to the workbench, where he sorted out chalks, candles, pieces of parchment, and other paraphernalia of the very crudest sort of magic.

Sarkoon gathered up all his equipment and returned to where Morgan hung. He squatted down to arrange the things on the floor at Morgan's feet, putting everything in its proper place.

Morgan decided it was time to quit fooling around. Though his mind was numb from the blank mind spell and he could not work magic, the spell affected only him. "Now," he said softly, and felt a weight pressing down on his shoulders, and heard a low, rumbling purr. Sarkoon must have heard it too, because he looked up, his eyes narrowing.

"Now, where the blazes did that thing come from?" he muttered. He started to rise, but Phoebus sprang down on him, his claws and teeth flashing, right at Sarkoon's throat. He struck true, biting and clawing, and suddenly there was blood all over the magician, dripping on the floor. But there was no scream. The man fell back from his half-crouch; the *vendra* cat gave one more kick with his hind legs, opening up Sarkoon's abdomen from rib cage to groin. He stepped off the corpse and looked up at Morgan.

"I was beginning to think you had forgotten me," he said.

"Just waiting for the right moment," Morgan answered. He felt his mind clear and his magical powers come back. He thought the spell to sever the straps holding him and dropped to the floor. His arms ached, as if he had been hanging there for more than just a few moments.

"You did a thorough job on him," he said, looking down at Sarkoon's mangled corpse.

"Well, after all, I *am* part cat," Phoebus said, starting to wash himself of Sarkoon's blood. "What about Tseraith?"

"I suspect that Sarkoon's death will release him, just as it released me. Now all I need is the stone."

He hadn't seen anything like it out in the open, so he went over to the cabinets and opened them one by one. It was in the fourth cabinet, on a shelf at eye level.

It was a round red stone not quite two inches in diameter, with the eye of Ghebr carved into it. There were scratches on it, as if it had once been held by prongs. It was the missing pommel of the dagger. He reached for it.

"Don't touch it!" Phoebus screamed from behind him. Morgan jerked his hand away and turned around to stare down at the cat, confused and badly startled. "Not yet," Phoebus added more calmly. He ran to the cabinet, jumped up onto the shelf but at the opposite end from the stone, then walked over to peer closely at it.

"You have assimilated the dagger," Phoebus said. "If you touch the stone with your bare hands, you'll draw it into you, too. And that would be fatal." He jumped down again, went over to the work bench and under it. He came back with a leather bag in his mouth. Morgan took it.

"Thanks," Morgan said. He turned the bag inside out, put his hand in it, and picked up the stone as if he were wearing a mitten. As quickly as he could, he turned the bag right side out again, over the stone, as if it were very hot.

"He knows you've found it," Phoebus said.

"Who, Tseraith?" Morgan asked, drawing the string tight.

"Michael," Phoebus said in a fading voice. Without transition, Morgan was standing in his room in the House of Aaron in Harborbeach.

PART EIGHT

There is much a demon can do in its own form, but much that it cannot. One way around this is for a demon to manifest itself in a physical avatar. Then it becomes visible to human or animal eyes, and it is able to manipulate the physical world to some extent. The form an avatar takes is not at the whim of the demon, but reflects in certain ways the form of the being itself. But that form is only a reflection, not the true thing.

Avatars, however, take a lot of energy to construct and maintain. An easier way and the only way Evil can enjoy the pleasures of the flesh is to inhabit an already existing body. This takes little energy, and the demon acquires, along with the body, its knowledge and ability to function in a purely physical world. It is limited in that, while in a body, the demon's abilities are severely curtailed. It is, for the time being, no longer in complete correspondence with the energy fields of its normal mode of existence.

Animals will do to a certain extent, but animal brains cannot fully accommodate an Intelligent being. Hence Humans and other sentient species are preferred, besides the fact that such a host will of necessity become a useful part of the Force of Evil.

A difficulty is that most people do not like being inhabited. It is not comfortable having one's personality and privacy and integrity violated.

If they resist the inhabiting demon, they are said to be possessed. Even animals protest. The demon imparts considerable mystic power, but the host must suffer the demon's constant presence and interference in his or her own pleasures.

Not all people resist being inhabited, of course. Some feel it is a great honor, or a duty, or fate. They share with the demon, to some extent, its powers, though they are only being used, as a kind of vehicle.

Chapter Forty

✤ ✤ ✤

MORGAN'S LEGS FELT watery, and his stomach was tied in knots, as if he had undergone severe psychic bruising.

"You have the stone," came a voice from behind him. Morgan spun and saw Michael sitting calmly in a chair. Michael's eyes were glued to the bag in Morgan's hand.

"How did you know I had the stone?" Morgan asked, trying to cover his startlement.

"Simple, really. When I sent you to Tower Venabile, I kept an astral link on you. When I felt you take the stone, I sent a pulse along that thread that immediately drew you back along it to me here in the real world. It takes a little time to set something like that up. Now, *give me the stone.*

"Where's Dana?" Morgan counterdemanded. "We made a deal."

"Let me have the stone," Michael said again, more sternly this time but more under control.

"In a pig's eye I will," Morgan said, backing away from where Michael sat. He had no illusions abut Michael giving up Dana if he got his hands on the stone first.

"Come, come, no need to be so rude." He had been ready to reach out, but now he relaxed again, although the toe of his left foot kept tapping the carpet.

"Bring Dana here, Michael, or I'll take the stone away."

"Indeed. And suppose I give you the girl, and the stone isn't in the bag. Then what?"

"Two things. First, you can snatch her back again with no trouble at all, and you know it. And second, you *know* the stone is in the bag. You can *feel* it. You should see your eyes, Michael. Such greed!"

The almost golden eyes, which had never left the leather bag, flicked up to Morgan's face. "I didn't know it showed."

"It's the most obvious thing about you. Now, where's Dana? If you've hurt her, I'll crush the stone."

Michael's face blanched and his toe stopped tapping. "I don't think you could do that. Besides, what good would that do you?"

"None, I suppose, but it would hurt you."

"You should be thankful I allow you to take such liberties. I have inflicted severe punishment on people who were much less impolite than you."

"Not on people holding the Eye in the Stone, you haven't." Morgan was drenched in sweat.

Michael's face went wooden. "I see. You can't know much more than that, but even that's too much. I said I wouldn't underestimate you, Morgan, but I nearly did. You'd think I would have learned by now. Well, well, let me see. I want the stone. You want Miss Kirkpatrick. Suppose, then, we make an exchange, one for the other."

"That was the agreement to begin with. Now, you *know* I have the stone. You can feel it." He jiggled the bag slightly, and Michael's eyes went right to it. "But I don't know anything about Dana. Where is she?"

"Nearby," Michael said, forcing himself to look back at Morgan's face.

"Come on, Michael, stop fiddling around. Where is she?"

"Right here," Michael said, and she was standing beside Michael's chair. She was naked, confused, startled, and stared around her as if she didn't know where she was.

"Dana," Morgan said, resisting an urge to move toward her. She saw him then, and her face cleared.

"Morgan, I—" She started to take a step, but something held her back.

"Wait, Dana," Morgan said. "Just wait a minute." He looked back at Michael. "It's not that I don't trust you, you understand."

"Of course not," Michael said dryly. Dana looked down at him and recoiled. She tried, once, to cover her nakedness with her hands, then decided it was more dignified not to bother.

"But this could be only an image," Morgan went on. "Or a simulacrum. I'll have to find out if it's really Dana, and if she's really here."

"As a matter of fact, I had her with me all along and only just now brought her forth for your inspection."

"I'm going to have to make a test," Morgan said. He didn't like Michael's attitude toward Dana, as if she were a piece of property.

"Do whatever you wish," Michael said.

Dana stood silently beside Michael's chair, watching Morgan watch her. He tried frantically to think of a test he could perform that would reveal her true nature. But everything he thought of could also be falsified.

Except for one thing—their bond. It still existed, though he had been unable to reach her through it since she'd been kidnapped. He felt the bond now, the link between them. And now he knew it was indeed she, here in the room with him. He smiled at her, and she smiled back.

"Are you satisfied?" Michael asked.

"Yes, I am," Morgan said. There was no way Michael or anyone else could falsify the bond.

"Then give me the stone," Michael said.

"Let her get dressed first," Morgan said. Michael's mouth tightened, but he didn't protest. Dana's clothes were where she'd left them. She quickly put them on and came over to stand beside Morgan.

"Now," Morgan said softly. There was no catly pressure on his shoulder. He hesitated a moment, then handed the bag to Michael.

Michael took the bag, opened it, and impossibly out of such a small space, Phoebus the *vendra* cat came howling and clawing, shredding Michael's face. Michael dropped the bag with a scream, folded away, and was gone. Phoebus, bristling, his tail huge, dropped to the floor and picked up the bag in his mouth, with the stone still inside.

Chapter Forty-one
✤ ✤ ✤

"Neat trick," Morgan said. "For a minute there I wasn't sure you were going to come."

Phoebus dropped the bag down at Morgan's feet and sat down behind it.

"Just waiting for the right moment," he said.

But Morgan wasn't paying any attention. Dana had come to him in a rush, and now he held her, trying to calm her. He could feel her relief, her fear, her anxiety.

Her stay in Michael's torture chamber had been psychologically damaging, even though the demidemons had done her no physical harm. She was trying to regain control of herself, but it wasn't easy. For a long time stone buildings and anything with more arms than it should have would be a shock and a torment to her.

"I was afraid you wouldn't make it," she said after a while, trying to keep her voice from breaking. "They were so sure—and so eager!"

"But I did make it, and now you're safe. And we still have the Eye in the Stone."

"It's a little soon to start celebrating," Phoebus said. "Michael will have other ways of getting to you, now that the stone is here. You both are in considerable danger."

"I wish this whole mess were all over with," Dana said. "I want us to stop being magicians for a while and just go off somewhere."

"Me too," Morgan said. "But we're not done with the stone yet." Reluctantly, he let go of Dana, picked up the bag with the stone in it, and sat down at the table. "It was the pommel of the dagger," he said, "but there's more to it than that." Gingerly, he opened the bag and let the stone roll out. It lay on the table, the eye staring balefully up at him. Dana sat down across from him, and Phoebus jumped up on the edge of the table.

"What are you going to do?" Dana asked.

"A psychometric trace. This thing was once a part of the dagger, and we have the dagger in us, so we should be able to learn more than a little."

They did not have to touch each other. Morgan and Dana were psychically linked through their bond with the dagger, and Phoebus, as Morgan's familiar, and now Dana's too, was linked with them both in the way peculiar to familiars.

They turned their attention inward, perceiving the Lattice and its intricate relatedness to all things. They perceived the stone, and though they were clumsy at first, and missed many details, they learned.

It had been made by powerful magicians long ago, who had sought control over certain of the demigods. They had called up Ghebr, an arch-demon, who was more arrogant then, and captured a small part of him and sealed it in the stone. How that was done Morgan and Dana could not tell, but it reduced Ghebr's status and power, confining him to the Earth.

Whoever had the Eye in the Stone and knew how to use it could call Ghebr at any time and make him do their will. Those magicians and their successors kept Ghebr on a string for several thousand years.

But Ghebr had not been helpless. After a while he disrupted the magicians who had organized to take advantage of the stone. For a time the stone passed from hand to hand, along with the then imperfect knowledge of how to make use of it.

About nine thousand years ago it passed out of the real world. Its history then became confused. Even Ghebr was no longer able to keep track of it. It had, apparently, been kept in places where Ghebr could not go. Churches and other holy places were usually totally shielded from him. Morgan could not determine what the mechanism was at Tower Venabile that kept Ghebr out, but he suspected it wasn't the tower so much as the whole world that was closed to Ghebr and to his Servants.

Ghebr had known where the stone was, as part of him was in it. He tried many times to recover it but, as a demon, he could not go there himself. He tried to send his Servants, but they were blocked too. He enlisted the aid of other mortals, enticing them with promises but not initiating them into his Service. Without the dagger they were unable to penetrate the magical defenses. Those few to whom he entrusted the dagger also failed, dying when they touched the stone. They were not strong enough, or clever enough, or competent enough. And then the dagger was lost, as a consequence of some other enterprise, just as Ghebr had finally figured out the right combination of characteristics necessary in someone who would be able to get the stone.

Morgan and Dana withdrew their minds from the stone and sat back looking at one another.

"This is more serious than I had thought," Morgan said. "If Ghebr gets hold of the stone, then all our work will go for nothing. He has been handicapped, all these years, and the stone will enable him to regain his full power."

"If Pickard could have gotten the stone," Dana said, "Ghebr would have exalted him above all other Servants. But first he had to have the dagger, because he couldn't touch the stone without the dagger's mediating magic. But didn't he understand, that as a Servant, he was bound to fail?"

"I don't think so. Desire and greed and lust for power prevented him from thinking clearly. And even though he had been a Servant here for a long time, Michael, the newcomer, got elevated to the Grand Mastership over him. I can imagine what that did to Pickard's pride."

"So Pickard tried to get you to get the dagger and the stone for him. But why all this charade about Michael being missing?"

"Michael said that you were too close to him, and so he dropped out of sight, fuddling the memories of anyone who would be concerned at his disappearance. And then I blundered in. And what an opportunity. I was a magician; I was not a Servant. I could get the dagger, and with it the stone, and eliminate you, a direct threat, and eliminate and punish Pickard, a rival, all at once. And when I was done, I would either be killed, or else so perverted that I could safely be made a member of the Lodge myself. And Michael, with Ghebr's favor, would have been above any retribution I might wish to exact."

"The frightening thought," Dana said, "is that

the demon Ghebr has been actively involved in this whole plot, not just directing it from the sidelines."

"What frightens me," Morgan said, "is the re-alization that Michael came so close to actually sucking me into the Lodge. I mean, you don't know about what I did with two Novices, to try to get them to tell me where you were. The feel-ing of power, of freedom to vent my anger, was so intoxicating, so tempting."

"If he could have won you over, you would more than make up for any number of other Servants who might be lost in the process," Dana said. "You would be a formidable enemy indeed."

"I don't even like to think about it. And there's still the fact that I committed a murder, however justifiable, while under the influence of the Lodge, however superficially. A price will have to be paid for that. I just hope I can live long enough to pay it in the mundane world in-stead of after."

"But if Michael wants this stone so badly," Dana asked, "why isn't he here, taking it from us?"

"Because I hurt him badly," Phoebus said. "He has been damaged, and needs to be healed."

"Yes," Morgan said, "but Ghebr is not like those demidemons who initiated me, or held Dana. He has a mind and a will of his own. Couldn't he come here in person, and take the stone?"

"I don't think he could," Phoebus said, "with-out some kind of pentagram of power, or other means of supporting his incorporeal self in real space."

"But what about those demidemons, then?" Dana asked.

"They were brought here by Michael," Morgan said, "or by Pickard, and kept in the real world by their magic."

" 'My demidemons,' " Phoebus murmured.

"What do you mean?" Morgan asked.

"Michael said, 'my demidemons,' didn't he once?"

"Yes, he did . . ."

"Are you thinking what I'm thinking?" Dana asked in the sudden silence.

"I am," Morgan said. "Michael's eyes. He wasn't just being guided by Ghebr from a distance. Ghebr was actually inhabiting him just now, here, in the room with us."

"We have all been closer to death than we have imagined," Dana said.

"I don't know as much about demons as I should," Morgan said softly, "but I know Ghebr is too proud to think mere mortals, such as ourselves, even trained magicians, could outdo him. It is his major failing."

"Do you think we're safe, then?" Dana asked.

"For a while, but I wouldn't waste any time. Michael has been injured, and will have to be healed, but there's still Nick Jones, who even if he's not Grand Master, is a Lodge Master now, and very powerful in his own right. We may have only a short while."

"Okay," Dana said, "so what do we do now?"

"I don't know," Phoebus said.

"The best thing," Morgan said slowly, "would be to take the stone to the Dreamer, and leave it with him in the Other House. The problem is, ever since I got to Harborbeach, I've been unable to contact the Dreamer."

"That would be the best place for it," Dana said. "I'm surprised you haven't asked the Dreamer's help before now."

"It isn't that I haven't tried," Morgan said, "it's that I *can't*. I've been cut off. . . . That is, I cut myself off."

"Vengeance," Phoebus said.

"You mean Morgan's desire for it?" Dana asked. "Yes, I guess that would do it. And murder doesn't help, however justified it might have been. And I'm involved in Pickard's death too. Morgan, you're not alone in this."

"I know, Dana, and it worries me. But right now a more urgent worry is this damn stone."

"We can't just leave it here," Dana said.

"I know, I know, but how do we get to the Other House?"

"The fact that you have the stone now might make a difference," Phoebus said.

"Yes, it might. I guess it's worth a try." He calmed himself and went through the ritual for Deity Communion. He expected either to be still cut off from the Dreamer, or for the spell to work and the Dreamer to speak to him. What happened was neither one.

"This is strange," he said. "All I'm getting is an image of a door, in what seems to be the cellar of the hotel, somewhere near the heating plant."

"Some kind of special portal?" Dana asked.

"I guess so." Using an ashtray, he rolled the stone back into the bag and picked it up. It seemed to be a lot heavier than he remembered.

"So when do we go?" Dana asked as they got

up from the table. Phoebus jumped onto her shoulder.

"Right now. Then we'll really have our hands full. After the stone is safe, Michael will want vengeance on me for hiding it again. I will have to do something about that, and though I hate the thought, I might even have to kill him. Even if I don't, the confrontation will be more than a little dangerous."

"Yes, I understand."

He kissed her, and Phoebus climbed from her shoulder to his.

"There's another problem," the cat said. "Ghebr will want vengeance too."

"I can't think about that right now," Morgan said, "or I'd be so frightened I couldn't do what I have to do. Let's just do this one step at a time."

Chapter Forty-two

✢ ✢ ✢

THEY LEFT HIS room and went down the rickety stairs to the basement. There was a maze of dingy corridors, disused serviceways, shutdown kitchen facilities. They wandered around for a few moments, then saw a sign giving directions to the central heating plant.

When they got there they found that the only corridor from the plant was the one by which they'd come. They backtracked, trying each door they came to. They were all locked. At the third door on the left Phoebus said, "This is the one." Morgan tried the handle; it pulled open. Beyond was only darkness. Morgan put his arm around Dana's shoulders. Together they stepped through.

They were in a large, dark hall, filled with columns standing seemingly at random on a floor of smooth stone. The ceiling was lost in shadow far overhead, and if there were walls, they could not be seen for the columns. The darkness was not quite absolute, but they could see quite well, as if by astral sight. This was the Other House, an astral realm just outside the edge of reality.

They looked around at the columns, trying to sense some order to their arrangement, but if there was any they could not find it. It was then they noticed that the door by which they had come in was no longer there.

"How will we get back?" Phoebus asked.

"I don't think we do," Morgan said, "until we've finished our business here. Notice something else. Feel the Lattice." There was a strange quality to it, as if it had somehow been stilled, made rigid. The bond between Morgan and Dana was unaffected, but it would be difficult, if it were possible at all, to cast a spell here. The tension in the Lattice almost seemed to ring.

"I seem to have lost track of which way we were facing when we came in," Dana said. Every direction seemed just like another.

"Do you suppose it matters?" Phoebus asked.

"I guess not. Nothing's going to change if we just stand here." They started walking in the direction they happened to be facing at the moment.

As they passed the first of the columns, they saw that it was elaborately carved in an intertwining lacework of vines, leaves, flowers, serpents, insects, birds, and small animals, all tangled together and yet all somehow in a pattern they could not quite follow. All the columns were so carved, each subtly different from the others.

They walked among the columns for about ten minutes, or so it seemed. It was difficult to be sure of the passage of time here. Sometimes it would seem that they had taken just a few steps; at others that they had been walking for quite a while.

They became aware of something in the dimness up ahead, something as yet invisible because of the intervening columns. They kept walking toward it until, at last, between the columns, they could make out what looked like shallow steps. The shadows were thick here, and what lay beyond the steps was still invisible.

At last they came around a column and saw that they were nearing a dais, raised in three low steps above the floor. If there were columns beyond the dais, they were obscured by darkness.

There was something on the dais, a shadow in the shadows, obscured by shadows. They could not see what it was, but it gave the feeling of size, bulkiness, a huge boxlike throne. It was rectangular, as big as a dump truck. There was something equally huge sitting on the boxy throne. Or maybe, Morgan thought, it was a part of it.

The quality of the dim light that allowed clarity of vision elsewhere in the hall did not operate here. After a moment or two, Morgan thought it might be just as well. Though he strained to see the thing on the dais, he could not make out anything more than vague impressions, and they were disquieting.

There was something like thick tentacles coiling and uncoiling, slowly and silently. He could not actually see them, but those were the only terms he had to describe his perceptions.

There seemed to be a large head of some sort, horse-shaped perhaps, or maybe round, rising from the coiling mass on a long, snakelike neck. It might not have been anything at all. Whatever it was, its position and movement could not be accurately interpreted.

Morgan found the thing, his inability to perceive it clearly, and the implications of what he could perceive, decidedly disturbing. He knew Dana and Phoebus felt the same way.

Phoebus moved from Morgan's shoulder to Dana's. Morgan reluctantly took his arm from around her and stepped up to the first step of the dais.

The seething tentacles—if that was what they were—quieted a bit without actually becoming still. The head—if it was a head—rose up on its long neck and waited. Even this near he could not make out what it truly was, only impressions, hints of its general form.

"May I speak with you a moment?" Morgan asked. His voice sounded painfully weak.

"Two points that swing on different plains," the nonvoice said from the shadowed throne, *"and passing near are almost with each other.*

Passing near yet separated by such times as cannot join them, cannot make them touch. Two points that stand beyond a line and never cross, their orbits never intersect. If they could meet, the spread of time might blend, but in their two dimensions, time can live without them."

"I—I'm afraid I don't understand," Morgan said. The voice had not come from the head, but from the center of the writhing mass. At least the Dreamer didn't seem to be angry or displeased with him.

"I think he's talking about you and Michael," Dana whispered.

"No," Phoebus said, "about himself and Ghebr." The Dreamer said nothing.

"I've brought you a certain thing," Morgan said, "called the Eye in the Stone." He held out the bag. "We'd like to leave it in your safekeeping."

"We hold this galling time and times and play our orchids, moving like some half-green stone to flutter where soft winds are breathing mushrooms, making towers of glass, and finding silver ladles hung where moonbeams bend to play our lonely days."

Morgan thought he caught the meaning of those cryptic words. It had seemed that the Dreamer had acknowledged the strain Morgan had been under, and had forgiven him for his weakness while accepting the responsibility of guarding the Eye in the Stone . . . he thought. He put the bag with the stone down on the top step of the dais.

The Dreamer did not respond at once, but just waited in silence. There was a slight churning of the tentacle-shapes in/on the great cubical

throne. Then—though it wasn't really a voice—
it spoke.

*"Come dream with me and sing soft yellow,
holding bright in hand and eyes a garnet grown
where songs are born, and bird dust trickles
slowly down to shade our days in everness."*

"Thank you," Dana said. Morgan was surprised, but he shouldn't have been. The
Dreamer had spoken to her, not to him. The
message had some meaning that he hadn't
grasped. She had found it reassuring and com-
forting.

"Is it all right?" Morgan asked her.

"Yes," she answered, "everything is fine." She
reached up and kissed him quickly. "Let's go,"
she said.

He turned once more to the Dreamer.

"These truths we know are fine," the Dreamer
said, *"and when the vultures fold their long and
blackly wings we breathe them, sing them purple, shape the chords to fire and wrap our minds
in dreams to break the days and hold our arms
and spin like song-dust softly always falling."*

The words seemed to buoy him up. Phoebus
leaped onto his shoulder, and with his pulse
pounding, Morgan turned away with Dana and
strode off through the columned hall.

Chapter Forty-three

✢ ✢ ✢

THEY WALKED THROUGH the dimness in the direction they thought they had come. As they passed the columns they tried to recognize one that they'd seen before. But though each column was different, each was also so elaborate that when they thought they remembered a bit of carving they soon saw that it was set among entirely different elements, and that this was not the same column after all.

After a while they became confused. Each column looked familiar and yet was not. They couldn't remember whether a particular serpent twining around an ivy branch was like one they had seen as they had gone toward the Dreamer, or if it was like one they'd seen coming away, if in fact it was one they'd seen before at all. Phoebus had no better idea than they where they were.

After about twenty minutes or so, as far as they could tell, they had to acknowledge that they had never been in this part of the Other House before. The columns were arranged so randomly that it was easy for them to have lost their way. They stopped and looked around, trying to decide whether to backtrack or not. There was no telling one direction from another. They started walking again, in the way they happened to be facing at the moment.

It was neither hot nor cold here. Time passed, or seemed to. They felt as if they'd been walking for hours, but they did not grow tired. Nei-

ther did they come to any wall or door that
might lead them out of this place. Then again,
it would seem as if they'd been walking only a
moment or so. It was then that they would stop
and check the nearest column to see if they
would recognize it. They never did.

"I think we've gotten lost enough," Morgan
said at last. They stopped where they were and
turned around and around slowly, trying to detect a sense of presence that would tell them
where the Dreamer was.

"I can't feel him at all," Dana said. "Can you,
Phoebus?"

"No," the cat said.

"Well, unless we want to just sit down on the
floor and wait forever," Morgan said, "the only
thing we can do is to keep walking."

"Sitting won't do us any good," Dana said.
"We'll find the door out of here when we find
it." They resigned themselves to the inevitable
and started walking again, in no particular direction.

A moment later, off through the columns to
their right, they caught sight of a wall. They
went to it.

It stretched away on either hand, between the
columns, off into the distance in both directions. But to the right, again, not far from where
they were, was a door. They reached it in a moment and stepped through it into an alleyway.

"Now, why here," Morgan wondered, "instead of back to the hotel?"

"I don't know," Dana said, "but it probably
was not an accident."

"That may be," Morgan said, "but we have to
go back there anyway. Between us and the dag-

ger, we have lots of magic, but we don't know how to use it all yet. We'll need my grimoire, and the sooner we get it the better. Michael is certain to come looking for us, now that we've hidden the stone again. Or Jones will, if Michael isn't healed yet. We're going to need strong spells, Dana, if we're going to win this fight."

They left the alley, Phoebus riding visibly on Morgan's shoulder. They were still in Harborbeach, and saw at once where they were. They walked back to the House of Aaron, four blocks away. It seemed to be about midmorning.

They went through the lobby and up the rickety stairs. They stepped into the seventh-floor hall and turned toward Morgan's door.

"Wait," an anxious whisper called to them from behind. They turned to see Gary Weiss, standing just beyond the stairwell door, in the other end of the hall.

"Gary?" Dana asked. "What are you doing here?"

"Be quiet," Gary whispered tensely. "There are people in your room—Morgan." He came up to them and reached out a hand as if to touch Dana, but let if fall again. "Are you all right?" he asked.

"Yes," Dana said softly.

"Then Morgan didn't kill you after all."

"He did, but he brought us both back to life again."

"Should we be standing here like this?" Morgan asked, keeping his voice low.

"No," Weiss said. "Let's get out of here." He started down the stairs ahead of them.

"What made you come to warn us?" Morgan asked as they reached the sixth-floor landing.

"I waited outside the Jurgen-Smiths' house for an hour," Weiss said. "When neither you nor Michael came out, I went back in. There was nobody there at all."

"Michael sent the Jurgen-Smiths to hell," Morgan said as they continued down the stairs. He quickly told Dana and Weiss what he had witnessed.

"Do you believe me?" he asked Weiss as they entered the lobby and crossed it toward the front door.

"It isn't easy, especially the part about Michael being the Grand Master." They stepped out onto the street in front of the hotel.

"But he is," Dana said. "He had me fooled, too."

"Do you know who they were, upstairs?" Morgan asked.

"No, but not all of them are human. After I left the Jurgen-Smiths I went to your car and did a trace. That's how I found out where you were staying. I came here, and when I went to your room I could hear people moving around inside. I was going to try to take you by surprise, so I listened. I didn't hear much, but it was obvious they were going to kill you—they had some nasty ideas."

"They were expecting us?" Dana asked.

"Of course they were, and they'll come looking for you when you don't show up."

"And my grimoire is up there," Morgan said, "out of reach. How about yours, Gary?"

"I haven't looked at it in years. I'm not even sure I could put my hands on it right away."

"Dana?"

"Mine doesn't have the kind of spells I think we'll need," she said. "And besides, I don't want Cindy to get involved in this."

"We may not have a choice," Morgan said. "And anything you've got would be a help. We might as well try; there's no place we can hide."

"Attack them first," Phoebus said, "while you have the initiative."

"You gotta be crazy!" Weiss said. "The three of us wouldn't stand a chance, and besides, there are demidemons up there, I think."

"Four of us," Morgan said, reaching up to scratch Phoebus under the chin, "but I think you're right, we're too vulnerable at the moment."

"You have the dagger," Phoebus insisted.

"Yes," Dana said, "but who's had time to study it?"

"What dagger?" Weiss asked.

"The one we assimilated," Morgan reminded him. Weiss's face twitched. "It's a powerful weapon, but we'd need weeks and months to learn how to use it properly, and we don't have that much time. We may have only moments."

"That's true," Dana said, "but there's no reason we can't try to work with the dagger even so. We won't need a grimoire if we can just get a handle on the spells contained in the dagger. The power's there."

"And what about me?" Weiss asked angrily. "Come on, my car's in the parking lot." They started to walk toward the side of the building. "Goddammit," he went on, "I feel about as useful as an extra leg."

"Anything you can do will be a help," Dana

said, reaching out to take his arm. "Especially now, when we have to feel our way in the dark."

"Hold it," Weiss said, stopping short just inside the parking lot. It was about half filled with cars. "There's somebody in my Buick."

"Where?" Morgan asked. He saw Weiss's car two rows over.

"In the backseat. You can't see them, but they set off one of my alarms."

"Let's get out of here," Dana said, and they turned and hurried away.

"We need defense," Morgan said as they crossed the street and left the vicinity of the hotel. "And now."

"You guys work on it," Weiss said, moving between them and taking an arm of each. "I'll steer."

Morgan and Dana, trusting Weiss to keep them from colliding with the other pedestrians, turned their thoughts inward, feeling deep into themselves for the magic of the dagger.

"The spells don't make any sense," Dana protested.

"Of course they do," Morgan said. "We just don't understand them. But we can make use of them. Think about it."

"Yes, I see what you mean. They're very strange," Dana went on distractedly, "and complicated. Can we make them work?"

"If we had the time to perform the rituals formally," Morgan said, "I'm sure we could, and then we'd understand them too."

"Worry about that later," Weiss muttered. "If you can get a good defense spell up, you'd better do it. I think we're going to have trouble."

"There are other powers in the dagger," Morgan murmured. "Can you feel them, Dana?"

"Ye-es, I think so. It feels like we can use them to cast the spells, even though we don't comprehend them yet."

"Well, do it," Weiss said, "do it!"

"All right, all right," Morgan said as they started to cross a street. Weiss's hand gripped his arm painfully. "Let me concentrate." He closed his eyes, to help him visualize the unfamiliar gestures and sigils.

I'm with you, he felt rather than heard Dana say. Her strength and perceptions were added to his, and they called up the spells.

"Goddammit!" Weiss yelled, bringing them to a sudden halt. They were in the middle of the busy business street, and a portal was opening in front of them. People turned and stared, cars skidded, there were shouts of surprise, and yells of fear. Bolts of energy came streaking out of the fiery ring of the portal, to shatter and coruscate luridly, red and yellow and black, Energy, Life, and Entropy, against the shields Morgan and Dana had just that instant erected. The portal winked out at once.

People milled around, yelling, some running toward them, some away. They had seen that Morgan with his cat, Dana, and Weiss had been the object of the bizarre attack, the center of the phenomena. They crowded up to them, curious, afraid, excited.

"That was too damn close," Weiss said, "and they'll try again." The growing crowd was hemming them in.

"Follow my lead," Dana said, and Morgan saw, in his mind, what she wanted to do. He worked the spell, according to her instructions, concentrating on it and on the power of the dagger itself at the same time.

It seemed to the people around them that Morgan, Dana, and Weiss were just other witnesses like themselves. They wondered and exclaimed, talked of UFOs and psychic phenomena and attacks from Russia. The three magicians just walked away from the scene of the incident, unhindered now, and unquestioned.

"Damn impressive," Weiss said, "but every Initiate and Novice in Harborbeach will be after us now."

"We've been too lucky so far," Morgan agreed, "and we can't count on it holding out."

"But the power is there," Dana said. "We're not fools, and we're not helpless. I think we can pull this thing off."

"Let's not get overconfident," Weiss cautioned. "This is just the calm before the storm. Come on, let's get out of sight."

He led them to an alley, and they went up it. It made a left angle turn halfway into the block. As they neared this interior corner, two men stepped around it and stopped, facing them. One of them was Nick Jones. Weiss, with Morgan and Dana right behind him, stopped too. They watched the Servants watching them.

"There are others behind us," Dana said. "I think they know we're magically protected, but I can feel their power."

"Demidemons," Phoebus said. "They're just over the edge of the astral realms, waiting until the time is right."

"I think we'd better do a little fast running," Morgan said, grabbing his two friends by the arms. With barely any effort at all they slid into the Lattice: white, magenta, lavender, pale blue. Morgan could sense Weiss's surprise and dismay as they began a lateral movement, trusting in the spells of the dagger. The problem was that, in the Lattice, Phoebus could be of no help to them, and Weiss, because of his inexperience, could be a hindrance.

The walls of the alleyway became smooth concrete instead of brick. The windows disappeared, the buildings shrank, and everything was rippling and shimmery, shifting and changing as they raced across potential realities.

Their enemies were after them, not so swiftly as they, but as surely, with their wake to guide them. They could feel the Initiates and demidemons "behind" them. Weiss steadied as they went through pale green, pale yellow, to the pale orange of Earth. They walked up to the end of the alley, though they could hardly distinguish it now among the shimmers of light and color, pure motion, unadulterated relatedness.

Morgan wanted to find a good place to fight, but the enemy was too numerous, and too strong with the demidemons to aid them. Though it went against his pride, there was only one thing for them to do.

They fled. The lights and shapes and motions around them flickered and twisted until they became giddy. They went through purple and violet to the blue of Animal, moved laterally as far as they could go, then shifted back down to the pink of Light. They walked through the coruscations following an oblique line.

They had never been this far into the meshes of the Lattice before, off the main line from white to black. There were knots in it, and they hadn't known that. They passed one nexus, then another. Then there was someone with them.

They lurched away from enveloping tangles as the Servant tried to cast a spell on them. They started to prepare a counterspell, but now there was someone else on the "other side."

The enemy closed in. Morgan and Dana—holding Weiss between them—shifted frantically. For a moment they were out from between their enemies, but then two more unseeable, only feelable, magicians appeared, and they were trapped.

Dana "grabbed" huge "handfuls" of the fabric of the Lattice, Morgan tried to separate them to find some shortcut to another part of reality, and Weiss twisted other strands to keep their attackers at bay. He was in a full paranoic rage now. He manipulated the Lattice, clumsily but forcefully, ripping one Initiate to shreds, and sending a demidemon into convulsions that broke it apart.

But the enemy was quick. The Initiates and demidemons closed in, taking advantage of Weiss's unfamiliarity with the Lattice. Morgan pushed him to one "side," fended off a counterstrike, then slid across the fabric of the Lattice, trying to get to a position where he could attack without endangering his friends.

As if that was what the enemy had been waiting for, they all turned away from Morgan and Weiss, and converged on Dana. Knowing no combat spells, she had had to watch and wait. She tried to twist away as the spells rippled

down the web with deceiving slowness. Morgan
was too far away to stop the unraveling.

But Weiss wasn't. With a distorted scream he
lurched toward the tearing edges, grabbing
them as he went, changing their course even as
he was torn apart. The recoil rebounded onto
the casters, shredding demidemon and Initiate
alike. Dana jerked "above" the resulting gap,
and stretched out toward Morgan. He in turn,
even as the surviving enemy recovered, reached
toward her, and together they fell through into
the gap and a confusion of color and sound.

PART NINE

All intelligence on Earth shares a common basic "self," so that if any intelligent being turns evil, it hurts the whole of Intelligence. Such a turning aside from Good adds weight to Evil's side of the scale, giving Evil the power it needs to pervert others.

The Tukhanox regards power as an end in itself. It does not seek pleasure, nor wealth, nor any of the things power can give to mortal beings. To its way of thinking, the highest expression of power is the total destruction of the system in which the power is exercised, be it social group, nation, world, star, or universe.

This is the objective and the goal of the Tukhanox, absolute power expressed in absolute destruction, and this is the end toward which it strives. More than one party, or community, or nation has gone down to destruction because of the Tukhanox. Its ambition is great, though it will content itself with more limited objectives temporarily. After all, its ability does not match its ambition by a billionth part, though that is enough to cause considerable suffering on the Earth.

What the Tukhanox offers its followers is as much power on a smaller scale as they want and dare to indulge in. Their exercise of that power serves the Tukhanox more than it does them. The fall of Nazi Germany was as much a part of the Tukhanox's plans as the destruction caused by the war.

328 ALLEN L. WOLD

Ghebr at one time was the Tukhanox's prime agent on Earth, the demigod most personally responsible for the furtherance of the Tukhanox's plans. Ghebr has had other names at other times, and in other cultures. Baalzebaal, Mephistopheles, they are all the same. Whatever Ghebr's potential might have been, in allowing a part of himself to be captured and placed in the stone, his status was reduced from that of archdemon with the ability to move from star to star and influence a whole world, to just that of a demon, bound as other demons are to certain astral zones in the world.

Chapter Forty-four

❖ ❖ ❖

"Dana," he screamed soundlessly, and lost control completely. The meshes of the Lattice writhed; his pursuers were lost. He felt the bond between them, pulled at it as if that would bring her to him. He felt a panicked response—but distant, oh, so distant.

He couldn't stop his fall. He didn't know which way he was going. Colors flickered around him. He tried to call to Dana again, but she was elsewhere.

And Phoebus—*vendra* could not travel the Lattice. Morgan was alone.

He continued to fall through the Lattice, but now he could feel he was sliding along a kind of line of least resistance. An image formed in his mind, of Gary Weiss, sacrificing himself for Dana. Morgan's motion changed. He was falling toward Weiss now. But Weiss was dead. If Morgan continued along this line, he would join his friend in death.

He thought about Earth instead, and Harbor-beach, and veered to the side. But that would take him back to the hands of his enemies. He thought about Dana, but she was nowhere, as he was, and his course through the Lattice did not change.

Nick Jones had led the attack, but Morgan didn't want Jones. He wanted Michael. He thought about his brother, with all the strength of his love for him turning to hatred. Again his fall changed slope.

Colors shifted down the scale toward the white end of the spectrum. He was able to see the outside world now. He was speeding laterally across the meshes of the Lattice. The city gave way to a forest, which grew up and was cut back. Another city appeared, became hypermodern, disappeared, and water rose to cover the land. Everywhere there was only ocean.

Except for an island, which grew, rose, then sank. Seaweed covered the water, then dry land again, then distant jungles, an immediate volcano that quickly eroded to low hills, then flatness and desolation, and a little way off, the burning ruin.

He came out of the Lattice and stood under the bright sunless sky, waiting for the Servants who had been pursuing him to make their appearance.

"I owe you one, Gary," he said in the silence of the desert. And more than one, he realized, feeling a subtle lifting of guilt from his soul. Morgan had owed for Pickard's death, and Weiss's death had paid the debt.

After ten minutes, nobody came. He had lost them completely when he'd fallen through the gap Weiss had torn in the Lattice. He felt inside himself for his bond with Dana, and found it, a thin thread, leading—somewhere. He tried to send a message to her, but the distance was too great. He knew only that she was alive. He turned toward the ruin and started walking.

As he neared the building he looked for his footprints in the sand. But that had been a dream, no matter how close to truth. There were no footprints here, though there might be, several miles away, at the spot where he'd first been sent.

He stood in front of the door, trying to think of what to do next. His thoughts of Michael had brought him here. What would his brother be doing in a place like this?

He didn't go into the building by the door, but instead went along the wall to the right to the courtyard gate and entered there. Across the yard were the kitchens and washhouse, just as he'd seen them in the dream, built against the back wall. They were burning, with greasy orange flames against the black smoke.

The fire wasn't natural, though part of the structure had fallen in. That was due to whatever had happened here originally. Whatever had been made of wood had long since been reduced to ash, but that was because of the original fire, not this mystic burning. All that was left to burn was stone, and burn it did, and had done so for uncounted ages.

There was a window in what had once been the kitchen. The roof above it had burned away, and it was through this opening that the smoke billowed. Flames burned within the building and around the sill of the window. On the sill lay what looked like a large scroll of vellum.

It was burning but unconsumed, protected by the magic fire that surrounded it. The fire had not been created for that purpose. This ruin had been here a very long time, and the fire had been burning equally long. The Servants had merely taken advantage of what was already available.

His thoughts of Michael had brought him to this ruin. Michael was not here in the flesh, he was sure. That meant that some other, more essential part of him was here instead.

Morgan looked at the scroll, so carefully preserved in this mystic fire. The thought came to him that maybe this was Michael's contract, a real contract. Not like the trivial forgery Morgan had signed, but one that gave power, in exchange for a soul.

And perhaps containing the soul for which the bargain had been made. Michael's soul, kept here in the scroll, as a constant reminder to Michael of what was in store for him when his usefulness to Ghebr and the Tukhanox was ended.

"Is that you, Brother Michael?" Morgan whispered at the scroll. But the flames did not answer.

Morgan knew that no hand could hook the contract out of the fire. Whoever tried would be instantly enveloped in flames and destroyed. So would any kind of stick or pole that might be used instead. Though apparently out in the open, for any who cared to look and see, the contract was as safe as if it had been buried a mile in the earth.

He found it ironic that his brother's contract should be hidden here, in the same place in which he had been marooned once before. Morgan had been thinking of his brother then, too, which could be why he had been brought here the first time. But all that was really academic. The important thing was to take advantage of this opportunity while he had it.

Morgan tried a fire spell on the flames, a reverse one that would quench them. But they were unaffected. He tried a levitation spell on the scroll, but the fire consumed the spell even as he cast it. He could not touch it with his hands; he could not touch it with his magic. But he had something else that might work. He had the dagger.

He and Dana had assimilated the dagger, so that it was no longer a physical thing, just an idea shared between them. And as such, it had a certain reality, and was not just a spell or the product of one, in spite of the spells it contained. The idea of the dagger retained certain qualities that its assimilation could not destroy.

The cold iron of the dagger, in concept only, quenched the flames on the scroll itself, leaving the rest of the fire unchanged. Morgan reached for the scroll, lifted it from the surrounding fire, and took no hurt.

He could feel the tremble through the Lattice as this simple action circumvented other powerful spells that had been set on this scroll to protect it. Ghebr, and Michael, would feel it too, and would know, or guess, what it meant.

He unrolled the vellum. It was indeed a contract, with Michael's signature in one lower corner, in blood. In the other corner was a different kind of mark, an obscene scrawl that could only be the "signature" of the Principle of Evil, or of its viceroy.

He didn't bother to read the contract. He didn't really want to know what conditions Michael had agreed to in exchange for his power. He rolled the scroll back up again, feeling his hatred change to an aching pity, then walked to the middle of the yard and sat down in the dust.

The contract could not be unsigned. Michael,

if he wished, if he had the moral strength, could repudiate it and die, but Morgan could not do that for him. All Morgan could do was destroy the contract.

And if he did that, and if Michael's essential self was actually contained within this scroll, then Michael's soul would be destroyed in the process. It would be as if Michael had never existed. History would not change, but there would be nothing of Michael to pass into true death.

On the other hand, he wouldn't be damned, either. Ghebr would then be without a host, and the Lodge without a Grand Master—at least for a little while.

There would still be Nick Jones to deal with, and an enraged Ghebr. They would most certainly put vengeance as their highest priority. Morgan could flee, but they would track him down, and punish him for what he had done.

But he would not be alone. When he returned to the real world, he would find Dana again, and with the dagger between them, they would be able—he hoped—to keep the enemy at bay until Ghebr lost interest. After all, there was still the stone, and though it was now safe, the demon would consider its recovery far more important than any trivial vengeance—he hoped.

He thought about his brother. Michael had tried to help him through those bad years when he'd been a street fighter. It had been Michael's advice, when the judge had offered Morgan three years in the marines or three years in a penitentiary, that had helped him make the choice that had changed his life for the better.

The back of Morgan's throat ached. He didn't really hate his brother after all.

He stood, pushed memories out of his mind, and held the scroll high in his left hand. He felt and found the power and the magic of the dagger.

"Michael," he called out to the still air, the rushing flames, the billowing smoke. "I know you can hear me, Michael." He knew that Ghebr was aware of him too. It was Ghebr he hated, not Michael. "I have your contract, Michael," he screamed at the empty building, the desolate land, the silence—the memories. "I'm sorry, Michael," he cried at the impossibly distant horizon, the too-blue sky, the sunless day. He loved his brother. "Oh, Michael," he whispered in the stillness. Then he drew upon the power of the dagger, and made new fire on the contract.

He held the contract high over his head, and it burned. The scroll turned to ashes, which drifted softly down around him. His hand was untouched.

Chapter Forty-five

❖ ❖ ❖

EVERYTHING AROUND HIM faded. There was only the plain, absolutely flat, with its infinite horizon, now not of sand, but of stark white dust. He had expected to return to the real world.

There was no magic here. Overhead, in a pale-yellow sky, was a green sun. It was not so bright that he could not look at it. Light rays streamed out from it, long and straight, inaudibly tinkling with a melodic sound he couldn't quite hear. They shifted and sang. The sun, itself, did not move.

A bit to one side of the sun was a point, and from that point there fell a shadow, dark against the pale-yellow sky, stretching out to infinity and beyond. But aside from that there was nothing.

A movement near his foot caught his eye. He looked down. There, on the white dust, was a little spider, no bigger than his hand. It was not a spider like those that live on Earth, but a spider of a different kind, black and brown and green, a spider with little hands at the end of each of its eight legs, a spider that danced in the dust.

Only in the dreams of the Dreamer did such spiders exist. Morgan knew where he was now.

This plain was beyond all magic, beyond time and space. This was the ultimate limit, spoken of, theorized about, written of in texts. But if ever it was seen at firsthand, the witness had never yet returned to tell of it. This was the intersection between the cosmos and the Abode of the Gods.

It was Ghebr's last stroke, retribution for Michael's death. In time, Morgan himself would be nothing. Just white dust indistinguishable from the rest of the plain, to be danced over by the spiders. Morgan saw a little pinch of dust fall from somewhere and settle down stark white on the dust already there.

The green sun overhead was not a true sun at

all, but something else that mortal minds could not grasp. There was no wind on the white space plain. Only the white dust of years long dead, the powdery ash of time.

Morgan's mind, overwhelmed by grief for his brother, whited out like the space plain that surrounded him. He looked down at the little spider, and watched it dancing. Like a child, he felt like dancing too. So he did, in time with the pulsing rays of the lost green sun overhead, and to its silent music.

As they danced, Morgan and the spider, they were joined by other spiders, dancing, playing with their snow goblets. Their dance turned the edges of the white space plain, which has no edges, and it sloped down to become the spiders' beach, on the edges of the Blackest Sea. One way was the realm of the gods. In the other way, across the Blackest Sea, was the cosmos.

Morgan danced with the spiders, and they danced with him, and among the spiders was another thing, much bigger than they, red and black. When he realized what it was, Morgan stopped dancing. The spiders all skipped away along the beach, and out of sight.

"Phoebus," Morgan said, "how did you get to me here?"

"The Dreamer sent me. Michael is dead."

"I know. And I might as well be."

"But Dana is still alive," Phoebus said. "At least until the Servants get to her."

"What can I do? No one has ever come back from here before."

"This is not the other side of true death," Phoebus said. "From there, no one returns, but I have visited here once or twice."

"You are a *vendra*."

"True. And you have a bond with Dana, a bond that still exists. Feel it."

Morgan did so. "It is so thin," he said.

"It is enough. Or, it can be. You cannot die yet. Ghebr has made Nick Jones the new Grand Master of the Lodge. You still have to battle them."

"But Phoebus, Ghebr sent me here. I'm a prisoner."

"You don't understand. That was what Ghebr had intended, but if you stay here, he will come for you. He is not denied this place, though the Point Upon a Star sends its Shadow down. If he meets you here, he will be in his power, while you will have nothing. You must confront him on more equitable terms."

"How can I fight a demon? Even with you to help me, he is too strong. The best I could hope for, with Dana's help, would be to stay out of his way, until his mind turns to other things. It's not that I'm afraid of death, Phoebus, you know that. But death at Ghebr's hands would be too horrible, and if I die, Dana will die too."

"True," Phoebus said. "And it is true that if you confront Ghebr, one of you *must* die. And Ghebr is immortal."

"He will come for me if I don't go to him. And as you say, here I would have no chance at all. In the real world, at least I could, perhaps, do him some damage. At least break his last hold on the Lodge. Perhaps."

"You always do what you have to do," Phoebus said. "Now, look there." He pointed with one paw. Morgan looked that way, out over the

Blackest Sea. There, so far away he could barely
see it, was a tiny patch of light. The universe.

"That's where Dana is," Phoebus said. "That
way lies home."

Chapter Forty-six
✣ ✣ ✣

WHAT A RISK! What a gamble! What an adven-
ture, to swim across the Blackest Sea and back
into reality. There were old stories that once,
aeons ago, the Dalra people had sailed the
Blackest Sea. But that, if it was true, was another time, and a different matter.

Morgan stared at the so distant point of light
that was the universe and thought of Dana. This
time, though the connection between them was
stretched to its very limits, he felt her answering response. He did not have to ask what to
do. He picked Phoebus up, put the cat on his
shoulder, walked down to the edge of the Blackest Sea, and stepped in. It was not wet, though
it was buoyant. And it was not cold. He had
expected it would be.

He went forward. The surface of the Blackest
Sea rose to his calves, to his knees, his hips, his
chest. He let himself down into it, as if into a
physical ocean, and reached out to start swimming, with Phoebus securely hanging on to his
back.

He felt the currents and took hold of them.
They were weak here, so far from the stars that

generated them, but they pulled him just the same. He moved slowly at first, but gradually faster, and faster, until at last he was spinning along the star-lines, racing down the space-lanes, until the Blackest Sea was all around him, and ahead was the patch of light that was the universe.

In time he came to the universe of mass and time and space and energy, with its stars and galaxies. He rushed headlong, letting the bond between him and Dana guide him, until he came at last to a spiral galaxy he knew was his own. He followed the ever-strengthening bond to a limb of the spiral, and to a cluster of stars there, and in toward his own solar system, past the planets, to the Earth, and down to the lawn in front of Michael's house.

Dana was waiting for him. They did not embrace. The bond between them was sufficient, for the moment.

"He's waiting for you," she said. She knew, as well as he, what was at risk.

"Does he know you're here?"

"Probably. But he's not come out, or made any move, and I'm ready to flee the instant he does."

"That's good, because if he got to you and killed you, I'd die too, without having done him any damage."

"That's why I've been careful. But then, I've got the Dreamer's help. Even Ghebr can't stop me from getting to the Other House if I have to run."

"Then Ghebr's the only one I have to worry about," Morgan said, reaching up to scritch Phoebus under the chin. The cat did not purr.

"Do you have any chance?" Dana asked.

"Somebody has to die," Morgan said, "and Ghebr is immortal."

"I know." She touched him now, fingers brushing his cheek.

"Whatever happens," Morgan said, looking down at her, "we'll be done with this. This pays all our dues in full."

"I know that, too." She smiled, then she stood up on her toes and kissed him once.

It was over too quickly. He stepped away from her and went up onto the porch, in through the double front door, through the entrance hall, and into the living room. Nick Jones was sitting in Michael's chair, smiling, his golden eyes bright. Somebody had to die, and Ghebr was immortal.

"I underestimated you again," Jones said, echoing Michael's words, watching as Phoebus, hackles up and tail huge, jumped down and moved to one side of the room. "You are indeed a wonder to behold. I wish you could have joined forces with me. In spite of your flaws, you would have been the most powerful force for Death this world has ever seen."

"I have no intention of ever joining you," Morgan said. He was not afraid. Dana was filling him with her courage, her hope, her energy.

"I'm quite reconciled to that now," Jones said. "There is no further need for you and I to struggle. Why have you come here?"

"You don't think that I believe for one minute you'd let me live after what I've done. The stone is out of your reach. So is the dagger. And your Grand Master, my brother, is dead. Surely you have some thoughts of revenge."

"That may be true," Jones said, "but after all this thrashing and struggling, you just walk in here to face me to the death? There can be no other way, you know. Step aside, go away, leave this foolishness be. If you and I fight, one of us *must* die. Do you know that?" His eyes were gold, the gold of Ghebr.

"I know that, Jones, but if I don't fight you now, you'll come for me later, when I'm unprepared. I may not have much chance now, but I'd have none then."

"But if you fight me, you will die. And Miss Kirkpatrick will die. You have so much potential, I'd much rather try to enlist you later. What's come over you?"

"You will never enlist me. Let's get this over with."

"Don't be silly. Think of yourself. Sure, if you leave this be, I will come out ahead, even if the stone is beyond my reach. But if you live, there is much that you could do. And there's no need for me to pursue you. I am not vindictive, even my enemies admit that. You've won your freedom, won it fairly. What more can I say? Why not go off with your paramour and let it be?"

"Don't slick at me with your smooth words. What good could I do if I fail to try to finish this off properly, whether I die or not? If I just walk away from you, you will have won your victory without any effort. I want to be done with you, Jones. Are you afraid of me?"

"Of course not," Jones said. "It was foolish of me to try to talk you out of it." He got to his feet, came over to Morgan, and put a hand on his shoulder. Morgan shrank from the touch.

Jones's body began to change. Morgan could

see, superimposed on Jones's human shape, another shape, hairy, serpentlike, with too many arms, the avatar of Ghebr the archdemon, the Cold Hand of Fear.

Morgan felt his throat scream, felt Dana, through his bond, recoiling at the same time. With his whole soul, he wanted only to get out of that place. His movement was instinctive.

But it was not flight. He threw himself on Jones, his hands reaching for Jones's throat. Man and archdemon, taken by surprise, lurched back, the transformation incomplete. Jones/Ghebr beat at Morgan with hairy, horny hands. Morgan felt spikes puncturing his skin, hooks tearing his flesh. He squeezed. The impetus of Morgan's attack bore man/demon over backward and down. They all fell to the floor.

Morgan was enveloped in the hideous stench of hot black copper. Spines penetrated his chest and abdomen; scaly coils twisted around his legs, wrenching muscle and sinew. His skin crawled as if thousands of insects were burrowing into it, but he held on, squeezed the still partially human throat, squeezed until the beating arms fluttered weakly and then were still.

In this confrontation, one had to die, and Ghebr was immortal. But Nick Jones was not. And Nick Jones was dead.

Ghebr fled. Only Jones's simply human body remained. Morgan lay on the corpse, then rolled off to free himself of the stench and the feel of the demon. His stomach heaved, and he threw up.

Jones was dead. Ghebr was gone—for a while. Morgan pushed himself up until he was leaning against the wall. His skin was blistered; he was bleeding from chest, back, arms, legs. His left thigh was broken.

Phoebus came up to him, avoiding Jones's body and the demon's blood. "Morgan," the cat said, its voice a frightened whine, "are you all right?"

"No," Morgan said. He wiped his mouth with a bloody hand. "No, I am badly hurt. Where's Dana?"

"I'll get her," Phoebus said.

"Yes, please." The cat turned and streaked out through the front door. It seemed a long moment before he returned again, a white and shaken Dana behind him.

She fell to her knees beside him. "I'm sorry," she said, tears streaming down her face to mingle with his blood.

"That's all right," Morgan told her as she started to work healing spells over his broken body. "We're out of it now."

"But Ghebr," Dana said, crying.

"Another time, another place," Morgan said, feeling her spells take hold, his body reknit. "And another hero. You and I, we're done fighting. We're going off somewhere. We've got some loving to do."

Phoebus just purred.

A THRILLING
SCIENCE FICTION TALE
FROM PAGEANT BOOKS!

NEENA
GATHERING

VALERIE NIEMAN COLANDER

It's the twenty-first century and America is no more. The U.S. has split into sections and destroyed itself with chemical warfare. A civilization based on technology, communications, mass transportation, factories, schools, culture, and medicine has ceased to exist. Forced to grow up quickly under such conditions, can Neena eke out a living while fighting off roving bands of survivors as well as the misguided attention of her uncle, Ted? Or will she choose to become the symbol of a reborn nation with the horribly scarred but loving Arden?

ISBN: 0-517-00643-X   Price: $2.95